STEVE ERICKSON'S
DAYS BETWEEN STATIONS

"The vision of a world where cultural memory has dried up and there is nothing left but a series of powerful, disconnected celluloid images.... Sometime in the not too distant future, the planet Earth is going rapidly to the dogs. Los Angeles is swept by sandstorms that darken the sky and send dunes crawling up the buildings. A pall of smoke hangs over Paris, where the lights have gone out and bonfires burn out of control. The canals of Venice have inexplicably dried up, and the streets, smelling of garbage, are periodically plunged into deep fog. The landscape is fabulous, bleak; the lovers who travel through it are just the opposite— romantically alienated and drunk on their own eroticism."
—*The New York Times Book Review*

"There isn't a risk that Steve Erickson hasn't taken in this novel; one gets the feeling that he's laid everything on the line."
—*The Los Angeles Times*

DAYS BETWEEN STATIONS

A NOVEL BY Steve Erickson

VINTAGE CONTEMPORARIES

VINTAGE BOOKS · A DIVISION OF RANDOM HOUSE · NEW YORK

First Vintage Books Edition, September 1986

Library of Congress Cataloging-in-Publication Data

Erickson, Steve.
  Days between stations.

  (Vintage contemporaries)
  I. Title.
[PS3555.R47D3 1986]   813'.54   86-40138
ISBN 0-394-74685-6 (pbk.)

Manufactured in the United States of America

Author photo copyright © 1985 by Alison Cobb

The traveler asks himself: if he lived out
a lifetime, pushing the distance away,
does he come back to the place where his
        grieving began:
squander his dose of identity again,
say his goodbyes again, and go?

PABLO NERUDA

DAYS BETWEEN STATIONS

When Lauren was a small girl, she would stand in the Kansan fields and call the cats. One by one they would come to her through the grass, across which lay the ice of the coming winter; and she could see them in the light of the moon. The shadows of the crossing clouds formed a thousand small dark junctions before her. The glint of the ice was like the glint of the cats' eyes, and that in turn was something like the glint of the stars through the clouds. She herself wondered why they came. They were wild and heeded no one else; their thrashing in the fields did the farmers no good; and Lauren's father hated the howl they invested in the night, like a thousand bleeding babies in the grass. But they came for her and it was certain therefore, because of that, that she was in some way special; and perhaps, she was to wonder twenty years later, they came for the same reason she came to them, which was that it was beautiful to see them, all the crucifixes of shadow and the array of lights like knives, and she was beautiful like that too.

Twenty years later, when she was making love to him, she thought of them, rather than of her husband on his bicycle riding a highway that led away from her. When he was far up inside her she cried a bit and held his black hair, and remembered stroking the fur of the wildest black cat in Kansas.

And then she looked at him in the dark and wondered where he'd come from. And knew he could never tell her, because he didn't know himself. They were both across the borderland of their youth, traveling with visas on the verge of expiration, imperiled by the pending truth of their trespasses.

She met her husband the summer she was seventeen. The smell of Asia was always in the air. When she saw him at a dance, he had already come back from the war, having gone and given the last anguish of adolescence. He never saw fighting, sitting on a boat off the coast and listening to the helicopters catch fire. He had no real sense of relief, because he wasn't wise enough to understand he could die. It never occurred to him. Any other man would have questioned skeptically the fortune that brought him back from the precipice of the jungle to an auditorium outside Saint Louis where she was waiting. They were introduced in murmurs; she loved him immediately, as he did her, but this guaranteed nothing. Later she would run across her father's porch, to the frantic glance of her mother and brothers, to watch him ride with his team past her father's farm; against the ash horizon the small determined line of figures moved like one gray runnel of water, with their metallic blue uniforms and helmets and their bodies horizontal above the bicycles—heads low and backsides high. She never waved to him from a wooden fence.

He was twenty. His name was Jason. He had straight blond hair, which was to grow longer. Later in San Francisco he would wear an earring and take off his shirt. He glowed with beauty, of course—like all the things and people she would surround herself with—towering over other men, rippling across rooms, everything about him precise and flawless. There was a sense of drive to him that resided somewhere in the upper part of his back, between his shoulders; and sometimes this part of him was close to his heart, and sometimes it moved him most powerfully when it wasn't obstructed by his heart at all. A girl waving to him from a wooden fence would have made the man in him feel important; but the child in him, which was the great part of him, would only have wondered what it meant. When she walked from the porch to the road and stood watching after him, he thought he felt the lines and colors of her reflection in his metallic blue helmet. But he looked to see, and he knew that in a field of blond Kansan beauties there was something about the splendor of her mouth that allowed him to presume she was his, even if he never identified it that specifically. They didn't wait to marry before making love, and she was as unsurprised as he that he should be her first; he didn't need to hear the small muffled scream to know that, just as he hadn't needed to look over his shoulder to know she was there on the road. She saw no reason to scream for his benefit. Without it, however, he felt something was missing when it was over.

He was considering whether to try for the Olympics in Mexico City when he came back from overseas; he decided to wait for Munich. This conclusion took the pressure off, and made marrying her easier. The night after the wedding they left for San Francisco; and on the plane, hypnotized by the roar of the takeoff, she knew instinctively she was pregnant with Jules. She stared out the window at the glossy runway, and dreamed that the wildest black cat in Kansas stalked the wing of the plane.

They lived on a secret street, which was entered through a small hallway at the top of a series of steps that ran up a hill. But for this hallway, the block was entirely closed, obscure to traffic and the knowledge of residents who had lived in the city their whole lives; the street wasn't on Lauren's map, nor in the local directory she bought her first day there, nor in an atlas in the library; the shutters of the windows banged open and shut by themselves, and the doorways were blank until the sun set, when darkness engulfed the street. There was one very old automobile at the end of the block, and she couldn't imagine how it had gotten there, unless it had been lowered from the sky. The sign on the building read Pauline Boulevard; and she was astonished when, two years later, they moved to Los Angeles and, after weeks of looking for a place, they were referred by an agency to an apartment in the Hollywood Hills at the address of twenty-seven Pauline Boulevard. They took the apartment. Pauline Boulevard in the Hollywood Hills was entered by a small passageway at the top of a flight of steps even longer than the flight of steps in San Francisco; and there were shutters that banged open and shut and not one face in the doorways. There was no automobile but rather a poster in mint condition of *Flesh and the Devil* with John Gilbert kissing Garbo. Three summers later, when Jason was in Europe training for Munich, Lauren went up to San Francisco for a weekend and looked for her old street, Pauline Boulevard. She never found it. Three hours that afternoon she walked back and forth along Columbus Street looking for the steps that ran up past an Italian deli; she looked for the turn she had made hundreds of times. The steps were nowhere to be seen. She asked neighbors, shopkeepers, patrolmen, mail deliverers; but none of them had ever heard of Pauline Boulevard. She asked the deli owner about the steps that once ran past his shop, but he had no recollection of them. She returned to Los Angeles in some despair, anxious that the Pauline Boulevard where she now lived in the Hollywood Hills would be gone as well, but it was still there waiting for her, and from her window on the top floor at the end of the street she remembered the corresponding view from her window in San Francisco where, staring down to Columbus Street far below her, she laid her fingers across the belly that still held Jules.

They had so little time together in San Francisco, where at evening she listened for the changing gears of his bicycle and looked for the flash of his helmet coming down the secret street. His first departure seemed to correspond with her revelation that she was four months pregnant. Two days later he was gone, moving from the place in the kitchen where he had been frozen by the news.

At night by a small desk near the window she wrote him; they didn't have the money to telephone. She looked for his replies; they came infrequently. The more infrequently his letters came the more often she wrote, as though to conjure some response that way; and so the letters mounted. She wrote one and then thought of another before mailing the first, so she wrote the second and put the first inside. Soon she was mailing five, six letters in one, then a dozen, then nineteen or twenty, until he was receiving in the mail huge Chinese-puzzle-box letters, opening one letter only to find another inside, and the second letter referring him to the third, letters inside of letters inside of letters. Digging his way to the core of the correspondence, he would throw the whole thing aside in disgust about the fourteenth or fifteenth letter. In his way he believed he loved her, and in his way he knew he needed her; but he was also transfixed by his freedom, and as in Vietnam, he never understood the expendables.

He did not come home when Jules was born.

She went through it alone, without anesthesia, and said aloud "Where are you?" to each contraction. The nurses and doctors, misunderstanding, would answer, "It's coming, hold on," not realizing that Lauren cared at that moment nothing about the baby, that if giving birth to a dead fetus would have brought Jason through the door of the delivery room she would have made that bargain willingly; and it was only as Jules was tearing his way out of her that she decided, in the pit of agony, she would never send Jason a letter again, let alone a Chinese puzzle box. She decided it without fury or vindictiveness; the pain was such as to clarify everything, and the decision was temperate, deliberate. She went home with Jules two days later, and slept by the window where she had written all the letters; a woman from down the hall moved the bed for her. Jules slept with her. He was put on a special formula, and the doctors told her not to breast-feed him. The first day, she and the baby slept constantly, on through the night. She was awakened the next afternoon by a clatter in the street below. It was a small cart being pulled along by several people, and a strange music was coming from it; a funnel was at the end of the cart, into which the people who lived on the street threw coins, all the people Lauren had never seen before. At some point she realized that in this cart was the body of a dead child being taken to burial; as the coins tumbled down the funnel a mannequin on top of the cart, in a red coat with gold buttons, and wide vacant eyes and a mirthless thin smile, raised an arm in salute. As the mannequin waved, all down the street the mannequins of small children appeared in the windows waving back, until the entire block was a row of mannequin arms swaying back and forth. At the sight of this Lauren quickly glanced down at Jules in horror, fully expecting him to be the child in the cart. But Jules was there sleeping on her chest in the afternoon sun, unmoved by the music below and the waving plastic arms.

Her breasts were sore from being full. She began going to the hospital so the nurses could take the milk and ease the pressure. They never explained why she couldn't breast-feed the baby. She tried not to think of Jason at all; the woman down the hall, whose name was Martha, helped her with the child, caring for him and cleaning him and feeding him; and Lauren relished the afternoons she could go out for a while by herself and walk to the bay.

She came home from one such walk one such afternoon, and in the doorway stopped to see Jason before her, without his shirt, and one earring glimmering in his hair. They stood watching each other, and she couldn't find it in her to resist him; she crumpled into his chest, his arms taking her and his face looking down on her while all she could mutter was "Beautiful. Beautiful," over and over, unaware she was saying it out loud. She knew at that moment that whatever delivery room oaths she made were futile, that she fatally loved his beauty more than she knew her own, that she loved the way other women looked at him and that she loved his godlike presence in their eyes; he made love to her then. Afterward she lay languidly in bed clawing at his chest, until a baby's cry caught her attention. She went down the hall and got Jules from Martha, and brought him into the room and held him up to her husband and said, "This is your son." From the bed Jason watched the baby wordlessly, and Lauren set Jules down at his father's feet. Jason stared at the child awhile, not having the vaguest idea how to react to him, as though having missed most of her pregnancy and the child's birth, Jason had negated in his own mind the recognition of his fatherhood; he knew he was the boy's father, but he didn't feel it.

Jason looked up from Jules to Lauren. "I have to go back east again."

"When?" she said, devastated.

"Soon." He watched the child and, never taking his eyes from him, said, "There's a race in Philadelphia, an important one. A good showing will be important." He may have been unwilling to say he was sorry, or he may have been unaware it was necessary. He was gone three weeks later. She began writing letters again. The days stretched to weeks, into the summer, the first of many summers without him. If it was difficult raising the baby alone, she realized that without Jules she would have fled the loneliness on Pauline Boulevard, where no one emerged except for the funerals of dead children. She sat with Jules in Martha's apartment, the baby on the floor and the television flickering before the three of them its images of one man stepping on the moon. That first moonwalk was played over and over, and it was the first time she ever noticed Jules' attention fixed on anything, on that television set and those images; and he watched alert and intent, absolutely still.

She received no letter from Jason for a long time; and then suddenly one night the telephone down the hall rang, and the call was for her. They talked awhile, exchanging news, but she was distantly certain that it wasn't a casual phone call, and it was when she kept asking him over and over, to no response, "When are you coming home?" that she knew he had called because he had something to tell her. "Jason," she said.

"It will be a while."

"Is it another race?" she asked, and it was then she found out that in his way, he was possessed of a stunning honesty.

"No, it's not a race," he said.

She was silent for half a minute before she said, "What then?"

"It's . . . a personal responsibility," he said, and he began talking, explaining, and in the middle of it she realized that she was still hearing it all distantly; she was nodding along with what he was saying to her. The hall light went off by itself—it did automatically after several minutes—and after several more minutes Martha came out and turned the light on, having heard Lauren's voice in the hall. Martha smiled and waved, but all of this transpired without Lauren seeing any of it, conscious of almost nothing. "It's my child," he said flatly. "I should be with her when the baby's born," and she answered, "Of course. Of course you should. It's the right thing to do," in a monotone. At some point, after he had stopped talking, she asked him, "Is she the one you want?" and he said no. "Of course," she repeated, "of course you should stay with her," and the light went out again, and he said, "I'll be back when I can," and she just nodded and didn't hear him at all. She put the phone on the hook. She stood in the dark a moment, and the light went on, and Martha was revealed again.

"Lauren?" said Martha.

Lauren turned in the hall and went back to the room, and didn't look at Jules or anything around her. She stood before the window and the lights of Columbus Street poured past her to the bay, and she finally took her wallet and put it in her purse and walked out of the room, leaving Jules on the bed. Martha was still in the hall. She asked if Lauren was all right. Lauren said nothing, and Martha looked back to the room. "Do you want me to watch the baby?" she said. Lauren didn't answer.

Forty minutes later Lauren was at the airport. She never remembered later how she got there. She bought a plane ticket. She assumed she was buying a ticket for Kansas. She sat in the lobby waiting for her flight, and as she heard him tell it all again, just as he had on the telephone, a voice cut in announcing her flight. She was in the airplane ten minutes later. An hour and ten minutes later she was in Los Angeles.

She walked out the terminal, somehow under the impression she was in Kansas. In the taxi she vaguely peered out the window and looked at the tall grass. At Sunset and La Cienega she got out of the taxi and began walking west along the Strip. It was one in the morning. She didn't know the time. In her head, over and over, as in the airport, she heard the things he'd said to her on the telephone; she didn't hear the jangling guitars, or the comments men made to her as she passed. She wasn't thinking so much about what he had said as simply hearing it again and again; she wasn't mulling over the betrayal of it, or becoming enraged that he should decide to stay for the birth of a child who was illegitimately his when he didn't care enough to be present for the birth of the child he had with his own wife. No. She walked the Strip at one in the morning as though the phone conversation had hurled her into her own time, when it was not one in the morning, or ten in the morning, or ten in the evening, or midnight. She was too brutalized by it to care much for the fine shadings of betrayal or bitterness or especially rage; rather she was somehow set on course toward the most foreign thing she could find, whatever that might be. Walking there on the Strip, with the shop windows passing her and the faces of strange men caught in the glow of their cigarettes, she was only vaguely aware of the danger, and not aggressively running from it or for it; she didn't care. She didn't care. She wanted only to walk away from whatever became too familiar to her too quickly; the moment she passed a shop window, it was as though she had stared into it forever. She wanted to walk away from the men and the stunning glow of their cigarettes. The clubs emptied, bottles rolled across the sidewalks, the bars glistened of bourbon. Like a torch, the blonde glided along the Strip under the gaze of a hundred men.

Another man called to her and then another, and a car pulled up alongside her. Somebody from the car whistled for her. She didn't answer, she didn't hear, she only heard Jason saying, over

and over, It's my child, I should be with her. She kept nodding
to this, and the more she knew it was an outrage, the more she
kept nodding. Only in the midst of this did she hear the whistle.
The car moved slowly alongside her down the street. She passed
another man; steps followed her. It's my child, I should be with
her, she kept hearing, and she kept nodding, until finally she
felt sick. She suddenly knew she felt very sick, and stopped at a
streetlight, and looked around her in a daze. The car stopped,
waiting.

She fell to her knees there on the street. When she was finished, she became utterly cold; she tried to move away from
where she had been sick, and instead stumbled. In the periphery
of her vision she was aware the car was still there, waiting, as
though the driver couldn't decide what he wanted to do with her.
She knew if he got out of the car and walked up to her, she
wouldn't be able to get away from him; but she didn't particularly
care about this. She didn't care about anything. She didn't care
about the hem of the long blue coat she saw in the corner of her
eye. She didn't know how long this man in the long blue coat
had been standing there; she didn't care about the ominous still-
ness of the hem of the coat, or its nearness. When she heard the
door of the car open and shut, and heard someone coming toward
her, she didn't care about that. Nor about the intensity of the
voices between the two men, when she realized they were arguing
over her.

An arm in the blue coat reached down and held her by the
wrist, roughly pulling her up. The blue coat's other arm reached
around her shoulder. He started taking her further up the Strip,
walking faster than she could keep up; when she tripped, she was
snapped back into step. The driver of the car was left behind.
She didn't have it in her to pull away, or to question where she
was being taken, or what was going to be done to her. She didn't
have it in her to look at him, or to talk to him. He said nothing.

She thought the police would come along soon; she could
occasionally see a black-and-white glide past her down the boulevard. But no one stopped.

At some point she was in a car, slumped against the door.
Each time the car stopped at a light, she realized she could easily

open the door and step out and get away, but she didn't. She was, through all of it, still hearing Jason's voice.

The car turned up off Sunset and went higher into the hills, up a winding road. The lights of the hills vanished. It became darker and, as she had hoped, more foreign, until even the moment was no longer familiar to her. And as each moment became unfamiliar even unto itself, she hoped the voice on the telephone would become a stranger's, and that it would speak to her in a language she didn't understand.

In a little dirt cove off the road, in the middle of nowhere, the car stopped. His arm reached across and locked her door. She felt his hands on her shoulders and his fingers across her face. In the darkness beyond the window she could see the Kansas fields blowing back and forth, as though the entire earth was rocking. On the horizon was the house where she grew up; a small figure darted from its shadow, running toward the hills. The wind purred in the grass, and just past her house, before the hills, surrounding the fields, there seemed to stretch a long obstruction, as though it might be a wall lining the distance. His body shifted in his coat and he pressed against her. He was still running his fingers over her face and looking at her; she continued staring out into the dark, never turning to face him. The shadow of his coat enveloped her, until she was lying across the seat beneath him, and she said, somewhat foolishly she imagined, but as a verbal reflex nonetheless, "It hurts." She never expected it to mean anything. She had, in fact, wondered only if he would kill her afterwards. So she was astonished when the small sound of her voice seemed to trigger a realization and fracture a trance — and the shadow lifted, altered position, dissipated.

He backed away, over to his side of the seat. She heard him catch his own breath and could see him, from the corner of her eye, raise his hand to his brow and turn to something outside the window. He started the car again, and something between them changed; he was not quite the same person. He pulled the car out of the dirt and started further along the road, into the dark.

After a while the car stopped again. She heard steps circle around the back. She looked around, with no idea where she was; the door opened and she was pulled out.

She realized she was being taken up some stairs, and she heard the jangling of keys.

Inside a light went on. She looked up at the walls. There were film posters, and everything was a blinding glare. She was led by the long blue coat into the bedroom. She was led past a large bed, and then into the bathroom.

She stared at the sink, and at the toilet bowl. She heard his voice now, low and tight. "Are y-y-y-y—" It stopped and took a deep breath. "Are y-y-you going to be s-sick again?" She would not have heard it at all, not over Jason's voice, except for the stammer, like an emergency message in code intercepting her frequency. She saw the arm of the blue coat slowly reach over to the sink and turn on the water. She watched the long blue arm reach to her face, and she stared at the water, waiting. She felt something around her mouth, wet, and realized he was wiping her lips with a cloth. He rinsed the cloth in the sink, and wiped her mouth again, and then her face.

"Are y-y-y—" Again he stopped, gasping.

"I'm not going to be sick," she said.

The long blue coat led her back into the bedroom and sat her down on the bed. She was there alone for several minutes. When he returned he pushed her back against the pillow. He put a tray in front of her. "C-Can you drink this?" he said. She took the cup and sipped at it.

Silence filled the room, except for the sound of the cup against her lips and the wind against the roof. She was now absolutely certain that she wasn't in Kansas at all, that there was no tall grass beyond the window, that if she was to step from the door and call the cats, none would come to her. There was a face on the wall staring at her; not Jason's, or her father's, or her mother's, but an old face with large white eyebrows and piercing eyes that might have been the very black of the black-and-white poster the face was staring from. She might have liked to imagine the eyes were looking at her, but like Jason's voice on the telephone the eyes seemed directed past her, to some place above her. Their glare was penetrating, and whatever they watched was focused clearly in the old man's mind; there was no ambivalence about the vision. Under the face was the name *Adolphe Sarre*. She had no idea who he was. The steam of the tea drifted up past her gaze, and his white hair seemed to float away.

Everything inside her felt depleted except for her chest, which was full of milk. In an exceptional moment of lucidity and concern she thought about Jules. She thought about Martha in the hall. She said to herself, I should not be wherever it is I am now. I should not be in a stranger's room, in a stranger's bed.

The Morse code came through again. "W-W-Would you l-l-l-l-l—" The voice stopped again, as it had before, breathing heavily. After a moment it resumed. "T-T-T-Tea. Would you c-c-care for more tea?"

She shook her head. She looked at the old man's eyes.

She put her hands on her breasts, holding them because they hurt. She lay there supporting them for several moments until she could feel him standing over her, and then she dropped her arms to her sides. She sank back in the pillow. "A-A-A-Are you all right?" she heard him say, never opening her eyes; and she could neither nod nor shake her head. She felt him sit on the bed beside her. He went on talking then, and she felt nothing but her full breasts and the warmth of the teacup through the tray on her lap; and the white flash of the walls seeped through her lids less and less. It flooded across her, in her moment of least resistance, the possibilities of the situation she was in—now when it was too late for her to leave, when she couldn't have lifted herself from the bed for even Jason, for even Jules. She didn't hear what he said, because the sound of his voice evened to a hum, the stammers smoothing to slurs and his tone dropping. She supposed he might be trying to hypnotize her. She was a pool of shifting currents: confusion and anxiety and, too late, fear that she might slip away and never wake; and beneath it the devastation of the phone call, and finally the resignation to where she was and whatever might happen. She listened and image after image spun before her; and his voice became calmer and slower, lulling her, threading through her like celluloid. She became too deeply lost in something else to understand what he was saying, and too deeply lost to hear in his voice the sadness. It was reasonable that she wouldn't hear that, that she wouldn't assume that of him—that would have been assuming so much.

She felt him unbutton her shirt, and she felt her large unmilked breasts fall free of the material; and she felt him unsnap her jeans and pull them from her legs. The palm of his hand brushed her thigh, and his own breath, which didn't stutter at all, was on her neck.

She knew he was there several seconds looking at her, and then she felt his mouth on hers. Then she felt him pull the blanket up over her.

She didn't think of him again. She didn't sleep but struggled fitfully with a dream that never quite arrived. When, early in the morning, just before dawn, she walked quietly from the apartment, past his sleeping form on the floor with a pillow beneath his black hair and his blue coat over his shoulders, she looked at him only once, his back to her and his face still unseen.

He woke nine years later remembering nothing. Not his name, nor what he was doing in a room in Paris, nor whatever it was that had occurred before he went to sleep that blotted out his identity. That was what it was, the obliteration of self-sense more than of mere memory; it wasn't so much that he couldn't remember, but rather as though it was gone, his life before that morning. He lay there quite a while looking around the room, his eyes traveling the ceiling to the corners, and listening to the traffic outside. Water dripped in the sink. The walls were pale and unadorned. There was a book by the side of the bed, *Les grands auteurs du cinéma*. He finally stumbled to the window and looked onto the street below.

He did hold on to one memory, going over and over it. He did this not out of any real panic or confusion; he was amazed, instead, by the sense of relief he felt, though of course he had no idea what it was that so relieved him, unless it was the obliteration itself. What he saw in his mind were twin boys, blond, standing on a stage before an auditorium of people. Lights were cast across their figures, and their hair shone. Their mouths were small and their eyes wide, and their hands, held before them, were shaking. Seated to the rear were several men and women, watching the two children and waiting. The audience was waiting.

He found an American passport in the drawer. He opened it and looked at the picture, and then looked at the face in the mirror. They were the same face, the same black hair. The name on the passport was Michel Sarasan. This surprised him, because a second before opening the passport the name Adrien ran across his mind. Even now, after reading Michel Sarasan, the name Adrien resounded. It felt familiar to him, as though it should have been written on the passport. Sex: M. Wife/husband: XXX. Age: 29. Birthplace: France. Bearer's address: Los Angeles.

A week later Jack Sarasan, a film producer in California, received a phone call. He immediately left the studio, got in his limousine and went home. At this moment, always conscious of those things that were his, he realized that one of the reasons he had never liked his nephew was that Michel wasn't his—not the way the chauffeur, or the limousine, or the house were his. Jack Sarasan drew the line on how far people could go and still be his, and the ones who slipped over the line he cut loose; but his nephew had cut himself loose long before. Jack was trying to calculate exactly how long by the time he got to the house. "Eight," he concluded aloud, to the stairs, lighting a cigar.

"Eight what?"

Jack looked up at the doctor coming toward him. He never liked the doctor either, but his wife claimed to trust him.

"Eight what," the doctor said again, taking his coat from the chair.

"Eight years," said Jack, after studying the doctor. "Since Michel disappeared."

"Well, he's back," said the doctor, glancing upstairs.

"I know he's back. What I want to know is why."

Michel had shown up at the door, which the maid answered. The maid had stood gawking at him until Judith Sarasan came up behind, who in turn gawked at the eyepatch Michel was wearing. He had gotten it that first day in Paris, after waking, and put it on so the anonymity of his face would match the anonymity of his memory. He had worn the patch in the streets, along the boulevard Saint-Michel, in restaurants and cafés, in shops and in the Métro, on the trains and on the airplane coming back; and somehow came to feel more and more assured when no one seemed to know him. To the recurring vision of the twin boys in the auditorium, he switched the patch from eye to eye, first watching one boy and then the other, dividing everything he saw in half. It was on the plane that a stewardess, more alert than the others, noted the patch covering the left eye when sometime earlier it had covered the right. She notified the pilot, who notified officials at LAX when the plane landed, who questioned Michel for three hours before allowing him to go. When he walked up the long drive from the taxi at the bottom of the hill, he stood at the door asking tentatively of his aunt, Do I know you? And do you know me?

Why are you wearing that patch? she wanted to know, and called the doctor.

"Why *is* he wearing a patch?" said Jack. "Is there something wrong with his eye?"

"No," the doctor said. He mulled it for a while, there in the entryway.

"Well?"

The doctor put his hand to his chin. "Nothing physically wrong with him at all," he said, shaking his head.

"What's that mean? Has he finally gone completely crazy?"

"He seems to have amnesia."

"Amnesia!"

The doctor put on his coat.

"Did somebody bump him on the head?"

"That happens in the movies."

"I know what happens in the movies," Jack said tersely.

"More likely to be emotional trauma," said the doctor. "A confrontation, a startling revelation. Something that makes the mind wipe everything out."

"He doesn't remember anything?"

"He talks about twins. You know anything about that?"

Jack was visibly stunned. He took the cigar from his mouth.

"You know anything about that?" the doctor repeated, peering at him.

Jack shrugged, and now he too looked upstairs. He shrugged again. "It's nothing, I suppose—"

"Of course it's not nothing. Of course it's something. So what is it?"

"Well, he had two older twin brothers," said Jack, "who drowned in France when Michel was very small. That was when his mother—my sister—sent Michel here to the States. I would have thought Michel was too young to remember any of that."

The doctor started for the door. "Well, I told your wife that my guess is it will all come back to him if and when he uncovers the trauma. I'm not an expert. You may want to get some help."

"Is your guess the best you can do?" Jack said.

"I know he's not physically affected. That's what I *know*," the doctor said. "Except the stuttering."

"What's that?"

"Your wife said he used to stutter."

Jack recalled this with distaste.

"Well, I've been talking with him for an hour, and Mrs. Sarasan has talked with him several hours, since he arrived. And neither of us has heard him stutter once."

Michel stood on the balcony upstairs looking over the grounds in back of his uncle's house. Since the doctor left he had been alone, and now he put the patch back on. He knew, of course, that nothing was wrong with his eyes; but he didn't suppose anything was wrong with his mind either. When the patch covered one eye he saw people all over the lawn: a nude woman on a huge turtle riding into the swimming pool, and horses on the far knoll screaming past in a herd. When he changed the patch over to the other eye no one was to be seen except the nude woman lying at the bottom of the pool and the turtle by the side, and a bloodied white horse lying dead beneath a tree. He kept changing the patch back and forth, watching the progression or, as it were, the deterioration.

When he walked down the marble stairs into the living room he saw his uncle sitting in a huge stuffed lavender chair, puffing on his cigar and surveying him. Michel didn't remember his uncle's face at all, and it seemed different from eye to eye, features broadening and the light changing, shifting from mundane to something unpleasant—a face out of kilter. Watching his nephew move the patch back and forth, Jack said, "What are you doing?"

"Uncle Jack?" said Michel, and it sounded false to him. He couldn't imagine having ever called him Uncle Jack. He was correct, it turned out.

"I thought your eyes were all right," said Jack.

"There's nothing wrong with them," said Michel.

There was a time, thought Jack, when it would have taken Michel a full minute just to spit out that one sentence. The words would have bounced around in his mouth like a pinball. "Can't you remember anything?" said Jack.

"Twins."

Jack nodded.

"Adrien."

"Adrien who?"

"I don't know. Just the name Adrien." Michel didn't need to remember anything to realize his uncle didn't like him, but because he remembered nothing he couldn't realize why. The following days he sat in his room staring out the doors that opened onto the balcony, watching the shadows that loomed over the yard. He became depressed and then slightly desperate; and the panic he'd warded off that first morning in Paris finally found him. He had come to California because the passport said to; he had expected, he thought it wasn't unreasonable to expect, that he'd be welcomed here, that he'd find the things he expected a home to offer him—answers and the immediate, insistent belonging that went with a family. But he was still left faceless by the hostility he felt from his uncle. It would have been enraging had he been equipped for rage. Because he was not equipped for rage, he wore the patch; he realized the things it made him see weren't really there, but he also realized that those things had been there once, that this eyepatch provided him glimpses into his own past. So he kept the patch because, branded faceless by something that had happened to him before he woke in Paris, he decided he should be faceless on his own terms, not until he remembered who he was but until he *knew* who he was, whether he remembered anything or not. His aunt could feel his despair. She didn't feel jealous of his opportunity to start over again; she was considerate enough, even perceptive enough, to understand that for someone like Michel, it wasn't an escape but a sentence— to have to start over. And the only time she ever really stood up to her husband, in over twenty-five years of being married to him, after the mistresses and the indifferences and the loud tawdriness of the marriage (she wasn't a loud tawdry woman at all), was a week after Michel had returned, and she caught Jack scowling at the image of his nephew standing on the balcony at night, Michel's one eye staring at the black of the sky and the other eye staring at the black of the patch that covered it. She said, "He's your sister's son."

"He's not my son," said Jack.

"That's not his fault. You hate him because he's like your father."

He was stunned to hear her talk to him like this. "Fuck you," he sputtered, as though that could deny it. Watching her turn and walk from the room, he thought to himself he'd about had enough from all of them, Michel and the doctor and now his wife. He looked once more at the form of Michel on the balcony and then called out after her: If he starts screaming I'm going to throw him out. But he didn't suppose Michel would scream anymore. It first happened the day Michel arrived from France as a little boy, sent by his crazy mother from a small French village on the Atlantic coast. Jack hadn't seen his sister since they themselves were children, long before the twins; but he'd happily anticipated in her son Michel a protégé of his own, to be groomed by the studios as Jack himself had been. The boy, however, was odd right off, like his mother, from the moment he came walking down the ramp of the plane too shy to even look up; his aunt took him by the hand and tried talking to him, though Michel understood only French. Jack hadn't spoken French in a long time, so the conversation among the three of them was limited to broken attempts at the language and the boy's frantic, painfully stuttered replies. The boy said very little at all, in fact; but that first afternoon, after arriving home, they could hear the child talking to himself up in his room in a torrent of discussion among myriad voices. When he talked to himself he didn't stutter at all; in fact he didn't sound like the same person. The two adults looked at each other; each had grave concern about anyone who talked to himself, particularly a child, as if the stuttering weren't disturbing enough. That night they got a much worse shock. Jack was throwing a little party for a number of people whose favor was important to him; the party was held on the back lawn. It was a warm pleasant evening, and everything was going along smoothly when a sound came from the house. The small boy was standing on the balcony in full view, staring not at the lawn but the night, spewing a stream of verbal abuse at something or someone; Jack remembered enough French for his hair to stand on end. The guests just looked up at the boy in awe and consternation; and Jack scrambled inside, located the hired help and instructed one woman to shut the boy up by whatever means were necessary. She ran up the stairs, followed by Michel's aunt; and the guests watched as the child was plucked from the balcony and disappeared from view.

This happened several more times: in school, the shy, deferential student would be suddenly seized by a compulsion to scream whatever French obscenities he was capable of conjuring at the age of seven or eight. The teachers were always shaken by the transformation; the tirades were always in French, even when he was otherwise speaking English; the violence of what he was saying was clear in his tone and his eyes. Finally the aunt and uncle took him to a number of doctors. They talked with the boy but didn't seem to find any answers. Though the stuttering was always evident, Michel never screamed for them. Jack told the doctors the stuttering was making the boy crazy; the doctors could find no indication the boy was actually insane, but there was something deep inside tormenting him, and it was this making him stutter, not the other way around. Rather than inhibit the boy and his conversation by making him more conscious of the stammer, the doctors felt the child should be encouraged to talk, stutter, even scream, in order to release whatever had a hold on him. By now the idea of listening to Michel at all drove Jack wild.

An incident later in the school auditorium was the last straw. That was when Jack did what he should have done all along, which was come down on the boy hard. The boy didn't scream after that. Jack's wife worried that Michel became despondent, perhaps broken; but Jack knew that was a lot of nonsense. Nevertheless, it was true that as Michel grew up, their relationship decomposed, and along with it Jack's hopes of molding an heir— a situation marked by constant disagreements and fights, and culminating in the boardroom confrontation they still whispered about around the studio. In Jack's boardroom, before Jack's directors, Jack's nephew exploded in the stammering, word-wrenching fury of his childhood, lacerating his uncle with his own wild spastic tongue that somehow rendered what he said not ridiculous but all the more humiliating. Absolutely shaking then, face stricken, Michel burst out the door and was gone. Over the next few years Michel made a small student film that won a prize in a festival; and then disappeared.

So if Michel began screaming there on that balcony, or so much as stuttered to his uncle once, Jack would cast him from the house. Michel was left to pursue his own discoveries as best he could. If he had in fact lost who he once was, there was no percentage in it for Jack to help Michel regain that past. Michel began wandering the city in the afternoon, peering in windows he supposed would remind him of something, looking in every face to see if that face recognized him. He still wore the eyepatch, unwilling to discard it. He walked along Hollywood Boulevard and Sunset Boulevard, through Venice, where the carnival would seem likely to yield at least one sign of the past. He waited for someone to call to him, for someone to grab him by the shoulders and shake him. He spent days in Echo Park walking across bridges, looking for his name among the graffiti on the walls.

He started going to movies.

One day he passed a theater on Wilshire Boulevard near Lafayette Park, and he looked at the billboard and something stirred. He realized then that he'd been avoiding the movie marquees out of some aversion more eloquent than disinterest—now this billboard was the first familiar thing he had found since waking in Paris that morning. He paid his money and bought a ticket, and went into the theater and sat, alone in his row, waiting for the lights to fall and the screen to flicker for him, and he knew that it was this moment he had avoided—that if this moment were to mean nothing to him, he would have felt more utterly lost than ever, he would have felt isolated in a way the preceding days could not even imply. So it was a moment of wild exhilaration for him when, as the film began, he felt great excitement and passion. But something even more remarkable took place. The credits rolled by and he watched them carefully, something turning behind his eyes, and the story started, and he remembered it. He remembered all of it. He knew, not out of cleverness or precalculation, that the man Joseph Cotten came to Vienna to find was not dead at all, but alive; he remembered Orson Welles in the doorway with the cat at his feet, and in the ferris wheel musing over the insignificance of the people below him, and running through the sewers with the police at his heels. And he remembered in detail, painfully as though it was some recast shard of his own childhood, Alida Valli walking down the road with the leaves falling around her passing Joseph Cotten in cool disdain, too violated by his treachery to acknowledge he was waiting for her. This all came to Michel there in the theater, within the first few minutes of the picture.

He went to another movie that evening but the same thing did not happen, and it dropped him into a sort of depression—but not enough to wipe out what had happened that afternoon. He learned that not all movies would do this to him. But he always had an inkling for the ones that would: He would pass a poster or a title and something would stir, like it had that first time; and he followed his hunches. He was almost always right. He remembered everything, and most clearly he remembered the faces: Oskar Werner's stunned expression when his best friend and the woman they loved drove off the bridge into the water; the electrifying close-up of Falconetti in her trial, sentence and martyrdom; and most of all Chaplin, the look of humiliation and ecstasy, rose between his fingers, before the woman who'd gained her sight and lost her innocence; and like her, Michel wondered if, when he could see it all again, it would make him regret the squandered virginity of his instincts.

Where he had lain in the bedroom of his uncle's house feeling like a man without a persona, passive and unmoved and uninterested, now he was equipped for the thing he'd been so inadequate for: the rage, which he needed. Whether he remembered anything at all, he was still who he was; and now he felt the flashes of rebellion and intensity that had always come so easily to him, no matter how obstructed by the stuttering the expression of those things had been. Of course he didn't know he had ever stuttered, he didn't know those things had come so easily. He raged first of all at himself. It was his natural inclination to do this, and he didn't know that either.

One night he went into Venice to see some student films. He sat through the first four or five without feeling anything whatsoever. Only a minute or two into the sixth, he was overcome with nausea. He didn't know why he felt this way. There was not, apparently, anything on the screen that would cause this reaction. The film was about an old woman who lived in a house somewhere in France; this was clear from the subtitles. She wandered from room to room, up and down the stairs, and outside the window one could see the sea. The entire film was of the old woman talking about her feelings in this house. She pointed out the rooms where her children had lived: three sons, she noted. The two oldest, who were twins, died when they were small. They went swimming one night where there was no moon, and in the morning she found the bodies on the beach. She went into town and bought two coffins, and put the bodies in the coffins herself; she showed with her arms how she lifted them up. Then she asked the men from the town to help her bury them. The old woman explained all of this in a monotone. Now she went on, she said, "living in the window, waiting to die in the window"—there was no window in the room, however, when she said this. Toward the end of the film, Michel thought he was going to be sick; nothing he saw before had affected him this way, his innards were churning. He was in a cold sweat when the picture ended, and the credit came on, "A film by Michel Sarre," and he sat stunned in the seat still watching the white screen even as the lights went up, because though the last name was different, he instinctively understood that this was his film.

On his way to the house that night, after leaving the theater, the streetlights went out one by one. At the top of the hill, he looked out over the basin of the city to see, suddenly, the rest of the lights vanish in a single moment. It was as though the earth itself had disappeared. The lights of his uncle's house went as well. He walked up to the dark porch, and felt a pang of loneliness at the realization that movie screens from one end of town to the other were black at this moment; and when he opened the door, his aunt was there to greet him with a burning candle in her hand. She held it up to his face, looking to see if he was still wearing the patch; and as the patch did for him, the candle illuminated everything around her only a little at a time: in this sense his perspective was no longer unique, at least not at that moment. "The lights have all gone out," he said; and she smiled. "What's funny?" he said. "You used to have so much trouble saying your l's," she answered. He didn't know what she meant. "It's the second time this year," she went on. "They'll be going out a lot."

"A lot?"

"From here on out."

From here on out? He didn't understand it was the last twenty years of the twentieth century. She lit another candle for him and he went up the stairs to his room. He stood on the balcony and now noticed, over in the yard behind the next house, a small, half-completed bridge that stretched across one of the knolls and ended in midair. Other nights he would see the bridge progress until it completed its arc. Across the hills other people were building bridges; and later, as the lights went out more often, as more nights lapsed into blackness, more bridges were built. Someone was to explain to him that these bridges were built for following the passage of the moon at night, that as more nights passed lightless, the moon was the only light there was; and in that light Michel could see the moon-glistened figures on the moonbridges in their backyards, staring into the night, following the white globe's journey. This is why all the bridges were built the same direction, because everyone watched the same journey; and across the city people stepped in time to the slide of the moon across the sky.

One year after informing his wife that another woman was having his child, Jason returned to the apartment on Pauline Boulevard in San Francisco. He walked into the living room and both Lauren and Jules looked at him as though he'd left only ten minutes before to get a newspaper or carton of milk. Lauren vaguely remembered, to whatever extent she remembered anything about their last conversation, that he had said he would come back, and remembering that had eliminated any doubt even as it broke her heart. She was convinced by now, in the way she was convinced those moments Jules was being born, that heartbroken was a state she would know forever and with which she would therefore learn how to live. What Jason was not prepared for was the same wounded stoicism in the eyes of his son; he thought it unreasonable that he should be so judged by an infant fifteen months old. He avoided eye contact. He bought a blue truck in Oakland. He drove his family and possessions down the middle of California to Los Angeles, where Lauren found everything mysteriously familiar. They found the other Pauline Boulevard and took an apartment. Later Lauren lost Jason many times, and never reclaimed him; he reclaimed her when he chose to. She lost Jules only once, in his sleep, when he was nine, for reasons no doctor ever knew. He closed his eyes at the exact moment that, thousands of miles away, another opened his to no name and white memory.

The months that followed Jules' death were a period of mute devastation. It was near the end of this time that Jason first saw the new neighbor. On his way up the stairs one night, Jason peered through the opened door of the third-floor apartment, which was still empty but for a few boxes and the occupant himself, who stood alone looking around him. He wore a long blue coat and had his hands in his pockets. Jason watched from the stairs and moved on just as the other man turned to face him; it wasn't until much later that Lauren saw the neighbor from the window of their truck. He was walking up the steps to Pauline Boulevard as they were driving down the street to Hollywood. In the dark she saw only the back of his coat, and the eyepatch was a blur of black, like a bit of the night caught in his eye.

• • •

She wouldn't meet him for over two years. Even when Jason was gone, racing on the East Coast, or in Europe or Australia, and she was alone, she didn't turn to the neighbor for a favor; innocent companionship would have been in order. Jason was incapable of being jealous, he was certain there could never be anyone else for her. It wasn't in him to feel the measure of her depths, which had now become very deep. She watched from her window as though looking for a procession of funeral mannequins on a street with nowhere to go. She saw the cats in the corners of the boulevard, in the porticos and against the curbs, slinking out at dusk along the walls, appearing and vanishing. She had a cat of her own for a while. They knew each other's presences, they could feel each other from other rooms; the sun through the window always settled where the cat had been, and from her pillow Lauren could see the ephemeral silhouette. When the cat was pregnant and it came time to give birth, Lauren was awakened in the night, opened her eyes to see the cat's eyes glowing at her. Then, moving to the closet, Lauren grabbed a flashlight from the dresser. She followed the cat into the closet, and in the beam of the light watched four kittens emerge, each in its little sack; then she watched the mother eat the sacks and the offspring uncoil before her. Of course she thought of Jules then, and it was too much to bear.

One could not say Jason actually cheated. There wasn't the duplicity involved to call it that. He was open about it. I fuck other women, he said, it isn't that I love them. It's the only way I know how to know them; knowing them, he told her, only makes me love you more. She answered, Well it doesn't make me love you more. It makes me love you less. He understood that it hurt her, but he must not have understood how much it hurt, or else he didn't care. It never occurred to him that he could lose her; he knew she was still madly in love with him, twelve years later.

She knew it was not emotionless relationships he had. Perhaps they did not involve his emotions, but they involved the emotions of the other women. These women called and begged to speak with him when Lauren answered the phone. They wrote him letters that Lauren found and read. Jason made no effort to hide them; it wasn't malice on his part, but the cruelty of indifference, which was worse than malice, because it didn't have malice's passion. It went on for years; he had sex with too many of them to count, and he had affairs that lasted months with five or six. He told her to go out with other men. She slept with two. She loved none. She saw no more of them.

When the kittens had grown a bit, the mother took them away. Lauren came to the closet to find them gone. One of the windows was open, where they had escaped. Lauren had assumed escape was not an issue, she had assumed the cats weren't prisoners. She watched sadly from her room, hoping for a glimpse of them in the street. The day after they left, Jason came back from northern California where he'd been racing. I used to be able to call all the cats when I was in Kansas, she told him. Yes, he said, but that was when you were young, long ago.

It didn't take long to find out about Jason's newest affair; she called that night. Jason asked Lauren to tell the woman he was out. On the third call the woman began crying. It didn't seem to matter to either Jason or the woman that the intermediary of this call was Jason's wife. Or if it occurred to the woman, she didn't care; she was that desperate; Lauren realized the woman assumed Lauren had already lost him. Lauren wasn't certain the woman was wrong.

She packed. She had done this before, but this time she was serious. She was leaving, she simply didn't love him anymore. Jason came into the bedroom and watched her put the clothes in the suitcase. He sat down on the bed and stared at the blouses, the nylons, the underwear. I'm leaving you, she said; I simply don't love you anymore. I'm serious this time. He said, You're not serious. He made her sit down while he talked to her. He put his hand on her arm. You love me, he said. You know you love me, and that you belong here. What is this bullshit, packing? We're supposed to be with each other, and it's always been that way. That other woman, I don't love her, he said. It's fucking, that's all.

She loves you, she said.

She doesn't know what she feels, he said. She thinks she loves me.

After a moment Lauren began to shake, pushing the palms of her hands into her eyes to stop it; she cried on through the night, and let him hold her. He kicked the suitcase onto the floor and took off her clothes. He had her; but whereas before, always before, she had rested on his chest never wanting to leave him or lose him, this time she blinked at the walls, listened to him sleep, and realized she had come very close to doing it.

He told her the next morning he was leaving again, for Texas this time. Another race.

Another dusk, and from the window she saw one of the kittens in the street, and ran down the stairs to the front door and stood in the long shadow of the block that touched her feet. In the setting sun the windows of the street gleamed like gold teeth, and first in a low din, ascending to something like sirens, she heard all the cats the way she used to in the fields. She opened her mouth to call them like she used to; she was so alone she couldn't stand it. She opened her mouth again, closed it again. She said nothing, looking up at all the cats watching her. She could see their eyes glimmering between the gold teeth of the buildings; the way they watched her she knew she didn't belong. One flash after another struck her. She stood in the light looking at all the cats far from her. She was terrified that she would call them and none of them would answer. After a while the cats turned from their posts and disappeared, leaving her there in the doorway.

There were still times she heard Jules' stuttering. Alone in bed at night it would wake her, and she always forgot, just for a moment, that he'd been dead two years. Then when she remembered, she would assume it was a dream. Then, after lying there several minutes and the stuttering didn't stop, she decided it was her conscience. It was to remind her it was her fault, which she had always known anyway, since the first time he talked. It had taken so long; months and months he had remained mute, passive. When he did speak, it was G-G-G-Goodbye. He wasn't going anywhere, but he was bidding her farewell anyway; he was planning to leave from the first.

Somehow, she associated it with the lost night. The lost night was the one in San Francisco when she walked out of the apartment, having just talked to Jason on the telephone, leaving the baby on the bed alone. The next thing she knew she was staring at the bay and it was afternoon, the sun shining and the water blue, and she reached in her pocket and found a used round-trip plane ticket to Los Angeles. The lost night was the first thing she thought of when Jules said G-G-G-Goodbye. When he died in his sleep—like belated crib death, one doctor said—Lauren realized it was the death he was supposed to die that night when she left him on the bed and went wherever she went. Nothing ever shook her from this conviction, and she could never tell it to Jason. So then she was alone without Jules, and without Jason most of the time, and without the cats, meaning without her childhood—all of this finally leaving her without the desire to be alive. This desire was so lacking in her that she was afraid to reach down inside herself for one passionate connection, because she was sure that passion would be just the thing by which she'd bring everything to a close; she didn't have even the passion for dying. She spent long hours smoking dope, and by seven at night when the fog came in from the sea she'd get up from the bed to open the window; and lying back on the bed she closed her eyes, perhaps lost consciousness, perhaps not—she didn't know how long it had been before she opened her eyes and saw, every night, the gray cloud hovering over in the light from the desk lamp, blooming like an ash rose and enfolding her. More marijuana; more fog; more guilt: and the shifting hejira into the longest lost night of all—that was where she was going. The wet heavy deadness was interrupted only by the floor, which seemed to hum; with everything wilting and cold, the floor swam beneath her like a smoking pond when all else was darkest. She often stared at the ceiling and the walls and the way the entire room seemed illuminated by the floor, though she knew there was no real light at all. It was something from beneath the floor, and then she remembered the neighbor lived down there.

Jason became more interested in the neighbor when he began going to clubs. Sometimes he took Lauren along; often he went out alone, his evenings always ending with somebody else. Lauren wearied of clinging to him simply to keep him faithful. She preferred just dying a bit. "You won't believe this," Jason said to her early one morning, having just gotten home.

She stared up at him in the dark, from far down in the center of the ash rose.

"The guy downstairs, with the eyepatch."

She did not remember an eyepatch.

"He runs the Blue Isosceles." She nodded. "I see him there all the time, up on the stairs behind the stage. I saw him tonight and said, You show up here a lot, and he said I'm the manager."

They both waited for him to say it.

"Well," he finally said, "we ought to go down and meet him sometime." He said it with the most barely discernible trace of anxiety in his voice. Lauren was mystified. She'd never heard anxiety in Jason's voice. But she felt something in her stomach when he said it. His face was far up there, beyond the petals. She nodded, and the flower closed.

The next morning she wasn't certain she'd heard it at all. And yet Jason mentioned it again, and though the anxiety was still there, he seemed to press it, as though it was something he wanted over with. She resisted, passively. Some weeks went by.

Jason took her to the Blue Isosceles one night, after months of leaving her alone in her room. Outside the club along the Sunset Strip were kids wearing leather and steel. Cop cars flashed in the street. The clanking of metal was everywhere, and in the dark of the club, cables lay like snakes. Girls with bare breasts in leather vests passed back and forth with trays of glasses, and in the unlit halls Lauren could see men covering their faces when someone lit a match. The smell of tequila and gasoline was in the air. The band onstage was fronted by a female lead singer who stared out at the audience with a deadness in her eyes, sweating beads of petrol; her voice, harmonically discordant, sounded full and extravagant in the heat, as though the song itself was wet and bloated. Fumes rose visibly from the stage. With every match struck, the club seemed on the verge of ignition. At one point Jason said to her, "There," and pointed to the stairs behind the stage.

The man stood on the balcony overlooking the club with his arms folded, tapping a high-heeled black shoe not to the music at all. He brushed the night-black hair from his left eye sometimes. Over his right eye he wore a black patch. Tell me about the owner, Jason said to the waitress. The waitress looked up at the man on the balcony. He isn't the owner, she said. He's the manager. You want to talk to the owner? No, said Jason, I was wondering about the manager. The waitress said, Do you want a drink? I don't know anything about the manager. No one knows anything about the manager. Jason said, How long's he been manager? The waitress said, Two years.

I'll have a beer, Jason said.

When she first saw him, she looked away, though she had no idea why. Now she watched him gaze over the crowd as though looking for someone he didn't really expect to find. She watched a woman alongside him hand him a drink, and then he leaned against the rail of the stairs gazing out into nowhere again, saying nothing. He was watching the lights sweep across the room and the people's heads; and as they swept back across him, his own head seemed momentarily afire: around him the conversation was rendered senseless, and everyone rendered a stranger.

Nothing appeared of interest to him. Not the people in the crowd hurling themselves into each other, nor the bouncers hurling them in turn out the back door. Nothing seemed to exhilarate or appall him, and the fact that, for a moment, all of these people became anonymous somehow made him less anonymous, standing there untouched by it and unimpressed. The light from above kept sweeping across the room, and it was in those moments when the light touched him that she really saw him, in a series of glances—but they were moments that negated the moments that preceded them and, in a way that was absolute and which she couldn't quite bring herself to challenge, negated all the moments before them. Suddenly she found herself stripped of every lost night she could remember. For a moment she thought perhaps he saw her; the light moved and he went dark, and she found herself caught there, waiting for the light to find him again. When it did, his face seemed only a haze, profile endlessly tangled. The light continued back and forth, and Lauren continued staring, waiting—and she saw him again and lost him again until, after this had happened three or four times, he was a sheer glow that she could have still seen had she shut her eyes, as though she had been staring at a hovering moon there in the tumultuous club. Then the light seemed to fade, and as he sank into dark for what she thought might be the last time, he looked straight at her, and she could see his one exposed eye glisten just as the sight of his face vanished.

She knew him.

She lay there in bed that night trying to place him, as Jason slept next to her. She went back over and over all the places from which she might have known him, charting coordinates across her heart for the telltale latitude or longitude that would reveal the secret to her. She thought maybe she met him with Jason, since Jason seemed interested in knowing more about him; but then she remembered Jason's mystification. This made her all the more curious and anxious, as though there was something about the neighbor Jason knew but Lauren did not; but this was countered by Jason's own apparent anxiety. No one knows anything about him, the waitress said.

She got up and went to the window, watching the street that ran before her; against the night sky the rise of the wind was spinning a row of weather vanes, and in a crossfire of gusts each vane swirled a new direction. She listened to the traffic on Sunset Boulevard at the bottom of the hill, and then she heard steps below her, a door opening and closing. Above the row of lights from the windows was a mad blur so frenzied the vanes seemed to rise from the rooftops in flight; she was sure they were cats with wings.

She heard the door of the apartment below open and close again.

Then she listened to the steps on the stairs, and heard them grow louder and louder. She found herself breathing quickly, saying to herself, Who are you? when the final word caught between her lips, at the knock on the door.

He knocked again. Jason stirred in the bed. "Jason," she said. A third knock. "Jason."

Jason sat up in bed, still more asleep than awake. He blinked at her stupidly. "What?"

"Somebody's knocking."

Jason sat listening. "I don't hear it," he finally said.

"Somebody knocked several times."

He turned the sheets aside and moved his legs to the floor. He went out into the other room. She heard the door open, and the exchange of voices that followed. A moment later Jason came back. "The guy downstairs," he said. "Do we have any spare fuses?"

"I don't remember," she said. "In the kitchen, perhaps. The drawer by the sink." She said, "What is it?"

"He needs a fuse," he said. "Why don't you come out?"

"Why?"

"Because it may take me a while to find the fuse. Come out and talk to him."

"Like this?"

He stared at her. "Put a robe on," he said. He went into the kitchen. She sat a moment and then put a robe on, and left the bedroom.

The neighbor was standing in the living room. He was wearing a long blue coat that looked very old. Like before, she had to look away at first. He looked up when she walked in, and watched her expectantly; she nodded and smiled casually. "No light?" she said. The one uncovered eye stared at her intently; she was still tying the robe around her waist. "What's that?" he said.

"The lights in your apartment."

He said, "At first I thought it was another blackout. It isn't a bulb, so I'm assuming it's a fuse." He added, "The clocks have all stopped."

There had always been an element of beauty in the things to which she was attracted; but he was not beautiful. His face was long and there was a hooded, almost dazed look to his eyes, or at least to the one exposed. "I'm sorry," he finally said, after a pause. "I didn't catch—"

"Lauren," she said. "You've met Jason, haven't you?"

"Yes." He looked around, almost sullenly.

She waited, and finally gave up. "You're—"

"Adrien," he said abruptly, as though hoping she wouldn't ask. She nodded, a little nonplussed, and said nothing. He breathed deeply. "Uh—" he started. He stopped and she looked back up at him. He watched her very closely, and she wasn't sure if she felt offended by it. He said, never moving his gaze, "Were you ever in Paris?"

"No."

He nodded, and now looked off a bit. He seemed a little perplexed.

"Are you French?" He didn't answer. "Adrien's a French name, I guess," she said.

He looked back, rather startled. "Adrien?" She blinked at him. "Why do you call me Adrien?" he asked excitedly.

This is a very strange conversation, she thought. "You just said your name is Adrien."

He laughed, and now she definitely felt offended. "No," he said. "My name isn't Adrien. I don't know why I said that. I said that? Uh," he shrugged, smiling. "It's Michel, actually." He nodded.

"Michel." She nodded back. "You're sure."

"Not at all," he said. "Not at all sure."

"Well, can I call you either one then?"

"That would be fine."

"Can I ask you something?"

"Yeah."

"Which eye is it that bothers you? Or is it one when you're Adrien and the other when you're Michel?"

He smiled. Jason was still knocking around in the kitchen, looking for a fuse. "That's it exactly," Michel said. He looked very impressed, for the first time that night. He looked down at his feet and then back at her when he said, "You know, yours is the first face I've seen in two years that looks exactly the same from either eye."

Jason came out with the fuse. "Is that good or bad?" said Lauren.

"Good," said Michel.

"Here's the fuse," said Jason.

"Thanks," said Michel. "Sorry if I woke you."

"Need a flashlight?"

"No. I have one."

"We were at the club tonight."

"I know," Michel said. He opened the door. "I owe you a fuse."

She stood there awhile looking at the door. Jason went back to bed. She listened to the door downstairs open and close again, and continued standing there until the sounds below waned. She stood there a few minutes when Jason's voice came from the bedroom. "Funny," she heard him say. "Guy couldn't wait until morning to borrow a fuse, when all he was probably going to do was go to sleep anyway." She sat in the bedroom awhile longer, wondering. In the hush of the night an answer came to her later, and she couldn't believe it.

Then, the first of the sandstorms came. She watched it from her window—a mild one, compared to the ones that would blow through the city later. It left a fine silt on the buildings, and took some of the paint off the cars. All the windows were left like round portholes, the sand filling the corners; and there was the slight rattle of sand on the roof. Sand fell with the opening and closing of doors, and in the dark people wore sunglasses to keep the sand out of their eyes. Since their apartment, and the window she watched from, faced the west toward the ocean, she could never see the storms approaching, coming from the deserts in the southeast as they did; but people began watching for them from their moonbridges in the day, sighting the black cloud far away on the edge of the Santa Ana Freeway, and from the bridges at night as the storms cast a gauze across the moon itself. The second and third storms came two weeks after the first, and they were worse. There were four blackouts in those two weeks; they had never before been so frequent. With the fourth storm one afternoon, she saw from her window the clock stop, the table light die, and caught the motion of cats scurrying; then the sky went brown, and the windows shook as if they would shatter. It was like that, with her back to the east—no warning; the storm suddenly upon her; it was terrifying like that.

Jason left again, and this time they had a terrible fight on the eve of his departure. He finally admitted to Lauren that there was no race this time, that he was going to see his son. You care more, she said, about that son than you ever cared about our son. It's the only son I have, he said; and she answered, I suppose you blame me for that. He walked out wordlessly.

Those weeks alone she thought about Michel. She listened to him come and go downstairs, and watched from the window when he walked down the street in his long blue coat. Alone, with nowhere to go, and no one with her, she went over and over the past in her mind, looking for his face in the places she had been, among the hours that were hers. She could never find him. When his door opened and closed below, she listened for his steps on the stairs, wondering if he might come talk to her. Once, twice, she thought she heard him approaching; but he never did, leaving only the trace of his form in the street below, gliding across the sand. And when Jason came back, and they muttered their ritual greetings to each other (the previous conflict never having been resolved), the first question he asked of her, the first one that was not ritual but of which he seemed to care about an answer, was of Michel, and whether she had seen him.

She was vaguely astonished. "No," she said. "Why would I see him?"

"He lives right below us," said Jason.

"He's lived right below us for two years," she said. "Why would I see him now?"

He shrugged. He seemed noticcably relieved. "I was just asking," he said. "I thought you might go down to the Isosceles with him, or something."

"Why would I do that?"

"I don't know!" He abruptly went back to unpacking. She had never seen him like this before.

"Do we know him from somewhere?" she said.

"I don't think so."

She just nodded.

That she somehow felt it important to talk to Michel again did not, in her own mind, in the rationale she presented to herself, imply more; so she couldn't explain why she felt as she did when Jason told her Michel had invited them to the Blue Isosceles as his guests. All day she prepared for it. She took her red velvet jacket and hung it in the shower, turning on the hot water so the steam would make the fabric glisten; for an hour the bathroom billowed, until the ceiling dripped and the walls ran with sweat. She took a bath exactly seven hours before they were to leave, for she had calculated her skin looked best not immediately after bathing but later, when it regained its glow, and her hair could dry in curls. All afternoon she took care not to mar herself; she stayed away from the window when the sun sank westward, so the glass would not make her perspire, and it was the sheerest coincidence that the one time she did go near the window she looked down into the street to see him standing there shaking a rug. He turned and looked up, and she backed away from the window quickly—surely soon enough not to be seen. She stared at clocks. She pressed her ear to them sometimes to make sure they hadn't stopped; she clicked on lights sometimes to make sure the power hadn't failed. She tried to read. She waited until her hair was dry to nap, and then propped herself up against the pillows so her curls would not be flat when she awoke. She couldn't sleep anyway. Some moments, only a few, she felt calm enough to realize that, for the first time since Jules had died, she felt she was alive. She didn't want to understand it.

At seven she put on lipstick. She hadn't worn it in years. At a quarter past seven she took off the lipstick and put on a different color. At seven-thirty she took off that lipstick and resolved to wear none. At seven-thirty-five she resolved to wear the lipstick after all.

She wondered if Jason noticed how she had doused herself in perfume. She panicked, thinking that perfume was too much. She considered bathing again. But then the hair would be undone. Then she put on more perfume. She held her jacket up to the light to see that it still glistened.

When they left, Jason watched her.

They didn't talk on the way to the club. She found herself forgetting Jason altogether. Something in her stomach tightened at the box office, when Jason gave the girl behind the glass his name. The girl looked on the list. She couldn't find his name, and something shot through Lauren. The girl found the name, and Lauren exhaled. There was even a complimentary tab, for drinks; they were led to a special table upstairs, overlooking the

dance floor below. The waitress came and took their order. Lauren
tried to sound casual when she looked across the table to Jason
and said, "Is Michel joining us?"

The waitress said, "The manager never drinks with guests."

Lauren sat through the first band hearing nothing. There was
the usual commotion on the floor below, the same smell of
gasoline. The waitress doesn't know, Lauren told herself. We're
Michel's guests. The set ended after forty minutes. The waitress
came again, and Jason ordered two more drinks. Lauren didn't
care if Jason saw her looking around the room. Jason seemed
calm and unperturbed, the way he usually did, as though nothing
could threaten him at all.

She was staring off into space when she suddenly turned and
there he was.

Michel and Jason talked. Michel signaled the waitress and
ordered a drink. "A landmark," the waitress said to Lauren. Jason
said he'd have another beer. Michel looked at Lauren for the
first time. "No, thank you," said Lauren, holding her glass. Michel
shrugged. The waitress left.

Jason went to the toilet. Michel and Lauren sat at the table,
neither saying anything. Lauren was afraid to look up, certain
he was staring at her; but when she did, she saw him just rubbing
his finger along his lip, looking at the people at the bar, gazing
past the rail to the stage. The patch was on the eye closest to
her, and it was clear he didn't realize she was there at all, he
was thoroughly indifferent to her. She became very aware of all
the perfume. She became aware of the slight red of the lipstick
on the rim of her glass, and she just watched it. Jason returned.

The second band came on. Somewhere into the second song,
Michel pushed back his chair, got up, made a casual farewell
gesture with his hand, and walked away. She stared after him.
She was sure he would come back. She was sure he had something
to say to her. He disappeared, and then near the end of the band's
encore, some thirty minutes later, she watched him reappear.
She hadn't moved her gaze at all. He was wearing the long blue
coat, and talking to a waitress, then talking to someone behind
the bar. He moved through the crowd, which was calling for
another encore. He spoke to someone at the door. He pointed

to the stage, pointed to the stairs. He was right below her, as he had been when he shook the rug beneath her window. He never looked up. Then he was gone.

After the show Jason took her to a bar. She had a kahlua and cream. He talked to her the entire time, sometimes watching the women who passed their table. She interrupted him at one point. "I want to go home," she said.

"Have another—"

"I want to go home."

In stately devastation she watched out the truck window on the way home, peeling with her front tooth the gloss on her lips. The night was pitch black, and nothing was illuminated but for what she believed to be a winged cat gliding over the buildings, though it could easily have been a hang glider who drifted in from the beach. As their truck ascended the hill to the steps that led up to Pauline Boulevard, there were frozen in the gutters people wearing heavy overcoats to protect themselves from the sand; only their heads pivoted slowly. The windshield of the truck was stained with salt. There was no moon and a low fog. They walked up the steps and the street was totally dark. "I thought we left on a light," said Jason, staring at their window. From the top of the steps overlooking the city could be seen a long line of headlights moving toward its destination very slowly—a procession in a city black and shrouded. Unlocking the outside door at the bottom of the building, Jason stepped in and touched the hall light switch. The hall remained dark. "Shit," said Jason. "Another blackout." Lauren leaned against the wall, silently staring before him. "What's the matter with you?" said Jason.

She shook her head.

"I'm going back to the truck to get the flashlight."

She nodded.

"Wait here," he said.

"I'll go on up."

"Wait until I get a light before you go up the stairs."

"I'll go on up," she said, pulling her arm from his hand. She could tell he was relieved that she was dead again. She moved up the stairs slowly, never holding the rail, her arms still folded. Everything about her that had lunged through the day stopped now. She didn't even have it in her to feel foolish or resentful. She was vaguely grateful for the dark. She was somewhat amazed that she felt like crying; it had been a long time since she'd done that. Not since Jules.

She got to the second level, and then moved onto the third. At the third she stepped around, onto the stairs to climb to the fourth and last, when some part of the night seemed less lost than the rest. It seemed to throb at the end of the corridor, a blackness not so muted but deeper than the blackness around it, as though it were a part of the night that had absorbed more light and was therefore exiled by the rest of the darkness around it, cast into something more forbidden. She stood on the stairs and looked at it, listening, and in a blackness that would not have allowed her the sight of her own hand inches from her eyes, she saw the exile move.

She said nothing. She didn't call to it. Outside the window some high-pitched tone came smuggled by the wind, and she couldn't decide if it was an animal or a squeal of brakes in the street. She listened for the sound of Jason returning, and she thought about the way she felt the first time she saw Michel. She felt now, there on the stairs, invulnerable to mundane clocks and the pending reflow of power that would set them humming again. The exile moved again, to some place close to her, and then its cessation stunned the room; she stood with nothing left to survey, nothing to touch, nothing outside to hear; and everything was exposed in the dark. She stood motionless, barely breathing, her toes on the edge of the stairs, with its surrendered steps and destination in nihilistic disarray, saying to herself, Do something, though she never wanted to leave here. She commanded herself up the stairs and disobeyed repeatedly; she never expected anything of him. That would have been assuming too much. He could not know that she'd lost Jason, since she didn't admit that to herself; he could not know she'd lost the ring on her finger, since she had taken it off herself; he could not have predicted the decisions she'd made, since she hadn't yet made them. She could not have thought that he would sense her own passages through halls of limbo, since she hadn't chosen the doors; rather, he would have to be attuned to the sort of sadness that no man she'd ever known had ever understood: certainly not Jason. She could not, in short, know he wasn't like Jason; and he, she assumed, could not know what Jason was like, and what therefore the marriage had done to her. Neither of them should have known these things except that now there was nothing left to survey, or touch, or hear outside, nothing to feel but the things that neither could know of the other; and therefore they felt everything. Not the details or the definitive traumas but the resulting carnage by which each had been ravaged. And when the sound of Jason's steps came up the street, she felt on her face one tear; and then her husband's footsteps slammed through the dark outside. She raised her fingers before her and felt a face inches before her eyes, and it was as though a line draped between them was yanked taut. There was the sound of Jason's voice; and she moved her fingers across the face lightly, till their tips touched the fabric over one eye, and if she thought to mutter anything at all he caught the sound of it in his mouth. When he would not break from the kiss and his face wouldn't leave hers, she took the palms of her hands from his bare chest and slid them to his bare shoulders, around his back, until she pulled him to her more. His fingers were in her hair. "Lauren," came Jason's voice from downstairs. A hand caressed her chin, and she turned her head slightly and bit the hand hard. It didn't move from her face. She looked everywhere in the dark for him, and she knew he was looking too. Both of them had known, the moment before he touched her, what it would be like, how it would feel. Both of them knew, the moment he kissed her, that in another time and place, they had done it before.

"Where do I know you from?" she heard him whisper.

"I don't know."

"But we've met before," she heard him say.

"Yes, we have."

"Two years I've never seen a living face that was anything but strange," she heard him say. "Then I saw yours, and I knew it. Like the faces I know in the movies."

"Lauren," came Jason's voice, and the hand moved from her face. She reached out to hold it. "Lauren!"

"Yes." The beam of Jason's flashlight slashed the staircase. Light flooded the hallway, and the city.

"Wouldn't you know it?" he said from the stairs. "No sooner get the flashlight and the power comes back." She stood on the same steps, looking at the corridor before her. It was empty. The neighbor's door was closed.

Jason's head appeared on the stairs. He looked at her. "Did you lose count?" he said. "We're another flight up."

She looked at the door, and nodded.

"Afraid of the dark?" he said.

"Afraid of the dark," she said.

She woke in the middle of the night wondering if it had happened. She lay on her side and stared at Jason's back. She listened for sounds from below. She tossed and turned and got up and went to the window like always, searching for an answer, like always. She wondered about the cats, and then went into the bedroom, looking in the mirror. Everything hummed; if it was a dream, no waking moment had ever touched it. Something leapt inside her when she saw, in the mirror, in her hair, something caught that had never been there. It came easily between her fingers, unattached: a short, thin strand, very dark, from a patch of black fabric.

Then she was in pain. It began with odd twinges that escalated to a long ripping throughout her womb; she felt it the rest of that evening. She ran to the toilet, hideously sick, blood and liquor streaming into the bowl beneath her.

The next day she thought of him. And the rest of the week, wondering when she would see him again. She thought of calling him at the club but did not. Then Jason left again, this time for the East Coast, from where he was to go on to Europe, and for once it seemed he departed reluctantly. On the morning after he was gone she knew she would go to Michel. There was a blackout. It was hot that day, and when the power came back on across the city she went through the refrigerator discarding spoiled food. She ignored the pain but was sick again that afternoon.

That night she lay in bed clutching her belly. She got up a half dozen times to go to the toilet. The last time she lay on the bathroom floor with her head against the porcelain seat, falling asleep and waking, looking at the electric heater with its grill and doubled coils. She had a dream about the coils, winding up her uterus; and she woke dreaming that the coils were skewering her insides.

She rose from the bathroom floor in terror. She went to the closet and pulled from the hanger a white cotton summer dress, and got it over her head. She thought about calling him. She said to herself, He won't want to deal with this, he'll hate me for imposing it on him. She had dialed the phone when it slipped from her hand and she slipped from the chair to the carpet.

That night he got off the bus one stop early, and walked. He cut up from Sunset and past the apartments, entering Pauline Boulevard from another direction, and walking the length of the street to his building at the other end. There was a light in her window. Though it was quite late, and there weren't many lights in the windows along the streets, there did come from each residence a glow from the television set. Ever since the blackouts started, the television stations had taken to showing old films of the first moonwalk. Now the stations ran the films over and over all the time, and people simply left their televisions on, since it took more power to turn them off. In window after window, as Michel walked home, he saw men and women holding their sleeping babies, staring at their living room screens without emotion, without recollection, as the moonwalk flickered on into the night.

Later in bed he heard a sandstorm blow in from the deserts, and the building swayed in the silt like a shipwrecked vessel hoisted onto its keel in the mud sea bottom. The sheen of dust scraped the barnacles on the sides. He had seen Jason leave the morning before and now his body didn't let him sleep. He tossed and turned and went to the window to see if the light of her apartment shone on the sand below. It was finally the steady muted scraping outside that made him drift off.

He awoke at five-thirty in the morning when it was still dark, and went to see if her light was still on the sand. When he saw that it was, he listened for something upstairs—a sound to let him know she was waiting for him, as though the hush of the dust was the sound of her thighs rustling together. He glared at the ceiling with his one free eye, as though he could drill a hole through her floor.

He lay in bed another hour.

When he rose, he pulled on his pants, opened his door, climbed the stairs and didn't knock. He merely turned the doorknob and stepped in. He closed the door behind him. He checked the patch and instinctively changed eyes, only to change it back—something he rarely did. He undid his clothes and dropped them to the floor. Lauren, he called.

She heard his voice somewhere just below her womb. She couldn't see anything but a fleshy gray, and she struggled to bring to mind a face to go with the voice. The voice was far away, of course. It was faint, tiny and drifted up to her in petals, like it was peeling off the walls of the tubes below her stomach. Her tubes and passages were lined with this voice, and because the petals were somewhat opaque, she couldn't be sure if what she saw was their color or the color of the walls behind them.

There were other sounds, a wreath of noises encircling the voice that came up to her—people chattering and something like the tapping of metal fingers, all of it a vague echo. She kept looking for a face, as though she thought the petals might fall in a pattern and form a visage she remembered from somewhere else. She sometimes thought she recognized the voice, but in the midst of the other sounds she wondered if she was imagining it. She could feel the voice in her tubes and her uterus, and the way it threaded up through her belly. It became closer if not louder, never particularly like words to her. It was a rolling syllable, somersaulting up to her in lopsided, unending pirouettes. It was when it became more distinct that she knew it was a stammer, a single letter sustained: a very long L. LLLLLLLLLLL-LLLLL. In her mind she finished the effort. L-L-Love, l-l-life, l-l-lonely, l-l-light, l-l-luminance, l-l-lascivious, l-l-lady of the l-l-lake, l-l-lately, l-l-lastly, l-l-long long ago.

L-L-L-L-L-L-L-Lauren.

She knew it was that all along, really. Lying there, wherever she was, she hadn't fooled herself. She was waiting to decide how she felt about it, whether the idea that this voice was trying to call her name frightened her, filled her with remorse or comforted her. She didn't feel threatened by it, but rather by the loss of what to answer to it.

It seemed ridiculous to her that he would be back inside her. Was he trying again? Was he giving her a second chance? She resented a second chance, because it confirmed the guilt she always believed anyway, and mainly because she wasn't confident she would do better the second time. And yet this seemed petty to her; she suspected herself of ingratitude; she recognized this was a rare offer of redemption. Wherever he was in her, she couldn't understand why he was hurting her this much, since she hadn't known he was there; it wasn't time for this kind of pain. She realized then he was trapped. The other noises seemed to go away.

LLLLLLLLLLLLLLLLLLLLLLLLLLLLLLL. Only more desperately now.

Lauren. She looked up, and it wasn't Jules after all. The voice was definitely blue. When he wore the patch over his left eye, she couldn't remember if he was Michel or Adrien.

Then she was gone again, and the petals scattered, and there was nothing to hear, and no voice to see.

•   •   •

She was in the hospital when she awoke, a window by her head overlooking a parking lot. On the wallpaper were long green vines and small yellow blossoms. The bed faced an open door. A nurse appeared and looked at her. "Are you with us?" she said.

"I think so," said Lauren.

The nurse left. From the hall Lauren could hear her. "She's awake, Doctor." There was an exchange. The doctor came in with the nurse, and Lauren was pleased that he was handsome like a soap-opera doctor. "You're awake," said the doctor. Lauren nodded.

"Am I O.K.?" she said.

"Tubular pregnancy. A bit longer and it would have ruptured." He raised the bed. "More?" Lauren said it was fine. The doctor said calmly, "It was very close."

"How did I get here?"

"Someone brought you."

"Someone?"

"Without an eye."

She almost said, Oh that phony. There's nothing wrong with his eye. Instead she said, "Close?"

"Maybe minutes."

She was dazed enough she still didn't get it for a while, until he left. Immodestly she pulled up her gown and looked at the scar above where her hair had been shaved. It had little staples in it, and she ran her fingers along them gently; it looked like a zipper. Actually, it amused her. She went to sleep and dreamed of open-heart surgery, and zippers beneath each breast.

There was some more pain, in the moments before she regained consciousness; and then, in the sun that lit her inner lids, his form took shape before her—very blue, like the petals, deepening to black at the top of him. When she saw him there, she knew that wherever and whenever she had seen him before she had seen him much like this, standing at the foot of her bed, perhaps in a long blue coat like that one. When she saw him there, she knew what she'd felt all along. "My one-eyed prince," she said sarcastically. "My cyclops rescuer." He watched her intently. She closed her eyes again for a moment and opened them, and looked over the side of the bed. "I'm really in a hospital."

He nodded, turning his head from wall to wall. "This is it."

"Where was I?"

"Where were you?"

"Was I in my apartment?"

"With the phone off the hook."

She waited for him to sit on the bed. She asked, "Are you going to kiss me?"

"Yeah, I am." He put his arm on the metal of the bed, and watched her someplace above her brow. She never closed her eyes as he lowered his face to hers. She reached up and put the palm of her hand on his head, and wondered if he was going to say something; his mouth moved as though something was on his lips, and he seemed to barely bite the lower one. I went crazy, he said. He took her in his hands and turned his mouth to hers, like on the stairs; when he did it again she gasped a bit, and thought of zippers. Without thinking she felt her breasts. Why? she said.

"Because I thought you were dead."

"So?"

He combed back her hair with his fingers.

"Did you put the phone back?" she said after a minute.

The one eye opened to her lazily, and he let nothing escape. "So I would not have liked it," he said, finally.

"Why?"

He shook his head. "Yes," he answered, almost grimly, "I put the phone back."

"I was calling you," she said, somewhat shocked because she hadn't planned to say so.

"I came for you."

"Would you have made love to me?"

"Yes."

"Would you have taken me if I resisted?"

"Yes."

"Would you have taken me if I resisted completely? If I fought back ferociously?"

"You would not have."

She shook her head. "No. I would not have."

"And would you have liked it?"

"Yes."

"I mean dying."

"What?"

"Would it have meant nothing to you if you were there on the floor dead?"

"I've felt dead a long time."

"Because of him?"

"Partly. Mostly."

He nodded.

"Close call, the doctor said."

He nodded.

"Who are you, Adrien? Michel."

He shrugged.

"Why did you ask if I was ever in Paris? Were you in Paris?"

"Yes."

"How long?"

He shifted on the bed.

"Jason has gone to Europe. Not Paris."

He nodded.

"To race."

"Is he a race car driver?"

"He races bicycles. Almost went to the Olympics in..." She thought. "Seventy-two? Munich."

"I don't think I was in Munich."

"I may meet him in Italy in a few months."

"I think I was there."

"You think?"

"France, Spain, Italy, Switzerland, Belgium." He stopped a moment, remembering his passport. "The Netherlands. England. I think."

"Jason would have won a silver medal. He filed the wrong papers on one of the preliminary meets, and was disqualified."

He said nothing.

"Does it bother you to hear about him?"

"Yes."

"He's my husband," she said. After a pause she added, "I can't leave him."

He said nothing.

"Are you French?"

"No."

"I thought—"

"I'm American. I was born in France."

"In Paris?"

"I don't know," he said.

"You don't?"

"No."

"You don't know where you were born?"

"No."

She just nodded.

"Odd, huh?" he said.

"You must have come to America when you were very little." She offered this idea as though it was something they could speculate on together.

"I think so, yes."

She continued nodding. "Is that why you have a French name?" she asked. "Michel. Adrien too, I suppose."

"That's why."

"Is your last name French?"

He stared at her in a funny way. He seemed to be looking over her face again, his one eye running up and down her. "Sarre," he said. "That's French."

She repeated it thoughtfully. Then, "Adrien?"

He smiled.

"Michel?"

"Yes?"

"Are you going to kiss me again?"

"At some risk," he answered.

"Why," she whispered, when his mouth was close to hers, "did you go crazy?"

"I don't know," he said.

"What would you have lost if you had lost me?" she whispered.

He didn't say, for he couldn't have explained it. Yet she knew, without him saying it; and as soon as she asked she hoped he didn't answer, for she couldn't have stood it for the same reason he couldn't have said it. And when he kissed her again, she only lay there without opening her eyes, hoping that when she did he would be gone, that he would have left without a trace: because she couldn't have stood his departure either. There was a twinge below her belly, and then a particularly bad contraction; and by reflex she did open her eyes, and he was gone. He had gone the way she wanted him to, and somehow she knew it was because had she watched him he couldn't have left her.

There was the spillage of blue and the red of dusk over the room—a sepia she had seen from her window a thousand dusks; the core of every object deepened in color and the edges streaked dazed and broken. With every glance everything in the room seemed to run and blend. And a thousand dusks had not been like this: there she lay carved, gutted and stapled; and yet not quite ever had she felt this whole. From her window she saw the trees bare and dripping with sand. Old buckets turned in the parking lot, and far beyond the street an old wooden fence leaned north. Several deserted cars lined the curbs; small ridges of the last storm crusted on the windshield wipers. After the amazed exhilaration faded she missed him horribly, once the lights of the hospital hallways shut down and she was alone in the dark. When she woke again at dawn, she was sad and somewhat shocked to find he wasn't there at the foot of her bed once more.

She ate breakfast and slept again; and this time she felt his fingers brush the top of her face, and she waited before waking for him to kiss her again. He wore the same blue coat, and had not moved the patch. He brought her a magazine. She made him a list of things she would like, toothpaste and shampoo. The nurse came to change the bed, and Lauren found herself, almost to her own surprise, clutching his arm as he was scurried out of the room. He returned that night and they watched the moonwalk together. He continued to run his fingers over her brow until it was the last thing she remembered. "He was here until midnight," the nurse told her later. "We had to make him leave." Once, as the doctor pushed the button to lower her bed, everything stopped, and a brief power shortage left her suspended between up and down. Tomorrow, the doctor told her, we walk.

Michel came when the doctor was helping Lauren out of bed. Together the three of them walked up and down the hall. She felt a bit of discomfort in her stomach but that was all. She asked the doctor if the staples might fall out before they were supposed to and he said it wasn't likely if she was careful. Michel stayed, and Lauren showed him the scar. He stared at it blankly and touched it with one finger, saying nothing. Michel said Jason had called. He had been trying their apartment for two days. Michel told him what happened.

"Where was he?"

"Pennsylvania. He leaves for Venice next week." Michel looked out the window. "Unless he decides to come home."

"Did you tell him everything?"

"No."

Lauren said, "The doctor told me to go home tomorrow."

"I'll take you."

She nodded. "I can't make love for three weeks."

Jason called that night. He said he would cancel his entry in the rally if Lauren wanted. Or he could get a flight a few weeks later, since the rally wasn't until the fall. Lauren said it wasn't necessary. There was nothing he could really do for her, she said. Jason sounded funny when he hung up. She thought: He knows. He has always known. He knew from the first, before any of us. We all know. It's why it took us two years to meet; it's why I felt it through the floor.

The following day Michel stood again at the foot of her bed in his blue coat, his black hair falling down over the patch, barely any expression on his face at all. Impassively he took her bag in one hand and put his other arm around her. They went down the elevator together; when the doors opened, she felt some pain. They walked slowly through the lobby. At the front of the hospital, she clutched at her stomach, felt to see if one of the staples had popped loose, looked to see if blood was spreading in a circle on her gown. There was nothing. The parking lot was streaked with long blue shadows running east.

He picked her up and carried her; she held the bag in her lap. He walked with her quickly through the automatic glass doors and out into the light. A haze was in the direction of the ocean and a slight wind moved her gown, and brushed her legs. She realized she didn't know where she was. Everything was still, as though in the time she was away from the world, it had slowed considerably. Are you all right, he said. She hung on with her face in his coat, her hands on the back of his neck. She could feel the buttons against her hair, and pulling herself to him his coat seemed to fall forever, hitting the ground and spreading along the asphalt, as though all this time he'd been wearing his own shadow. Can you stand? he said, just for a moment—and he put her down and she didn't take her face from his coat but waited. He fumbled in his pocket for the keys. When he got the car door open, he took the bag from her and placed it in the back. He lifted her again to put her on the seat. She took his hair with one hand and his lapel with the other. "I love you, Adrien-Michel," she whispered. "I don't want to, but I do." He looked at her, his mouth never moving, no response on his lips at all; he put her in the car and stood there for a moment still looking at her. He closed the door. He walked around the car, opened the other door, considered and hesitated; he was still. Then, before getting in, he took the patch off his head and dropped it to the ground, where the gust that had rippled past her gown carried it across the lot and past the blank trees until it was no more than a small dark dot.

He took her home, put her in bed, lifted her gown over her head. He made her some tea and sat and watched her drink it. She kept staring at his face that seemed naked. The extra blueness of the extra eye disturbed her. Aware of it, self-conscious now, he kept glancing down. Then she looked back to the tea.

At night he took off his clothes and took her in his arms and only then, in the dark, did he begin to talk. He talked about the years they had been neighbors, and all the times he had seen Jason leaving, and how he had wondered whether she felt alone. He admitted, as she did to him, that he'd avoided her, though he never understood why. She'd become something of a mystery to him, as he had to her, the two of them stranded within their rooms, coming and going invisibly. But when he had seen her there in the crowd at the Blue Isosceles, he knew it wasn't for the first time, as she had known it wasn't the first time she saw him.

It was almost too late, he said. He had come to accept the idea, after two years of looking for a face he knew, that there would never be such a face; and after he came to accept it, he came to depend on it. After being afraid he'd never find it, he became afraid he would. His secret life became safe and comfortable; and when he saw her the first thing he thought was that she was someone who knew more about him than he did—which turned his blood cold, like the movie had done.

The movie? she said.

And he told her about the movie, running from the theater at the sight, he realized later, of his own mother, and at the knowledge, he somehow knew immediately, that this was his own work. So he knew, from that and the dream-memories he had, that he was the son of a French woman, born somewhere in France, and that when he was very young two brothers, twins, had drowned one night. And his mother's brother was a producer in Hollywood who hated him for a reason no one would tell him. And the hostility of his uncle and the terror of his aunt had compelled him to leave as soon as possible, which he had. She asked him if he'd ever seen the film again. He told her no, but he could any time, because it fell into his possession when he came across a trunk of personal effects, and there it was, in its dull metal canister beneath the books and papers. He thought of destroying it that day, and he had thought of destroying it every day since; but instead he stared at it on a shelf, like it was a possessed object which would hurl him across the room at the touch of it.

So she told him about the cats. In the dawn she pulled him naked from the bed and they sat in the window and waited. At the first gleam of the sun on the far building of the street, there emerged one cat and then another. They were only seen for a moment, before they disappeared around another corner, down another narrow canyon between two more buildings. She told him how when she was young she could call them in the fields, and they would respond in herds, struck and spellbound. Michel said, You ought to call them again. But that, Lauren answered, was when I was young, long long ago.

He stayed with her the entire time, bringing her groceries and cleaning her apartment. He did everything but answer the telephone when it rang in the mornings. Then, when she sank into each conversation with Jason like a reverie, Michel stepped quietly out of the apartment and stood in the hall staring at the banister that ran alongside the steps. He stood waiting, trying not to think, until after a while the door opened behind him and there she was, finished. She looked at him with his hands in his pockets and he looked much younger without the patch, but for the eyes that always looked old. He didn't look at her but glanced over her shoulder at the phone returned to its cradle, and then staring at the ground stepped once more into her world.

A white haunted lull filled the following days. They watched it pass beyond the window, from her bed where they lay together saying nothing. The sand stopped awhile, the city scraped raw by the recent storms—white blotches on the buildings of Pauline Boulevard where the paint and plaster had been torn away. All the windows were scratched, long intricate webs across the glass. It was quiet. There wasn't the sound of traffic but for a few buses and the bulldozers moving the sand where it had piled high. The moonbridges which Michel had seen when he first returned to the States were now smooth white mounds with only an occasional railing still visible. People went out, life in general went on, but it wasn't clear whether this calm was courage or concession. The sky was white all the time. The wind moved the sand slowly across the horizon in large masses like clouds. Electricity went off and on all the time now. People didn't buy anything they had to keep in their refrigerators. They wore wristwatches because clocks couldn't be trusted. The owners of the Blue Isosceles now closed the club four nights a week. On his way to and from the club Michel saw the streets strewn with stranded cars. Televisions blinked erratically in the dark. Jason was in Europe; he did not call again.

Michel would come home from the club to find her still awake, a lamp beside her bed if the current was running, a candle burning if it was not. In bed she touched him dangerously. She ran her hands up his legs and across his chest and his stomach, and then dropped her fingers to feel him, to run one finger up and down him. He had been celibate since that morning in Paris. He didn't know if he had made love before that morning. He didn't know if there'd been women in Paris, or Los Angeles—actresses or bohemians or lunatics in bookshops. Where the other instincts had returned to him even as he woke selfless in Paris, the instinct to take a woman was something he only rationally understood. He hadn't been touched by it directly, the way he'd been touched by hunger or fatigue. He never stripped naked before any woman since that day; it was the vulnerability he couldn't accept. He couldn't accept the notion of risking that much. In other words he entertained the possibility that he had never had a woman. In other words, in terms of who he was now, he might as well have never had a woman. But now she touched him this way in a fashion that surprised even her, and not only did he respond to the touch, but he felt his heart release a dark dangerous ink in his soul, as though each ventricle was the arm of a squid. When it flooded him, he knew he was capable of just about anything.

A black seeping dark filled those days, then: a craziness he was compelled to contain even as it threatened to gush first from him, then from their bed, then swell within the room lapping at the corners and pushing against the window. As he tried to turn from her, for her sake more than his own, she pursued the craze; she tormented him with her hands and pressed herself against him, pushing her breasts up against his shoulders and stroking him until his knuckles were white from gripping the springs beneath him. It occurred to her that this was her revenge against Jason; and then she thought of the voice stuttering in her uterus, and it occurred to her that this was her revenge against Jules. Before she fell asleep, as the lull outside ended and the first of the new storms was arriving from the east, it occurred to her that for a reason she didn't know, rooted in an incident she could not recall, this was her revenge against Michel himself.

They woke at morning to a black sky. In the course of the day the sky went from black to gray at noon and then deepened to brown to black again by sunset. The first storm lasted thirty-six hours; it blew high above the ground, leaving only a hiss on the rooftops along with the distant sound of the wind. This storm subsided and the afternoon was still; by night the second sandstorm arrived. It was closer to the ground, and while it wasn't as long as the first it bombarded everything violently; the next morning, in its aftermath, the streets were ranges of sand, sloped against doorways and all but burying the first levels of the buildings. Michel gazed out the bedroom window. "I have to go to the club," he said.

"Nobody will be at the club tonight," said Lauren.

"I have to go at any rate," he said, "and make sure." At the steps that led down from Pauline Boulevard they came upon a sandy incline too steep to descend, so they were forced to take the long way, following one of the other streets that went winding down the hill. At the club, the band Michel had scheduled for that evening was waiting in back of the building by the stage door. Michel told them he was thinking about closing. The singer, a girl with short blond hair and leather bands around her wrists, protested that the gig was too valuable to lose and asked if Michel would at least wait and see what kind of crowd they drew. Michel reluctantly agreed that if a reasonable crowd arrived, he would let the group go on. By sunset, when the sand on the boulevard was glistening a rosy light and there was a break of blue out over the ocean, neither Michel's cook nor bartender had shown up. Up in his office back behind the stage Michel could see from the window an ominous black cloud in the east, above the desert that lay just before Nevada. Again Michel considered closing the club; by now he was certain no one would show. One ticket seller wandered in. Lauren sat in a corner, resting from the twinges of pain, her eyes wandering out past the office window like they did so often in her bedroom. She would turn the dial on the radio sometimes; sometimes she would get something. We'll be out of here by ten, said Michel, unless the weather worsens, in which case we'll stay the night.

But by seven-thirty Michel realized he was wrong. People were starting to appear on the walk outside, waiting for the doors to open. By eight-thirty, there were so many Michel had to open the doors and instruct the ticket seller to begin business. The people poured in and by nine the club was mobbed, packed to the walls, and they kept coming, filling the dance floor and pushing aside the tables in back of the room, until the club couldn't accommodate them all. Michel couldn't imagine where they were coming from. This crowd was even stranger than usual; at times they looked altogether different from anyone who'd come to the club before. It wasn't the hard leather-and-steel regalia but the subterranean contortion of their faces, as though they had unearthed themselves, waiting in the sand for the hour when they could converge here, climbing molelike from underground between storms. Since there was no bartender they began helping themselves to the beer in the coolers, passing them down the line into the crowd. The free beer didn't placate them long; it was warm from the power having gone out so often. It was clear to Michel these people held any generosity of shelter or sustenance in contempt.

Now he wished he hadn't opened the doors at all, because the atmosphere was explosive and he knew no way of short-circuiting the charge, least of all with music. It was possible that the music would leave the crowd spent and satisfied, it was also possible it would leave them in a frenzy; but if the band didn't go on he knew there'd be havoc. Michel decided to start the show, but now even the band, which was used to tough crowds, was wary of this one; hesitantly they marched out on stage through the glass, bottle-ends crunching under their feet. A roar met them but it was insistent and threatening, not friendly.

The band began playing and the songs blinked on and off like lights, power surging through the club and then sporadically stopped, speakers and instruments and backstage strobes cutting out and then returning in sync. For a while the audience seemed amused by this, dancing frantically off the walls and freezing like statues in the blasts of dark and silence. But then they became impatient with it, and in the same dark and silence there was the crash of more glass, and ultimatums voiced from the tables upstairs. With each return of light and sound the singer appeared more visibly anxious, glancing around at her fellow musicians as though waiting for a signal to bolt. The wind outside could now be heard scraping against the walls. It set the crowd on edge even more. When the power failed for what must have been the tenth time, there was the sound of even more glass and bottles rocketing across the room; and then Michel heard one long cry in the dark that withered to a moan. Voices rose from the floor, random shouts, and when the lights came back the band's singer was covered with blood and on her knees, hunched over, the ends of her blond hair dragging in the pale pink human tissue on the stage before her.

Michel was standing next to Lauren who had watched from the balcony behind the stage. He pushed her back down the upstairs hall toward the office. Get in the back room and lock the door, he said. She stood there, staring past him, out toward the stage. Go on! he said, and her head seemed to jerk at the sound of his voice; she stepped back three, four steps. The band deserted the stage and their singer, leaving her where she knelt as the circle of blood around her widened. She did not move at all. Michel turned on the houselights; the crowd, at this point, was in the throes of glee, dancing and whooping before the motionless girl and her face lying at her knees. Bottles were flying everywhere and people were getting hit; and on the landing above, the railing gave completely, several bodies tumbling over the side. The crowd seemed prepared to dismantle the club from the floor up and the ceiling down, meeting somewhere in the middle. In the midst of it all, the blonde onstage never moved; and where at first the crowd appeared like it might descend on her and leave nothing, now they seemed to just move around her, as though having offered her as a sacrifice they understood she was no longer theirs.

When the final blackout came and the revelry did not stop but rather raised in pitch, heated by the dark, Michel began backing out, up the stairs of the stage; at the top he turned for the hall and decided to get Lauren and get out. The sound of the wind rose in the tumult; he wasn't certain whether the wind or the mob would raze the club first. In the hall he saw the window before him crackling around the edges, slivering in a crystalline pattern, and he could imagine all of them suddenly obliterated by glass; he wondered what moment he'd be shredded in an explosion of sand. Even in the night the sand could be seen hanging in the sky like an ashen hail, the blizzard cutting across the roof and the grit rattling within the building's innards. He got to the office door to find it unlocked, and stepped through as the window exploded and the glass sprayed through the club; he looked over his shoulder to see it stop in midair and then float down like silver confetti. He fell to the floor waiting for the office window to shatter too. He called out to her to drop. He called again.

She was not in the office.

He sat awhile, under the desk, trying to think. He was waiting for the wind to die; he couldn't hear himself at all, and he didn't see the point of calling for her. His great fear was that she'd gone back out into the club, and he felt worse about this possibility when he remembered the way she looked at the girl on the stage— as though, like the girl, and perhaps at the same moment, she had been stunned into oblivion. But now he sat there afraid of going back out into the club and what he might find, the wounded and the glass; and he didn't imagine she'd have gone back out there anyway. Rather he supposed she was in a closet somewhere, like the closets into which she had followed cats in labor.

When he did move he had to dig the sand away from the desk in order to get out; that was when he realized the office window had been open. In his mind he constructed this scenario: that perhaps she had even considered leaving the building, through the window, but seeing how serious the storm had become, and how far a drop it was to the ground below, she changed her mind and went to another room in the club. It didn't occur to him that she might have actually gone out the window.

Michel trudged through the sand in the room and slowly moved the door open, pushing away the sand that had mounted against it. In the hall there was more sand. It was pitch black so he couldn't really see clearly, and he could only discern the forms lying on the ground. He could smell the blood; but what froze the flow of his own veins was that there wasn't a sound at all from the club: not a murmur or a groan or a cry. It was absolutely still: not a stirring or a footstep. Lauren, he said. No one answered. He turned in the doorway and in the moonlight saw the sand fall from the ledges above the corners.

He went to the window. The moon was rising over the dunes and they looked like the waves of the Atlantic, as he had seen them before he returned from France.

He realized then that the sand had piled high against the building so that it wasn't a drop at all from the window. If there had been footprints, they were buried by now.

Disgusted, he turned from the window, went back into the hall and called again. Again there was no answer. The entire building seemed to be shifting, and a door broke open and swayed. Part of the ceiling gave and the sand fell through; he saw the dark sky beyond the torn ceiling; the wind was dead and the night was clearing.

In a heated and frightened fury, he returned to the window and stood: then he went through. Everything was still: the branches of the trees against the moon were bare but for white clumps of sand that occasionally shook loose; and standing knee-deep he saw nothing move. He watched the sandtrees for some minutes until one shuddered from something unknown, a breeze he didn't feel or the weight of the sand on a high branch. It was only then, from far away, he heard it; as he listened he realized it was bells in the night. Churches and homes are ringing their bells now that the storm is over, he said to himself; but in fact, in the black lightless city it sounded at first like the voices of children. The landscape shuddered again, the stripped white forms of the sand-trees drooling over the curbs in the moonlight.

That was when he felt it at his feet, soft and fine. He looked down and he saw the seaweed, there on the sand. He stared at it in the light as it glistened yellow-brown on the dune beneath the window. He wanted to go back at that moment, though he never believed in signs or visions. He stood watching it several minutes, and finally bent to touch it. He pulled gently at it; and when it didn't come up, he saw it was rooted, stretching a foot, two feet. He felt stupid, realizing it wasn't seaweed at all, but human hair.

Beneath the sand, she had been listening to him.

It was like in the hospital, when she had listened to her womb talk to her, only now it seemed a bit the other way around, that she was the one enveloped. She was in some kind of pocket; she could breathe, she could see, she felt like she had room, as though she could have gotten up and put on her clothes there under the sand. She had no idea what happened to her clothes; she felt the sand drift beneath her belly, between her breasts, down her legs. The sand was warm, to her surprise. Everything seemed calm. Because she remembered in the back of her mind she wasn't allowed to make love, and because she felt so nakedly suspended here, she had the sense of being absolutely virginal, free from any sort of gravity, unbound by any sort of temporal concerns. The wind that buried her here was gone, she could hear it, through the earth, miles away by now, nearing the ocean; she too could hear the bells though they sounded like nothing but a high tone struck off the rim of a glass in space.

She listened to him somewhere above her, and felt him pull at her hair. She knew it was him. In this state of hers, his touch was like a violation and it thrilled her. She thought of him standing over her in the sand, and in her mind pictured him against the the jagged blue edges of the window. The only thing she couldn't quite see were his eyes, because she hadn't gotten used to the missing patch; when she saw his face his eyes were replaced by dark patches of the sky, so it wasn't possible to tell what he was thinking or feeling, since the rest of his features were so impassive. She knew he was going to take her. She knew that from the way his shoulders sloped and the predatory way his fingers curled. She still couldn't see him but that didn't matter; it wasn't necessary that she actually see him. He stood in the sand and she knew when he pulled apart the buttons of his pants and dropped his shirt to his side, and poised himself naked above her.

She felt the sand shift around her, and the displacement from his knees dropping to the ground on each side of her; when he dug away the sand around her she felt his fingers inside her legs, and the sand slip down between her. Finally he had cleared away all the sand from her waist to her thighs, and once again she felt him pull her hair, until he had wrestled free her face from the dune. The breeze that lifted and died across the landscape was very slight; bits of bark blew by, and before her the moon pulled from the trees and drifted higher. He touched her around her legs and the small of her back. He held her hair with one hand and felt her face with the other, running his fingers across her brow. She remembered she wasn't supposed to do this, the doctors had said; but she understood that he wouldn't be stopped. She was pinned to the sand and she was thinking of one black cat in particular, and she was remembering the way she brushed its fur in a field on just such a night as this one, when each star was visible and the moon was a white cold hole throbbing above her: she was thinking of this when she felt him place his fingers just inside her and then follow with the rest of him. This was when she realized just how hungry both of them were. It was a movement so driven and unhesitant that she responded with a spasm. The sort of bliss in which she'd rested felt aborted. She attempted to pull away, she tried to twist around to face him; but his presence that far up inside her left her caught and wriggling.

He forced his legs inside hers, prying her apart; then he pulled at her hair again until she was forced onto her knees and hands. She tried to get a grip on the sand and kept slipping. If she turned her neck just a bit, she could see him from the corner of her eye, caught in the light and gazing to the east. Her hair was wrapped around his hands and she resigned herself to letting him take it. He dropped her hair for the moment and held her below the waist, pulling her to him so he was deeper in her; they seemed to go on in waves. She could feel his fingers press into her sides, down to her legs; stunned by the sight of her white smooth back, he became harder and faster, pulling her closer and driving himself deeper until it didn't seem enough for him. He brought his hands up her belly and took her breasts, and leaning forward fell in frenzy across her back, and her arms gave way. She felt herself being driven across the sand, clawing at the ground trying to accommodate him, pulling herself across the dune while he held her by her breasts. When her whimpers became cries it seemed to make him crazier, and she put her hand in her mouth to silence herself; but she cried out louder. She was begging him no, no, but he tore at her on the sand until she collapsed beneath him motionlessly, with the sand in her mouth and the night in her eyes, and the recognition of that which she'd tried to crawl away from: and that was that she wanted him to go on doing this until he consumed her. Almost unconsciously she said, It hurts, Michel. It was simple and hopeless the way she said it; she never expected it would mean anything to him. Perhaps it was its hopelessness that made him stop, as though struck, and look down at her. Everything came to a halt, the enflamed momentum of it shut off. She looked up at him and he looked away for a moment, down at himself caught inside her. He started to withdraw, but she contracted and held him. Don't, she said, and she contracted and released over and over; and when he came it was as though he had never felt it before; he could not have looked more amazed. They lay together there awhile. The wind rose and the moon moved higher. She was almost asleep, just vaguely aware of him picking her up and carrying her up the slope to the broken window from where they had come.

When she woke, she could see through the door someone's arm. She got up and crossed the office and peered through, and she could see all the bodies. Had she been more conscious she would have screamed, but she only went back to his side. Their clothes were in a neat little pile nearby, where he'd put them. Somewhere far off she could hear a truck.

They dressed and left; he had awakened with all the bodies falling in the back of his mind. They went through the window, and down the slope. There were sirens far away and smoke on the horizon. They crossed to a deserted gas station and used the toilet. The toilet and the faucets released a small flow of muddy water; the pay telephone didn't work. Sunset Boulevard was glass and sand and white buildings. Michel finally found a telephone and dialed the police; the switchboard was impossible to get through.

They took the freeway going back. It was empty. At the interchange Michel and Lauren descended into a maze; small campfires burned in the distance. There were vagabonds around the fires, a vast hobo city. Both of them were thinking different things. Lauren couldn't help it that Jason crossed her mind; she couldn't help wondering where he was, what news he was hearing, what he'd be thinking. Michel kept trying to call the police from phones along the way. He tried calling hospitals and the National Guard. For all the sirens, he never saw anyone but the helicopters above them when they came out of the interchange. They walked down Vine Street.

Pauline Boulevard was not as hard hit. Whole sides of buildings were stark white in the sun, and there were no signs of life, no rustling about in the street; but no windows were broken and everything seemed bolted and latched. The sand wasn't as deep, certainly not piled to the second or third levels. In this last catastrophic storm the street slipped away on its own, not unwounded but unaffected.

He stopped her at the door. She turned and looked at him, her eyes wide. "I want you to call them," he said.

She bit her lower lip. "No."

"You can. You always could." He stepped behind and took her by the shoulders; he faced her toward the street. "You always could."

She exhaled, and looked from building to building; she couldn't see even one. What if there was none left? What if they were all buried under the sand? But she knew that hadn't happened, because somehow Pauline Boulevard had slipped away when the sand came last night, and they had slipped away with it. "I'll make you a bargain," she said.

He waited.

"I'll call them if you'll look at your movie again."

"I can't look at the movie."

"Then I can't call them."

She felt him behind her, pressed to her. "All right."

"A bargain?"

"Yeah."

"Promise?"

"Yeah."

She called. She called the way she used to in Kansas. She didn't call them by their names of course; that would have been preposterous. She called them with a code she had known. It was nothing precise like a chant or a ritual; she was talking to them, not conjuring them. It was the level of her voice, and an implicit trust; and, as he had implied, it was the degree to which she believed they would answer. She called and nothing happened, and she called again. A minute went by, and she sort of sagged in his arms with defeat; he could feel it. Call them again, he said. They're not coming, she said. But she called once more and her voice carried in the street, somewhat flat and indistinct; but, though she hadn't spoken loudly at all, anyone on the street, in the lowest cellar or the highest attic, would have heard the voice.

The street was so still that at first it seemed illusory, neither of them could really tell what had stirred: no door had opened, nor a window; but because everything was that still, the slightest motion caused a ripple—a vague, undetermined buckling. Michel narrowed his eyes. She shook her head. Then she felt something soft against her ankles, and she looked down and there was the cat. The cat was looking up at her, crying to her. It was the cat who had lived with her, the birth of whose kittens Lauren had witnessed in the closet. And when Lauren and Michel looked up from this cat, there, before them, filling the street from curb to curb, were hundreds of them. They were slinking out of passages, emerging from shadows; some were climbing up out of the sand. Some were dropping from the rooftops or uncurling themselves from hidden ledges. Slowly, cautiously, they moved to her like a Kansan field itself, their footprints spotting the sand in the street behind them. They came until Lauren and Michel were enveloped with them; everywhere the two of them looked, the cats were waiting—at their feet and at their sides and above them on the buildings, all sitting and waiting. Lauren looked at Michel and looked back at the cats, and in his arms she broke down and cried.

On the last June night of the nineteenth century, he was left with his brother at the bottom of the steps that led up to the Pont Neuf. A tramp sleeping on the quay woke to see a woman put them there, and got up to approach the small white bundle. He was surprised to find there were two of them. He took one and started weaving down the side of the river, unsure what to do until apparently, for no reason whatsoever, he decided to toss the child in. This was seen by a woman named Marthe from the boulevard above the river, and she ran down the steps to pull the baby from the arms of the tramp. There was a scuffle. The tramp may have even gone into the water himself; Marthe didn't remember later, so intent had she been on rescuing the child. She walked back up the river to the steps beneath the bridge, only to find the other infant gone.

The women at the house where Marthe lived and worked reacted to the baby with predictable enthusiasm; only the madam was dubious. A note had been left with the two children, crumpled down in the blanket behind the one's left ear; it read: "They are Maurice and Adolphe, both born of the same mother on 20 April of this year, near the village of Sarre." There was discussion about this note. The madam, who could already see where things were headed, suggested that the mother really wanted the children returned—like a would-be suicide who wants to be stopped at the penultimate moment. The other women disputed this: despite the mother's apparent wish to impart some identity to the children, they had been abandoned ominously close to the river; one had come close to drowning, the other probably had, and the mother had clearly left the matter to fate. The second point of controversy was: which was this one, Maurice or Adolphe? Logically everyone understood it shouldn't matter; but intuitively they all somehow felt it did, that to make a mistake of this sort would start everything off on the wrong foot. No one could decide.

They raised him there in the house, Number Seventeen on the rue de Sacrifice, not far from Montparnasse. Number Seventeen was by far the most exclusive of what were called the Houses of Unwoken Dreams there on the boulevard. It was not open to a general clientele but stood as a *maison privée*, owned by one of the wealthiest men in Paris, who had dealings with coal in America and was involved in the construction of the Métro, scheduled to open the following year. He would bring to the house friends and business associates, or send clients with a reference; otherwise no man could buy his way through the door, no matter how many thousands of francs he might offer. The eight women who lived and entertained in Number Seventeen were imperatively ravishing: six brunettes, two of them sisters, and two blondes. They ranged in age from seventeen, the youngest, to thirty-six. The seventeen-year-old had only recently arrived, brought personally by Monsieur Monsieur—as he called himself for purposes of discretion—from Tunisia, where he bought her on the auction block; brought naked before the bidders, the spectacle of a blond Tunisian nearly provoked a riot. Monsieur Monsieur made a bid with which no one could hope to compete. He called her *lumière de Tunisie*—light of Tunisia—which got shortened to Lulu. When Lulu held the child that Marthe brought home from the Pont Neuf, everyone understood that in a family of eight equal mothers, Lulu would somehow be most equal of all.

Lulu looked into the eyes of the baby and tried to decide for herself whether this was Maurice or Adolphe. She called him one or the other, to see which got a reaction; this went on over a year, the women calling the child Maurice or Adolphe depending on their own preference or whichever came most quickly to mind. During this time, they raised the child in the secret room. Number Seventeen had been built some hundred and thirty years before, when unrest in France and particularly Paris was rampant; a room had been added behind what was the study. Revolutionaries hid there from the troops of Louis XVI; later, after Louis' decapitation, when the revolution was devouring itself with frequency, revolutionaries hid there from other revolutionaries. It was a wonder everyone in Paris didn't know about this room. But in fact the room had been forgotten, so that even Monsieur Monsieur didn't know about it when he bought the house; one of the women had discovered it on her own. In a moment of truth, the madam of the house had to decide whether to tell Monsieur Monsieur about the room or enter into a conspiracy with the other women; she decided it made sense to have one secret that the master of the house did not share. So the room belonged to the women, and its silence and invisibility belonged to them as well. That was where they kept the child, hurrying him behind the panels in the study when Monsieur Monsieur arrived in the evening with his guests. The child, as though intuitive of secrets in a way deeper and wiser than his young life, almost never cried when in the sanctuary.

Lulu was privately Monsieur Monsieur's in a way none of the other seven had been; she was reserved for only him, she was never offered by him to his friends or associates. It couldn't be said that he slept with only her, but he slept with her when having a woman seemed to matter most to him. All of them suspected he was in love with her. It never could have occurred to her to love him in return, because he was much older and not particularly attractive. He was kind and never beat her. He even once suggested to the madam the possibility of divorcing his wife and marrying Lulu, a suggestion that astonished her and probably himself as well. He dismissed the notion almost as soon as he said it. But it's not likely he would have even thought of it if he didn't think that in this way he could acquire of her something he didn't have, which was her love. When Adolphe-Maurice was three and Lulu was twenty, she became pregnant. This had happened to a couple of the other women in the house, and without any deliberation they had been compelled to abort. But Monsieur Monsieur couldn't bring himself to have Lulu abort, and this had more to do with something deeper than just the privileges of possession. Lulu had the child.

It was a girl, and named Janine. She was blond like Lulu, not quite as dark but with her mother's brown eyes. She was raised in a house that was just getting over the tribulations of raising another baby; Adolphe-Maurice accepted the other presence fatalistically, even with fascination. After a year, when Adolphe-Maurice was four, Janine's first word was not for her mother, or any of the small animate objects that first attract children; it was rather a garbled, but recognizable, version of the name Adolphe, to which the boy responded for the first time in a definite, comprehending way. He was always Adolphe after that, and it made perfect sense to everyone in the house that a new baby would understand which name was right in a way everyone else had not. Lulu liked, rather romantically, to call him Adolphe de Sarre.

Years later, he would still vividly remember those things from that world of which he was first conscious: the voluptuous blues of the fabric, the glint of the mirrors at night just before he was escorted off to the secret room, the supple marble of the stairs leading up through the center of the house and the sound of footsteps up and down the stairs all night. He would recall the paintings, diminutive and understated, streaked with strange passions in which each seduction was a phantasm; and the music he heard through the walls was wrathful and haunting—Debussy's silhouette symphonies and the parlor-tunes-gone-mad of Satie. At dawn when he ventured out from the room, Number Seventeen's interiors glittered with the light of its crazy windows, their colored panes flickering on the floor. Creeping past each room, peering through each door ajar, he caught each of his surrogate mothers in a different pose of sleep—reclined on blue sofas, slumped languidly in velvet chairs, faces buried in white fur rugs now streaked with rouge. Outside in the street he heard the clanging of the ice truck and the huge frozen blocks that were dropped with a thud in the doorways; and even through the unopened gate of Number Seventeen came the smell of bread. All the suppressed child-rearing instincts of the women in the house were vicariously satisfied through Adolphe and Janine; the boy was clothed and fed and entertained, so he only hungered for two things. The first was real movement, which was carefully restricted: raised in secret, every bit of freedom was purloined by dark escapes out the back and over the wall of Number Seventeen's private courtyard. Otherwise he spent most of his childhood in this house, and most of his evenings in the room. Leaving him to hunger for her.

It was not so much a question of beauty. She wasn't the most beautiful girl he would ever see—beyond twelve she would never really change anymore; tall though she already was, her body would not fill out much, and still and fathomless though her eyes looked, they would never look wiser or sadder. Since she had begun bleeding at the age of eight, sitting there on the bidet in one of the rooms upstairs staring silently at the dark thick blood on her fingers, the look in her eyes had been like that; she looked up from the blood to him in the doorway, a weary knowing smile somewhere in the corner of her mouth. She sat looking at him and he stood watching her, and a wind came in from the courtyard. It caught her face in a blur of blond, and when he was a young man on the Champs-Elysées he would look at the bare tangle of branches on top of the trees and see within them her brown eyes and full plum-red mouth, and remember that first day she bled. As a girl growing up in Number Seventeen, she had no reason to do so secretly, and so of course she chose not to grow up with Adolphe; he listened to her voice beyond the walls, and caught of her blond hair every glimpse offered to him by chance opportunity, and did so till he was sixteen, wondering if he would ever get out.

He never questioned why he had to spend all his time in this room; this was for two reasons. The first was that he hadn't known anything else, he hadn't been given any reason to think it was unusual. The second reason, which extended from the first, was that he finally decided this was the way men lived their lives, as opposed to women, who obviously had the run of the place. He had grown up the only male in a house full of, now, nine females, and the fact that he of the lot had to stay in this room was logically due to being a male. Whenever men visited the house in the evenings, they were immediately taken off to rooms of their own— even Monsieur Monsieur disappeared with Lulu. Adolphe assumed Lulu was his mother. For this reason he assumed Janine was his sister, which complicated and darkened his feelings for her and the way he watched her from the room. By the time he recognized the instinct for what it was, he still wasn't clear whether it was right or wrong to desire his sister, or whether in fact it was his right, as her brother, to have her. All these things derived from growing up in this room no one else seemed to know, and from the inevitable conclusion that men were meant to live in these rooms, always secured from the knowledge and trespasses of other men, the entrances and exits of which were clearly determined by women. Barely five years later, when at the age of twenty he began the work that would consume his entire life, scenes always took place in rooms of destiny and exile, transcendence and madness, moments seized and murders pending.

By the time he was sixteen and Janine was thirteen, he felt like a caged animal. She had enough of her mother's brownness to glow there in the hallways at night, when she walked bare into the bath of gaslight from beyond the corridor beams. Sometimes she came to see him when she was lonely; she didn't notice the way he cowered by the wall staring at her. She blithely laughed at her own sentences, occasionally glancing at him carelessly in order to acknowledge she wasn't talking to herself. Lulu didn't know what to do with her; she noticed the way Monsieur Monsieur's son looked at her when the father brought him to the house. She contrived secret plans to smuggle the girl somewhere else, beyond the reach of the men who came here. She didn't dare share these plans with the other women; the fact of the matter was Monsieur Monsieur owned Janine as he owned Lulu, and what the mother considered for her own daughter was dangerous, a breach that could never be justified; this was more than simply relations, this was a matter of property.

Monsieur Monsieur's son, called Jean-Thomas, was almost thirty, though he seemed younger; not a line of maturity graced his face. He was good-looking in a somewhat offhanded and vacant way, and always well dressed. The women of Number Seventeen loathed him. Monsieur Monsieur had begun bringing Jean-Thomas some years before, when his own capacity for lovemaking had shown signs of diminishing. In this sense the master now kept the house for his son; and just as there was a generational transition between the two men, so there was among the women, older ones suddenly, inexplicably changed for newer ones. Where the older ones went Adolphe never knew. Where the new ones came from he didn't know either. The number of women, excepting Janine, was always kept at eight.

Janine, nonetheless, was clearly the one Jean-Thomas watched with transparent lust—though not transparent enough for the father to see it. Had he realized his son wanted his daughter, and a daughter only thirteen years old at that, he never would have brought Jean-Thomas again. The women saw it with a sort of heart-stopping clarity, but had no idea how to tell the father. Lulu saw it each time Jean-Thomas arrived at the house, sometimes with his friends. After manhandling whatever women he selected for the evening, Jean-Thomas would sit in Number Seventeen's foyer watching Janine.

Even Adolphe saw it, from around corners and through peepholes. Growing up in this room he was left to perceptions and insights that developed in isolation from the rest of the world; in this way some of his understanding was stunted, undeveloped. In other ways his understanding became keener, even extraordinary; in this room he learned to peer past everything that was immediate to and readily grasped by others. While other people's comprehension of things developed in a manner that was linear, his own comprehension became circuitous, spiraling, lifted and carried in patterns of its own by hidden currents, like the light in this room. Absolutely blocked off from any access to the outside, the room nevertheless had a light that was from no lamp or candle, and sitting on his bed he could see the dust rise from an unknown breeze. Nothing else stirred this room; its various clocks and bottles and figurines had been here when the room was discovered and could well have been, indeed were assumed to have been, here since the house was built. There were even two flintlock pistols on the wall, crossing each other. The light was the same Adolphe had seen in the street, on the rue de Sacrifice, moments after the sun set beyond the river, when the sidewalks were filled with men passing among the Houses of Unwoken Dreams, Number Five and Number Twelve and Number Twenty-six—always eying the forbidden Number Seventeen to which few were ever admitted. Adolphe himself would walk past the bals musettes and the other clubs, the houses marked Belles Chinoises and Belles Negres, and the nude artists' balls where rich Parisian debutantes could dance with tall muscular Africans, and well-to-do stylish gentlemen with other gentlemen. The light on the street at this hour, just as the rue de Sacrifice came alive, was a swirling smoky mix of the dusk from the river and the gaslamps only now beginning to smolder. Sneaking back to Number Seventeen at dark, Adolphe found the light in his room the same as the light from the street. On into the night this light persisted, and on the gray walls Adolphe watched a hundred shadows from the years this house had stood. When he placed a candle on the shelf across the room from him and lit its wick, he came to realize that in fact everything he saw was a flat surface, like a screen—that in fact dimension was an illusion. Everything was a flat surface and the pinpoints of light, whether from a candle on the shelf or a gaslamp above the street, were punctures in that surface—gashes made by somebody behind the screen. He realized then that beyond everything he saw there was an entire realm of blazing sunfire, and that colors were only the silhouettes of people in that realm—walking, eating, dancing, doing whatever they were doing behind the screen. It astonished Adolphe that everyone failed to realize they were just figures on a tapestry, the shadows of something else. He was therefore amused by the conceit of women, for instance, who admired the creamy color of their skin when in fact it was only the haze of some other woman behind the vast screen staring into a mirror. Adolphe could explain all of this to himself in this way, but he could not explain Janine: Janine wasn't the same as the others. Janine was like their mother; and Adolphe decided that Lulu was from this place beyond the surface, and she had, perhaps when she was a little girl, slipped through. Adolphe wondered why Lulu hadn't told them about this, and then realized she probably would when she thought they were old enough to understand it. He could see it wasn't something one would tell a child too soon. But on that particular night, Adolphe wanted to tell Janine, when she came hiding from Jean-Thomas. He watched her huddling there in the dusk of the room. What is it? he said.

Monsieur Monsieur's son, she said.

Beyond the walls of the room they could hear his voice calling her. Having decided to wait no longer, he became louder and louder, crashing around in the other rooms; Janine and Adolphe could now hear the other women's voices. There was a furor. As always, Janine was only barely aware of Adolphe, her large brown eyes directed intently at the disguised door, her breath caught in her throat. Adolphe's breath was caught as well, but for different reasons. Rather, he was feeling something dark inside him, spreading like ink from the ventricles of his heart; and he knew he wanted her too, the way Jean-Thomas did. He couldn't reconcile himself to feeling this way, because he knew the darkness was only a shadow cast by someone else on the other side of the screen. He crawled toward her, carefully, and as he reached toward her shoulder, as the shadow of his hand stretched across the wall and he reassured himself it wasn't his hand at all, as she then turned to him finally and saw, instantly, in his eyes, what had been there all along, and as she acknowledged it in a way that seared his memory forever, then the door-in-disguise burst open and Monsieur Monsieur's son stood there looking at them.

There was something askew about him; his features seemed lopsided in the way his hair fell across his forehead, and the way his face was wet. His eyes darted around the room with vague amusement, and the clothes he wore, those of the young dandy, were disheveled. He looked at the girl and then at the boy, smiled drunkenly. Who are you? he said to Adolphe, who didn't answer. Jean-Thomas didn't really care. He reached over and took Janine by the wrist and pulled her to her feet. "You can't take her," said Adolphe, in an even voice.

"Why not?"

"I'm her brother."

Jean-Thomas looked at Adolphe, distantly baffled, and then laughed. "Really?" he said. "So am I."

Adolphe remained crouched on the floor looking in Jean-Thomas' eyes, which regarded him one last fleeting moment before turning with the girl and disappearing from the light.

From that light, which belonged to the room itself, to the sound of Jean-Thomas' steps as they moved to a room somewhere above him, to Janine's cries in the stairwell of the house, Adolphe watched the light change, move, travel across the room. And when he heard the door close, and could feel the ripple of the ceiling from the thump of the bed as she was thrown across it, he saw the light fall, until the sight of it seemed to hum in his head. He told himself to go. He told himself that he couldn't wait anymore, that there was nothing after all that physically held him—no bolt was on the door, no key was in a lock. He could reach for the door, fling it open as Monsieur Monsieur's son had done, and be free of the room forever, the way Monsieur Monsieur's son was apparently free of rooms and could, unlike other men, travel between them at will, dragging a woman behind him rather than following one before him. But Adolphe was held there. He was there on two knees and one set of five fingers, the other hand still reaching for her shoulder. Only now the shadow of it was gone, and he knew that behind the flat surface, someone had moved. He knew that just as he could travel from room to room at will, he wasn't subject to the shadows of those behind the screen, that he could fling his own shadow away from any light, or grasp it in his hands and lock it away. There was no other issue then but courage; and he watched the door; and he listened to her above him as Monsieur Monsieur's son had her, the legs of the bed jumping across the ceiling. He was dismayed by how silent she was, and how loud Jean-Thomas was: it was something that, years later, he would remember indelibly, never allowing an utterance to leave his lips when he made love to a woman, and silently ravaging her until she screamed. He would never make love to a woman who didn't cry out, because of that night; he would never allow himself the moan of climax, because of that night. With every crash of the bed upstairs into the walls, with every sound of the ceiling reverberating from their movements, the light continued to ebb within the room, every color muted and every shade reduced to chiaroscuro: the effect was alternately stark, and like smoke. Nothing, he thought, could have moved him from the room, until he heard the one sound he never expected. He heard her laugh. Breathless and expectant. The slightest betrayal, and the sound of conquest.

That was when he bolted. He pulled the door open, ran through the hallways he had never run at night, past men looking up at him in bewilderment and the faces of women he knew so well, but who he'd never seen look quite like this: wet mouths and eyes like rivers; up the stairs hearing them call his name below, throwing open the door of one room, then another, interrupted couples in his wake, until at the final room down the hall he found the two of them. Jean-Thomas never turned around to look at him, too lost as he was in his grinding. But Janine looked up, to see Adolphe, small for his sixteen years, pull Jean-Thomas away from her and push him through the third-level window.

And because the rush was over, then there was that false sense of everything halted: Janine and Adolphe were both at the window looking out over the street, where Jean-Thomas lay. A crowd of men ran over, and Janine pulled Adolphe away. She watched the scene below and listened to the excited voices. She could see Jean-Thomas move, slightly, in the dark. The room was filled with the other women. Adolphe stood back by the wall, thinking, as they stared into the street.

Slowly they turned to him. He stared back at them. Lulu was in the doorway, looking like a dead woman. He's still alive, said one of the women by the window: the flurry of voices rose from outside. Adolphe stared at the floor. You have to leave, said Lulu. The madam of the house rushed into the room, looked at the women, looked out the window at Jean-Thomas below, looked at the women again, then at Adolphe. He has to leave, said Lulu again, to the madam. She was speaking as though he was actually her son.

He left. The women got some money together, and one of them gave Adolphe the address of a friend in Tours. Adolphe left by the back, as he had always done when he was escaping this house. As he had always done when he was escaping this house, he went through the courtyard; he never stopped to take it all in one last time. He would have taken Janine but he kept hearing her laugh. Finally, on the highway south out of Paris, Number Seventeen and its unknown room were behind him.

He went to war not long after that. The soldiers picked him up by a stone bridge over a small stream, on the road to Tours; there was not a sixteen-year-old boy who wasn't in the war. He gave his name as Adolphe Sarre. The troops debated among themselves whether the small Adolphe Sarre was sixteen or not; when he said he wasn't sure, they enlisted him on the spot. All of them were going to Verdun; soldiers went in waves. Winter came. The soldiers built bonfires in the opened bellies of dead horses, and draped themselves on the hot barrels of recently fired cannons.

When the food was gone they sat in the trenches gnawing at the chrome of their rifles. As he had in the room at Number Seventeen, Adolphe stared at the lights exploding in the sky pulled taut across the horizon: bombs left the sky in tatters, large gaping holes of light showing through. By the following year the siege was over and the French were marching to Lorraine. By then Adolphe seemed to feel nothing, too mesmerized by the light. One final gash in the clouds left him blind; they carried him on a stretcher into the ward of the wounded, and left him propped on a cot. He heard nurses' voices talking to him, but saw only white; in his mind he pictured the faces of the women of Number Seventeen, and to each voice that he heard he attached a face. There was no voice for Janine, there was no laugh that approximated Janine's laugh. After a while, there in the ward of the wounded, he began drawing his own lines on the white; he formed his own shapes. To each shape he called her name, and heard her laugh in return. He traveled, in this mesmerized state, between deep doubt and awed exhilaration: his instincts and understanding amazed him, and left him alone. At some point the white faded to gray; he thought he was losing the vision. One morning he woke and everything was dark; he thought he had lost the vision. He thought that he'd never see again through the surface of things. This went on for a week, two weeks, during which he sank into despair, until one afternoon he heard a terrific bomb overhead, the blast of which seared a hole right in his own darkness. At that point, he peered through the hole and still saw bonfires lit in the bodies of gutted dead animals, and men eating their rifles. He realized then that what was behind the screen was no better than what was before it, and there was no purpose to waiting for the moment when he could step through, to where he always figured he rightly belonged, as he always planned to someday do. He realized that carnage was carnage, defeat was defeat, and the dead would always die, and nothing was better over there, nothing was different. At that moment he grew up. At that moment he seized, somewhere inside him, the essence of what would drive him later: his drives were only awaiting some form to take. After that he went to sleep. The nurses couldn't wake him for weeks; to the doctors his coma appeared indefinite and probably unending. It wasn't until the eleventh hour of the eleventh day of the eleventh month of that year, at the very moment the Armistice was being signed, that he opened his eyes and could see again.

When Marshal Foch led the victorious French troops into the city, it was Adolphe Sarre's first real vision of Paris, having only seen before the rue de Sacrifice and a few outlying alleys. It never occurred to him, walking in the streets with the rest of the soldiers as the crowds cheered wildly, that the facades of the buildings were constructed from the ground up; rather he assumed the city had been formed like a canyon, centuries of rain and fire carving it out of the ground, and the river running through the canyon's core. He couldn't imagine that the Grand Palais overlooking the Seine was the invention of the same sort of living beings that lay dying and butchered on battlefields just kilometers away. Had he known this before going to war, he might have felt more compassion and revulsion and sense of misery for the wounded and dead; he might not have been so readily fatalistic. It was amazing to him to see men happily standing along the streets rather than in rooms or trenches; it was amazing to him to see women who were old and plain rather than beautiful and rouged and young. The citadels of Paris rose like chiseled cliffs and the windows glittered like caves in which fires had been set and stoked—small gouges in the screen, their distance an illusion.

In his uniform, he had only to stand gazing at something with the slightest look of longing or interest for someone to grab him by the elbow, acclaim him a hero and invite him to partake. In this way he was fed, sheltered, squired about the town. Being a soldier was a young man's ticket in those first days after the war; and the first night he marched into Paris, he had dinner in a small excellent restaurant, was offered a place to sleep by an old couple with tears in their eyes, and was given free admission to the Opéra, which was showing an American motion picture called *The Birth of a Nation* by D.W. Griffith.

He had no idea what a motion picture was. Of course the idea intrigued him: paintings he remembered from Number Seventeen skipped in animation across his mind. But the figures in this motion picture were exact images, not replicas or characterizations, and the action flickered at him rather than flowing past— and for all the buzz of the audience throughout the film, the idea of pictures that moved ultimately didn't surprise him, or cause him to marvel. Rather what stunned him was the sweep of it, the huge scope of General Sherman's march (though he wasn't at all sure just who General Sherman was), and how closely it approximated in logistics, if not horror, the war he had just seen. And when the Klan rode, and the Opéra itself seemed to shake from the hooves in the dirt, he was also stunned by the force of it. He walked out of the theater feeling he intuitively understood the language of what he had seen, as though the magic that had brought the entire audience to its feet at the end of it, that had shocked them into a frenzied abandon which equalled the same response the troops marching back from war had elicited—the magic of that was secondhand to him; it wasn't really magic at all. It was only the sight of something he had been looking for all along, peering behind the surface of things as he had, trying to see the blinding light.

Adolphe watched *The Birth of a Nation* many more times, and then one night wandered up to the theater's projection booth. This may have startled the man running the film, but Adolphe was still in uniform and therefore still a hero; so if he wished to sit in the projection booth awhile, it seemed a small favor to grant. In fact Adolphe wound up staying several days in the booth, sleeping on the floor and accepting a sandwich and some wine which the projectionist would bring him in the afternoon. While the projectionist might have thought it odd that Adolphe showed no real interest in leaving the small room, it was a perfectly natural situation for a young man who spent years in a small room on the rue de Sacrifice: what held Adolphe was the way the square gray clicking box slashed a white rip across the world to reveal the other world hidden behind.

Around the fourth day, a man from Pathé Studios came to the theater with several reels of film; Pathé distributed not only French films but foreign products as well. Adolphe asked if he could ride with the man back to the Pathé lot on the outskirts of Paris. At Pathé, Adolphe got a job unloading equipment, changing sets and running errands; he also watched transfixed as Pathé turned out hundreds of movies from one- and two-reelers to larger prestige productions. The other people on the lot generally found Adolphe a bit unusual but not unpleasant. He was polite and particularly deferential to the starlets, who reminded him of the women he had lived with before the war. He was regarded as attentive if also a bit absorbed, and often people took the time to explain things to him. The editors in the cutting room took him on as something of an apprentice; and when he'd acquired their trust, he was given a key to the room which he would use at night, long after everyone was gone. Then he would stand at the end of the cutting room and, with a single bare light burning, watch the strips of film that hung above the tables like falling water freezing before his eyes, until the room seemed to him a cave of glittering icicles.

After a while, Adolphe was allowed to edit a segment of film which comprised several scenes. He did not cut the scenes as the director of the film had instructed, fashioning instead a segment of frantic and abrupt juxtapositions that baffled his superiors and infuriated them. He was informed that he had no talent for cutting and removed from the department. One of the cutters, however, suggested to the executives that while he didn't particularly care for what Adolphe had done with his scenes, he thought the young man had a number of ideas and should perhaps be writing scripts. This argument wasn't entirely persuasive to the people running Pathé Studios, but if there was anything they needed it was ideas and scripts and so they put Adolphe in the script department. As with film cutting, Adolphe began essentially as an apprentice and contributed to a script which Pathé found acceptable after revisions. He contributed to two other scripts and then wrote another by himself which Pathé professed to like. But when Adolphe saw the rough footage of his story, he insisted on a meeting with the producer and director during which he explained to them that their version was nothing like what he'd seen in his head; he had written a dream and they had shot stultified theater. In turn the producer and director explained to Adolphe that Pathé was the largest studio in the world, bigger than even the ones in Hollywood, and that they knew all about picture making, but if he thought he knew more about picture making than they, he was free to go to any one of the smaller independent studios in Paris, which were many in number and utterly insignificant, like gnats buzzing around the face of the Pathé lion.

He returned that night to the rue de Sacrifice. He went at that hour of the day that had always meant most to him when he lived there, just after the sun had fallen and before the sky was black. Nothing about it had changed; in many ways the street was wilder and more astonishing than it had ever been. He did not choose to do wild and astonishing things. He chose to sit in a café within view of Number Seventeen and watch the front of the house and those who came and went. One or two of them he recognized; most of them were strangers. After two hours and several cognacs, Adolphe was drunk for the first time in his life and waved down one of the customers leaving Number Seventeen. There is a girl, he slurred. Her hair is the tangle of the trees on the Champs-Elysées and her body has not changed since she was twelve; her mouth is plum red. The other man had no idea what he was talking about, and as he walked on, Adolphe put his head on the table and wept in his own arms. The waiter brought a bill.

One morning ten months later, Claude Avril walked from his apartment where he lived alone, caught a carriage to the Métro and the train to north of the city, and sat in his office vaguely dissatisfied, as though it was any other day, thinking about motion pictures. Avril was a barrel-chested man in his forties, born of the French working class, who had raised himself rather tentatively to something higher; not a blowhard, he had still not figured things out, a fact he freely acknowledged and which he felt left him open to new options. He had become bored with other business ventures in which he'd been only moderately successful (because his ambitions in those areas were constrained by his boredom), and so he turned to pictures a few years before, attracted by the gamble of them. He regarded himself, correctly, as something of a financial adventurer; he didn't think of himself as an entrepreneur, let alone a producer. His small studio, located on a piece of land where there had previously stood one of the many flea markets that dotted the suburbs, had limited itself to the one- and two-reelers for which Avril could acquire financial backing; men with money regarded the whole picture nonsense as a novelty, a gimmick, the only thing about it not nonsense

being the ways in which it could be exploited while it lasted.
Avril himself, in no way a creative or artistic man, had this idea
that motion pictures might become big. If it was seen as something barbaric by others, to which mainly barbarians were attracted, like Americans for instance, Avril nevertheless figured
out barbarity was the order of the day; he had begun having that
feeling most profoundly not during the war but in its aftermath.
He was looking out his office window at the lot, watching the
frail ridiculous sets wheeled around, watching the small company
of actors playing pretend like large children in the dirt, when his
assistant came in and said there was a boy to see him.

"A boy?"

"He can't be more than eighteen."

"What does the boy want?"

"To talk to you about a picture."

Well, of course. Monsieur Avril shook his head, she exited,
and he sat there looking at the scene being shot, and realized he
was bored again. He got up from behind his desk, went out of
his office, passed the assistant and opened the door. He caught
up with the boy on the stairs. "You," Avril said to him, from the
top step.

The boy turned. He had pitch black hair, and the look in his
eyes was resolute and alarming.

"Did you have something you wanted to see me about? I'm
Monsieur Avril."

"I'm Adolphe Sarre."

"How old are you?" said Avril.

There was a pause. "Twenty perhaps, maybe a year or two
older. A year or two younger."

"You don't know how old you are?"

"When I went to war they decided I was sixteen. That was
three and a half years ago."

Well then at any rate I will stop calling you a boy, thought
Avril. In the office the two of them sat staring at each other across
the desk. A manuscript was placed before Avril. This is an outline
for a picture, said Adolphe. The manuscript was titled *La Morte
de Marat*. Quite an outline, Avril said, flipping through the
pages. He sat reading for several minutes. He immediately re-

alized the potential in a picture about the French Revolution; but they were talking along the lines of more than a two-reeler. Avril looked up at Adolphe, who was patiently waiting. "Well," said Avril. "It's quite impressive. You've spent a good deal of time and effort on this."

"Ten months," said Adolphe.

"Let me ask you. Have you been to Pathé with it? They might be quite interested."

"Aren't you interested?"

"I didn't say I wasn't."

"I don't want to go to Pathé."

"Why not?"

"I don't want them to take my story away from me."

Avril leaned back, then put his flat hands on the table. He said, "What is it that you want? Do you want to make this picture yourself?"

"Yes."

"Have you ever made a picture?"

"No." Adolphe waited a moment. "I know it's presumptuous."

"I would have to raise a lot of money for this. So, it's more than presumptuous, really. You see what I mean?"

"Yes."

"Do you know Jean-Baptiste Bernard?"

"No."

"He has directed a number of pictures for me."

"You want him to direct this picture?" said Adolphe.

"I don't want to take it away from you," said Avril. "Ten months on the outline alone. We make thirty or forty pictures in that time."

"I know it's presumptuous," Adolphe repeated. "Could you hire me as an assistant to Monsieur Bernard?"

Avril handed the manuscript back to Adolphe. "Come back in three weeks," he said.

Avril talked to Jean-Baptiste Bernard. Some thirty years before, Bernard had made a name for himself staging successful programs for the Opéra; now, nearing seventy, he had been hired on by Avril Studios as someone who knew actors and might maneuver them through the motions. Obviously he was no longer a success in the theater to be squandering his time on pictures; and Avril wasn't really sure that Bernard had a feel for pictures, but he was too unsure of his own feel not to go with someone who at least had some theatrical experience. Bernard listened to Avril's description of the picture he had in mind; as usual, he seemed neither fired nor inspired, only comprehending.

Bernard was all Avril really had to go with. Avril did some investigating, and was somewhat astonished to learn that Pathé didn't have its own French Revolution picture in the works. Avril talked to his investors. They insisted on guarantees, of course, though to Avril's way of thinking this was a business that offered no guarantees; that was what made the possible payoffs so enticing. Then, Avril had a stroke of luck when, at a dinner orchestrated by a mutual acquaintance, he persuaded Marie Rinteuil, one of the Opéra's most prominent actresses, to take the part of Charlotte Corday, the murderess of Marat; she in turn enlisted Paul Cottard, something of a matinee idol in France on the balsmusette circuit, to play the role of Marat himself. The investors were more impressed, and committed an initial outlay of funds toward beginning production of the picture. When Adolphe Sarre returned to the studio in three weeks, to the day, Avril bought the script outright, and hired him on as an assistant producer. Adolphe did seem a bit disconcerted that an actress in her early forties would play the twenty-four-year-old Charlotte, and that a cabaret star was portraying the revolutionary zealot Marat.

The following week Bernard began shooting some interiors. Avril was hunting down costume and set designers for the larger-scale scenes to come, as well as hiring a research team to authenticate period touches for the film. Despite the fact that there was now a considerable buzz in the industry, particularly at Pathé, about the new project over at Avril Studios, Avril himself was oddly depressed. The speculation was whether Avril could pull off such an undertaking, since his operation was puny compared to Pathé and not equipped for something of these proportions; Avril was affected by this nay-saying, even secretly shared the doubts. He had the feeling the equation was all wrong, and when he stopped by the set at times to see how things were progressing—

something he'd never done with the earlier shorts—and watched
Bernard laboriously moving Rinteuil and Cottard through the
paces, with the young Sarre sitting in the corner mute, his sense
of misgiving wasn't abated. A month went by; Avril was still hiring
set designers and running into people from Pathé who approached
and inquired cautiously. He was alarmed that rumors were already circulating the picture was floundering; he closed the set
completely, and locked the gates of the studio to anyone not
associated with the project—which only fueled the rumors more.
Avril summoned Bernard, and told him he wanted to see what
had already been shot.

They met at the back of the lot, in a vacant room where they
kept the backdrops from the shorts they had made over the previous years. They all sat together in the dark: the two stars, several
production assistants, the cameraman, the costume designers,
the set designers, the director, the producer. Afterward the stars
proclaimed themselves satisfied, the production assistants nodded, the costume designers commented on changes that would
be made in the wardrobe; the director, Bernard, shuffled about
listlessly. The cameraman, a Dane named Erik Rode, was silent,
studying the wall long after the images had disappeared. Avril sat
for a while, saying nothing, then slapped his knees and thanked
everyone for coming, asked if anyone had anything else to say,
and dismissed them. They filed out wordlessly; Adolphe sat in
the back of the room. When only the two of them were left,
Avril closed the door. "So," he said. Adolphe looked past Avril
at the wall, much like the cameraman Rode had done. "Nothing
seems to happen," Avril said. He motioned with his hand.

"It's all wrong," said Adolphe. "It has no movement. The
people move but the scene doesn't."

"Why is that?"

"Because the camera doesn't move."

"The camera can't move."

"Griffith moves the camera."

"Yes, well, Griffith."

"Bernard's all wrong about it. He directs like it's a play. The
actors are all wrong for it. They act as though it's a play. It's not

a play. These are moving pictures. They should move."

Avril looked at him. "What is it that attracts you to this?" he said. "Are you a student of history?"

"I don't know anything about history."

"Well then, the character of Marat?"

"It's not Marat."

"No? The events themselves, then."

"Their shadows."

Avril blinked as though he would fall asleep. "Their shadows?"

"Yes."

"Say you were directing this picture. What would you do different? Move the camera?"

"Yes."

"Fire Rinteuil and Cottard?"

"Yes."

"You realize it's Rinteuil and Cottard that got me the financial backing for this. Without them—" He stopped.

"But the money's been committed," said Adolphe.

"On the basis of Rinteuil and Cottard's being in the picture."

"Can they withdraw their commitment if Rinteuil and Cottard are dropped?"

"You're thinking quite a lot, aren't you, Sarre? You're not just sitting over there appearing mysterious after all. I don't know if they can withdraw the commitment, but they can refrain from making other commitments. We'll need those other commitments. We can't make the movie on an initial investment."

"But it *is* an investment," said Adolphe. "They'll have to decide at some point to either take a loss or invest more, hoping to eventually recoup the loss if not make a profit. At that point, it will be up to us to convince them to continue."

"Rinteuil and Cottard are two of our most successful actors, you know."

"We don't want actors. We want faces. I can tell them what to do, how to do it. I can tell them when it's too much or when I need more from them. Rinteuil and Cottard have the wrong faces. We need faces no one's ever seen, and that no one will forget once they've seen them."

"You can tell them what to do, how to do it?"

"Yes."

"You talk as though you're already this picture's director."

"We were speaking hypothetically."

"You know all about this movie stuff, don't you?"

"No."

Avril paced the room. "I've always thought of myself as a gambler, you know? But this frightens me, a little studio like mine in something like this. We're speaking of something grand."

"I know I'm young."

"Yes, well," Avril shrugged, "it's a young industry, all the American directors are young. Griffith's an exception, what, forty-something? The rest are all failed actors, writers, tramps, railroad workers, lawyers. What are you failed at, Sarre?"

Adolphe watched the other man. "I saw a picture last night," he said. "I'd like you to come see it."

So the two of them went to the picture that night, and afterwards walked together by the river. In the early morning hours they were still walking, as the lights on the street began to dim and the clocks shone like numbered moons above the curbs; on the quays below, the tramps slept in rows beside the water. "Well," Avril said, "I thought it was a rather unremarkable picture."

"But you do remember," said Adolphe, "the blind girl in the first part, when we first meet the sailor on the bridge?"

"Yes."

"She was a blonde, with a very sad mouth that turned slightly."

"Yes, right."

"She had brown eyes, and a glow to her skin."

Avril stopped, his hands in his pockets, looking at the young man. "I couldn't tell that from the black-and-white, but I'll take your word for it."

"She was rather sad sometimes, as though she had always been sad."

"I remember. What about her?"

"Charlotte."

"You think so?"

"That's the face."

"And Marat?"

"We'll find him."

They walked awhile longer. "Shadows, you say."

"The shadows," said Adolphe.

The next morning Avril fired Jean-Baptiste Bernard, and hired Adolphe Sarre to direct *La Mort de Marat*. It was clear to almost everyone, in and out of the picture business, that this was simply a huge publicity stunt, a hoax. A shoestring operation like Avril's announcing production of a very large-scale picture, directed by a boy no one had ever heard of and who'd never directed a picture before. The investors were thrown into a state of panic, then fury when they realized Avril had already tied up their money. Avril pleaded that they give Adolphe a chance to see what he could do. He announced to the press in a statement issued from his studio office that it was his solemn and deeply held conviction Sarre was a genius. Adolphe himself decided to get out of Paris awhile. He was going to film *Marat* somewhere else; he wanted to find a place that not only hadn't changed much in a hundred and fifty years—that in itself was easy, France was filled with villages that hadn't changed in a thousand years—but also a location with its own drama, suitable for both Charlotte Corday's late-adolescent madness and Marat's exiles from Paris. (In fact, Marat spent his exiles in England, but Adolphe, his "exacting" research notwithstanding, chose to pay no attention to this.) Adolphe decided to place Corday and Marat in the same proximity several years before Marat's death. He decided he wanted a place near the sea, preferably with either woods or mountains nearby. So, though Charlotte Corday was from the Normandy region of France, Adolphe left not for Normandy but the Bay of Biscay, a tumultuous Paris in his wake; he almost felt as though he was traveling into exile himself.

He went directly to a village called Wyndeaux, without deliberation or question. He would always wonder why later. Avril received the telegram: "Start production here. Send company." Several days later, he stood on the station platform at dawn; a crowd of villagers was already beginning to gather. The train arrived out of the mist, its windows filled with actors and cameramen and technicians, production assistants and creative consultants, writers and researchers and set designers and costume designers, musicians to provide the appropriate mood for the actors during particularly dramatic scenes (these musicians would be dispensed with shortly: Adolphe would provide the mood himself, not second-rate violinists). The passengers seemed to the townspeople like foreigners transported from another time; even the train had a reflective metallic sheen in which were caught images of the future. As the train drew to a sleek halt, the film company poured from the doorways and there was a bustle of activity like the village had not seen, the crowd surging into the city with crates and props and costumes, arcs and tripods and light bridges and mattes and the American Bell and Howells, right past Adolphe Sarre, who was mistaken by all for another village son. He watched them move by, impressed and awed himself: Avril, he thought, didn't get all these people off the backlot of his studio. He followed them on down the town's main road, listening to the laughter and excitement. The next day, from behind the city's fortified gates, he sent for her.

She left Paris like a fugitive in the dead of night, taking a carriage to the Gare de l'Est. Snow was on the tracks as the train moved south. The next morning, as the train pulled into the station, she watched from the cabin window. She had heard he was a young man, back from the war with the rest of the troops only a year earlier. She read in the papers how he lay in a coma in a hospital ward some time before the Armistice; nothing was known of his birth or family. The truth just never occurred to her.

The train came to a stop, and she pulled her one bag from the rack and maneuvered down the aisle of the car. She stepped from the door into the snow and saw no one; above her was an old sign with peeling green letters that read WYNDEAUX. She trudged slowly across the platform toward the building, pulling the bag behind her. When she got inside, she heard, behind her, someone call her name.

She turned to him. He stepped from behind a beam and she saw a blue light through the window cast across his face. For a moment she just watched, the expression in her eyes quizzical, then both suspicious and wondering. Adolphe, she finally said. She shook her head, and then wondered why, how, she could not have remembered. Adolphe de Sarre, her mother had called him.

He stepped forward and took her bag. He stood there a moment, his smile slightly sad. He didn't seem the same as she remembered him. She realized he wasn't supposed to. Let me take your bag, he said, after he already had.

She was not that much different, she was not that much older. She'd done all her growing and changing that morning she was eight years old on the bidet. They walked in silence to the hotel, and he showed her to the room. From her window she could see much of the city to the south: the castle walls jagged and massive, with grisly ramparts and parapets immediately beyond which was the sea. Boats docked along the wharfs just outside the walls, and there were cafés and small dives where the sailors drank at night; lanterns hung in the windows. The ramparts were blue, everything in the city was blue, because the wind blew the salt from the sea across the city; iced and hardened, everything turned blue. On the other side of the city was a forest, and the trees hung pale blue and heavy with salt.

Months later, both of them would wonder, when they were alone or silent together, if all along they had intended to make happen what did happen; it seemed clear to Adolphe that he must have. He knew he hadn't forgotten anything about the rue de Sacrifice. She, on the other hand, would have forgotten the rue de Sacrifice for anything; she would have forgotten Paris for anything, even for making a picture. She didn't care that much about making pictures; she had only made the one a couple of years before, when she was spotted by a producer who came to Number Seventeen one night. She told Adolphe this but nothing more, except that nobody could know she was in Wyndeaux, and if it was announced in Paris that she was to appear in this picture, and was in Wyndeaux filming it, she would depart immediately, she told Adolphe, for either the Alps or the Pyrenees. If he would keep this secret, she would do what he wanted; it didn't matter to her.

The blue was so subtle that she often sat staring at the sheets, the pages of books, the ceiling above her, trying to decide whether they were really blue, or whether the color had so permeated her vision that she was the one who brought the blue to everything she laid eyes on. Within four days of her arrival, even as the company was still preparing for production forty-eight hours away, she sat in the middle of the night staring at the blue; it awakened her. It had been on the backs of her eyelids and on the film of her pupils, and when she rolled over and put her mouth to the pillow, she tasted it. The texture of it was thick like cognac, but the taste was of metal. She sat up and put her head in her hands, clutched the blanket to her chest, and looked through the shutters of the window to the sea and the lights of the boats. She didn't notice, when she called him, that he was there immediately, as though he'd been sleeping outside her door. He pulled her to him and it was only about ten minutes later, so fixed was she on the blue and the shutters and the sea, that she realized he was inside her. Afterwards, with the lamp burning on the writing table, the blue didn't seem so bad; and when she stared into his hair she didn't see the blue at all. She asked him about it, and so he talked about the blue light on into the night, that he had seen it right off when he first arrived, and thought he could use it. He asked if she remembered the light of his room at Number Seventeen, how the room had its own light; that was the way it was here, he said. She hadn't really noticed the light, and he was secretly disappointed. Perhaps she sensed this when she asked why he'd wanted her to make this picture. He told her he had seen her face in the trees on the Champs-Elysées; what he didn't tell her was that he still remembered, had never gotten out of his mind all the time he lay blind among the wounded during the war, how she laughed when Jean-Thomas took her. Adolphe knew he would never forgive the way she laughed, that the laugh itself was a violation of his memory and vision of her; and so he would use that too, like he would use the light of the village. A woman who laughed that way could kill Marat, he told himself.

They always slept together like that afterwards, she clinging to his unblue hair and he wondering if it was the light that had brought him to Wyndeaux. But he didn't really think so.

One night they walked out past the village gates along the water and the boats. They could hear the sounds of the bars on one side and the water lapping against the hulls of the other side.

There was a deep blackness toward the direction of Spain, framing a house on the hill at the end of the beach, which shone even in the night and stole Janine's heart. Will we live in that house someday? she asked Adolphe; and the night was the color of night, not blue—until they came to one café in particular. It glowed the same blue as the village, only more intensely, as though the blue light of the entire village could have emanated from this one café, which hummed and throbbed like a generator. When Janine pulled back, Adolphe pulled forward, his arms in hers, and explained that if they went into this café perhaps she wouldn't be afraid of the blue anymore; but at the door he touched the knob hesitantly, as though it might give off a charge.

The café's interior was like a huge lantern, the walls curved and opaque, shivering with malevolent shadows. At the tables around the room sat perhaps two dozen ancient sailors with full white beards and gleaming white pipes. There was talking and laughing but all of it low, almost hushed; and the way each sailor nodded his head at another's story was very slow and deliberate, and the smiles took forever to form, and even then were never realized fully. On the tables behind the bar were the bottles. There were wine bottles, brandy bottles, whisky bottles, cognac bottles—hundreds of them around the room, lining the walls, on the floors and stacked in corners, rolling to and fro by the feet of the sailors; and all of them, even the ones that appeared discarded, were corked and secured. Inside each and every one burned a blazing blue. All burned so brightly that the entire room was cast in blue. When Adolphe and Janine entered, a number of heads looked up; many of the sailors just went on talking. Adolphe whispered something to Janine; she turned to hear him better; and then saw he was gone from her side. She looked all around her, then back at the sailors in something of a panic. One of them called to her, and someone gave her a glass of brandy. She would have thought it was going to be blue as well, but it was the light brown of brandy. The sailors went on talking; and she was going to leave but the secondary conversations dwindled to nothing and the attention of the room was turning to a very old sailor, perhaps the oldest of them all, who wore a wreath

of ivory around his shoulders and had the longest fingers Janine
had ever seen. He was taking each bottle, uncorking it slowly,
and then raising its mouth to that of a large empty cognac bottle
with a long neck. This bottle had no blue whatsoever, until the
old sailor seemed to pour into it the blue of the other bottles.
He did this with all the bottles, pouring the blue light of each
one into the one cognac bottle until, after several minutes, the
old sailor cried out, warning all those in the room that the glass
might shatter from its livid heat. The old sailors just laughed as
though they'd seen this trick before. But Janine was caught up
by it, mesmerized, and the ancient sailor saw she was; he turned
to a very young sailor sitting by him—a boy really, and the only
one in the café—and winked. To her amazement, Janine saw it
was Adolphe, in a blue and white striped sailor's shirt. He winked
back, and the old man stepped forward to Janine and presented
her with the cognac bottle. He told her to go ahead and take it,
it was cool now and she could touch it. She held it before her,
and with a gasp of wonder, saw that inside the bottle were two
blue eyes. They blinked at her.

All the sailors laughed and started hitting the tables. She looked
up at them and laughed back. She looked at Adolphe but he
wasn't there; and then she had another drink of brandy, and
another. She was feeling drunk and wonderful when she realized
Adolphe hadn't come back, and went out to find him.

Adolphe had been out by the water waiting. He didn't know
why he left the way he did; but when he had gone into the café
with Janine, suddenly something seemed too close—suddenly
whatever had drawn him to Wyndcaux was too imminent. It
must be the light, he said to himself. He was considering returning to the hotel alone when she came up behind him in the
dark, tickling his ear. She laughed when he turned to her. "Yo
ho ho," she said.

"Are you a pirate now?"

"You can make a pirate movie next," she said. "Or make Marat
a pirate. With an eyepatch." She tugged at his shirt. "I so liked
your little sailor suit."

"My little what?"

She laughed. "Look, Adolphe. He gave me the bottle. You went away so quickly you didn't give me a chance to show you. How did he do that?"

He looked at the eyes in the bottle. They blinked at him.

"I mean, I know they can't be real eyes. But it's a wonderful effect."

He led her back to the hotel, as she laughed and babbled on about eyes and sailor suits and how she was sure he'd be a superb sailor if he wasn't a movie director. Once or twice, she seemed groggy as though she would fall asleep on him; and, crossing the last of a series of bridges that led to the city's walls, she stumbled and the bottle landed in the water. Adolphe reached down from the bridge but the bottle drifted just beyond his fingertips, and headed out to sea. "My bottle," Janine said plaintively. They watched it go. "Goodbye," she murmured, and then was lost in his arms.

That season in Wyndeaux, the war that had consumed the world only two years before was but a rumor. History leapfrogged the village most of its thousand winters: the Black Death that seared across the middle of the fourteenth century, eliminating a third of its inhabitants and swallowing up whole towns, never whispered its name in Wyndeaux. If it was true that the plague halved time itself, slicing away the Middle Ages from the Modern, then Wyndeaux was left stranded on the other side, its gargoyles and belfries sighting no demons and housing no prophets, its fortress garrets repelling no invaders, its steeples unbloodied and its corridors providing refuge from no cataclysm. The town remained anonymous to the English who captured the coast from Louis VIII: Wyndeaux persisted French. Remained ignorant of both Catholics and Huguenots in the late sixteenth century: Wyndeaux persisted in its own private zealotry. Remained inviolable before Richelieu's siege in the seventeenth: Wyndeaux persisted unconquered. The revolution passed virtually unnoted, Bonaparte was a name of no interest; and in another two decades' time from this particular point, as Vichy spread German U-boats from one port to the next, Wyndeaux would persist hidden, enveloped in the curtain that world events could never lift.

The people of Wyndeaux, then, had stayed resolutely untouched and unimpressed with the rest of the world right up to the moment the movies came to their village. Avril Productions and *La Mort de Marat* wreaked a bedazzled and virgin havoc. Almost effortlessly, Wyndeaux was transformed overnight, its own facades mingling with newer, more disposable ones, its own scenes clashing with ones shot through with looking-glass light. The film company became a community within a community, and then as the days passed, the communities mixed like uneasily flowing colors—the garish and stunning trickling through the muted and dimly blue. The townspeople felt overrun and threatened until, to their own horror, they found themselves feeling privileged and exhilarated instead, leaning from the windows and stepping from the doors where they'd peered suspiciously at the outset. The company itself, in the meantime, was waiting.

They still weren't certain who they were waiting for. Sometimes, at night, in the window of his hotel, he could be seen

standing and watching over the city; he appeared quite young
and had wild black hair—slightly arrogant and terrified. Occasionally someone would say he saw the young man walking the
docks late at night with a blonde on his arm. The guess was this
was Adolphe Sarre. Directives were issued daily through associates. No shooting had yet begun. Like the rest of the industry
back in Paris, many of these professionals were skeptical. Night
after night they could see him pull the curtain of his window
aside and just stand there looking out, a small light burning
somewhere behind him. The company began to question if they
were going to make a film at all.

Then one day Erik Rode received a summons to Sarre's room.
He arrived at the room to find the black-haired young man standing in the corner; he knew the young man as Jean-Baptiste Bernard's former assistant. Adolphe didn't greet Rode or shake his
hand. They exchanged no pleasantries. Adolphe hid in the shadow
of the corner as though afraid to step into the light. After several
silent moments he blurted from out of the dark his dissatisfaction
with the work Rode had done for Bernard. He told Rode the film
had no depth and that everything looked flat. He stopped and
Rode just waited, brows arched. Adolphe shuffled his feet a bit;
he held his arms folded, as though he was chilled. I'm sorry, he
began again.

Rode interrupted him. "Monsieur Bernard wanted to shoot
everything at high noon," he said. "That kind of direct light will
flatten everything out. The man didn't know much about pictures."

Adolphe asked whether it was possible to shoot either earlier
in the day or later, and Rode said this was just fine with him.
He said that shooting about seven-thirty in the morning or five
in the afternoon would give the kind of three-quarter light the
director wanted for his exteriors. It would also leave the middle
of the day, or even night, for shooting interiors. Do you know
what I want? said Adolphe.

"I'm not sure." Rode waited. "Do you know what you want?"
I'm pretending I do, Adolphe answered. Then Adolphe and
Rode talked a long while. Rode told the director that other than
the cameraman, the two key people in translating to film what

the director wanted were the art director and film editor. Rode recommended a Dutchman who had worked as an art director on several recent German productions. The Dutchman turned out to be available and arrived within a week. After discussing the picture Adolphe and the Dutchman both came to the conclusion that their sets and mattes weren't right. They determined to reconstruct new sets according not to real life proportions but rather "the proportions of the mind," as the art director called them. Consequently a lot of the detail material the research team had come up with in the interest of authenticity was thrown out; a strict reality was binding and, in a sense, less real than an illusion which communicated more directly to the audience's emotions. Moreover, because of the way Adolphe wanted to light the film, whole surfaces of the mattes weren't worth completing at all—they would only be cast into shadow later.

The film editor turned out to be a young American woman from New York who had apprenticed with a couple of D. W. Griffith pictures, as well as directors like Rex Ingram and Maurice Tourneur. Working with Tourneur had brought her to Paris, and like everyone she was intrigued with what was already becoming a sort of dubious, even notorious *Marat* legend. She came to Wyndeaux about a month after the picture had already begun shooting. She learned what the other professionals had already found out—that Adolphe had a good idea what he wanted after all. Years later Rode would tell people that Sarre knew nothing about movie-making but everything about making movies, because he didn't make movies as such: "He filmed," said Rode, "his dreams." His eye and his instincts were right. He had a feeling for throwing foreground figures into shadow while sharpening the focus of the background, creating a riveting effect in the process. Adolphe didn't do this by using complicated lighting but rather by simplifying the lighting—using one or two lamps instead of six. Adolphe also saw the effect of this without ever looking through a camera; and in fact he refused to look through Rode's camera: he seemed to have a contempt for and fear of men's machinations. It was clear even to Rode, who understood little else about Adolphe, that the young man viewed things from a different place on the abyss, where the view was dimensionally altered and schematically dialectic; and that if Adolphe ever paused long enough to look at all of it through a lens, he would lose the vision. For this reason Adolphe needed his technicians desperately: yet he was reassured, for instance, that Rode still worked with a hand-crank camera rather than the modern motorized ones; that his editor disdained the new animated viewers and instead cut the film in the hand, holding it up to the light. Within six weeks of shooting—a time frame in which many films were completed—there were still weeks of work ahead of them. Yet Rode and the others felt the young director was onto something.

In Paris Claude Avril continued to finesse the film's finances. Marie Rinteuil and Paul Cottard told the press that while they found the notion of being directed by a twenty-year-old boy out of the ordinary, they were nonetheless ready to begin shooting. But once production was under way in Wyndeaux, Avril informed them that they too had been released from the picture. Now the picture's investors were murderous. *Marat* was a joke in the papers; and Avril hid in his apartment, communicating with the outside world through desperate telegrams to Adolphe about the picture's progress. Each day he waited nervously for an answer that never came. Finally, after two months passed, the police came to his apartment. The investors were prepared to press charges of fraud against him. Avril met with the investors and asked if they would at least look at what Sarre had done. He sent one more wire to Adolphe which read: "I will go to prison if you do not return immediately with picture."

Avril set up a screening at the back of the studio much like the one that had taken place several months before. The representatives of the principal investors arrived—three of them—and one of them brought a tall and rather aristocratic American who happened to be visiting Paris at the time. They waited for Adolphe until twenty minutes past the appointed hour. Repeatedly Avril would walk to the door and stare out into the dark. "Where's the genius?" the investors asked. Then he was there in the doorway without a word, just looking at them; under his coat he clutched the reels of the picture. The only thing that seemed to catch his attention was the aristocratic American in the corner; Avril could see something in Adolphe's eyes go slightly awestruck. Adolphe crossed the room and ran the film through the projector. When the lights were raised forty minutes later, everyone looked from the screen to each other. Adolphe stared at the empty seat from where the American had already left. The door was ajar.

Hurriedly Adolphe packed up the film in the canisters, not even rewinding. Everyone watched as though waiting for an explanation; when he ran from the room, someone finally called out, "Why isn't it like other pictures?" With the director gone, Avril was left to face the questions. "Why is it so dark?" said someone else. "Yes," said another, "the actors are always in the shadows." Asked the first, "He keeps moving the camera. Why doesn't he just keep the camera in one place?" The second said, "I kept getting dizzy, all that moving around."

Avril ran from the room too. By the time he got to his apartment, he realized he was ruined; now his only concern was whether he would have to go to prison. At the top of the stairs he found Adolphe huddled outside the door; suddenly he looked like a boy again, younger than he had ever looked. Adolphe glanced up at Avril wildly and got to his feet. "You can't let them take my movie away," he said. Avril just looked at him in the dark of the hall; he tore the boy's hands from his coat. He said, "I may go to prison."

"Did you think it was so bad?" said Adolphe.

Avril just shook his head.

"Did you think it was so—"

"It doesn't matter! I don't know what's good or bad. It wasn't like anything else, that's all I know. Why do you ask me? I don't want to go to prison, that's all I know." He paused. The young director looked shattered. "Do *you* think it's bad?" he said to him.

"No," said Adolphe.

"Then why did you leave?"

"Because *he* left."

"Who?"

"Didn't you see him in the corner?"

"The American?"

Adolphe looked at him amazed; he exploded with it. "It was Griffith!"

"Griffith?" Now Avril was flabbergasted. Adolphe was leaning against the wall, staring down the stairs. He still held the film close to him. Griffith walked out of my picture, he just said vacantly. Avril sighed deeply and took him by the arm. He put the key in the door and opened it. "Come inside," he muttered, "none of it matters now."

Inside, Adolphe crumpled into a corner on a pillow. When Avril woke the next morning, he was gone, and had taken the picture with him. Avril knew instantly that Adolphe had gone back to Wyndeaux to continue making the picture: when he returned to the village Adolphe told neither Janine nor the crew anything about the difficulties. Rather he explained that things had gone well, the screening had been received enthusiastically, and the picture now had to be completed as soon as possible. Adolphe knew, in fact, that this was not possible; he had only scratched the surface with what he had done so far. The company in Wyndeaux began shooting around the clock, hurried by the conclusion Adolphe knew was approaching down the railroad tracks. When he looked up one afternoon, several days after his departure from Paris, to see Claude Avril walking toward him, he dismissed the crew at once and walked with Avril into an alley out of earshot. Adolphe collapsed by the window of a patisserie. I won't give up my picture, he said.

"Adolphe," said Avril, "look." He shoved into his hands a copy of *Le Figaro*. On the front page was an exclusive interview with the great American motion picture director, D. W. Griffith, in which Griffith was quoted talking about European movies. He was citing the advances of the art in Germany, Italy, Scandinavia, Russia, and France. He was talking about how just the other evening he had seen an unfinished picture about the French Revolution by a young man named Sarre. The interviewer asked incredulously whether Griffith actually meant *La Mort de Marat* by Adolphe Sarre, explaining that there had been a great deal of controversy about the picture, that in fact most observers considered *Marat* a joke. Sarre, after all, was practically a boy who had never made a picture. "That's impossible," answered Griffith. "He has made many pictures, that's obvious to me. He has intuitive picture-making talents. Let me tell you, I went home that evening and woke seeing the faces in this picture, particularly the girl, and the way this Sarre moves her in and out of light. The fact that he's young means nothing, of course. Old men don't make pictures." He laughed. "I am the only old man who makes pictures." Is Sarre a genius then? asked the interviewer. "I don't know what a genius is in this business," Griffith said. "Let's say he's an original."

With the Griffith interview, *Marat*, though no less controversial, became a controversy to be taken seriously; the world's greatest movie director had said so. Pathé wired Avril offering to resolve whatever financial problems existed in completing the film. Avril, pulled from the edge of ruin, was not about to quibble over pride and independence; he accepted Pathé's offer, in essence turning his studio over to them while still retaining his role as executive producer. Adolphe plunged into the movie, fevered and impatient, and the news of the Griffith interview charged the company as well. Renting a very old theater on the edge of the village for the scenes where the revolutionary tribunal assembled and Marat met both intermittent triumph and setback, Adolphe packed the floor and the galleries with large crowds of townspeople, portraying the masses caught up in smoldering rhetoric. The director and Erik Rode got their best effect by hitching cameras to three perambulators that moved overhead along an intricate network of cables. Taxiing back and forth above, the cameras themselves provoked in the faces of the townspeople the mix of majesty and terror that Adolphe wanted. Over and over they did the scene, the heat in the hall intensifying with the light, the pressure building, makeup people dashing back and forth dabbing at faces and reapplying paint, costume people running through the crowd to rearrange a collar or a sleeve seen as askew from the galleries where Adolphe was giving directions. Over and over Adolphe exhorted both his company and the townspeople; he wanted to wear them down, push them to an edge. When he finally announced it was a take, the people on the floor turned to him and cheered, and the boy stood there astounded.

Avril told Adolphe that since the article in *Le Figaro* people in Paris had been asking about the new actress, wanting to know who she was. They are asking about you, Adolphe told Janine down by the water one night, and she threw herself into his arms and clung to him. "Don't let them take me back to Paris," she said, "please don't let them." From this place by the water, they had watched, as the evenings passed, one old woman who stood alone in a long black cloak gazing out to sea. As the evenings passed they had watched the sleeves of her cloak become entwined in the vines of the ramparts, and now Adolphe looked up from where he stood with Janine to see the cloak completely woven into the vines, the hood still raised, arms still extended, poised in the same stance as always: only now the old woman herself was gone. Of course I won't let them take you, he said. "You can't tell them who I am," she said, "promise me you won't." I won't tell them, he said, against the black sea.

He could no longer delay resolving the problem of casting Marat. He had sometimes walked along the docks, in the bars and cafés, to find the face he wanted. He decided he would now have to return to Paris, and took an evening train with Avril; it was a pleasant trip almost all the way, each of them still feeling a glow of success and good fortune. But outside Paris they had a terrible disagreement. Adolphe told Avril he had to find a Marat soon, for a number of reasons. "Of course," said Avril, "you can't very well make a picture about Marat without having a Marat."

"It's more than that," said Adolphe, watching out the window as the sun rose over France.

"What, then?"

"Janine will have to take time off." Adolphe turned to him from the window. "She's pregnant."

Avril sat for a few moments in irritation. "Tell me the truth, Adolphe," he finally demanded. "You've known this woman all along, haven't you. From the beginning you knew her, before you ever saw her in that other picture, before you ever cast her in this role."

"Of course," answered Adolphe. "She's my sister."

Avril went white. His mouth fell and the words seemed to gurgle up. "My God," he choked, almost inaudibly. "My God."

Adolphe flushed. For a moment he didn't say anything and then he jumped up from the seat and took his suitcase down from the rack. "Fuck you, Claude," he said, leaning over Avril, his face just inches from the other's. "Don't try to tell me men never take their sisters. Don't try to tell me that." His face was contorted with rage. He slammed open the door of the cabin, stepped out, and slammed it closed again. He moved down the hall and stood in the aisle the remaining thirty minutes into Paris while Avril sat absolutely motionless, afraid to stir, as though the shock fired into him had lodged near an artery and would tear through his heart at the slightest murmur of sound or body.

He was drawn to Wyndeaux; he still didn't understand why. Spring came and the blue light faded, and in the hours when he wasn't shooting, when he still felt drawn, he went to the water and stared into it. With the glimmer of sunlight on the water he tried to peer through again, to see what was behind; but he didn't seem able to do that anymore. He watched the sailboats and houseboats bobbing by the docks and felt, inside him, the pull, and tried to fathom it.

He had found his Marat in Paris, an Irishman reading poetry in an English bookshop near the Deux Magots. His name was Terry Tonay, and while Adolphe was amused by the irony of an Irishman playing the great Frenchman Marat, he decided to change the poet's name to Thierry Touraine. Within a month after Touraine had returned with Adolphe to Wyndeaux to shoot, it became clear to the director that his star was a bit disturbed; Touraine's eyes took on a gleam too luminescent, and Adolphe, who had always understood well the meaning of light, understood that something in the poet's head was afire, the brain was crackling. Summer came and then autumn, and now there was beginning to be trouble again. The sensation of the Griffith interview had become old hat, old questions were being raised anew; there was the suggestion that perhaps Griffith, who was coming to be regarded as old hat himself, was a little too easily taken in by Sarre. No one was calling Adolphe a joke anymore; but a lot of suspicious people held that in fact he was neither a genius nor an original but a shrewd con artist, who could not, when all was said and done, deliver. It was unheard of to spend this much time on a movie. Pathé wanted to see rushes. Janine was about to have the child, and Avril was trying to keep it undercover, certain he was sitting atop a horrible scandal that would wreck everything.

They named the child Jacques. Janine adored him from the moment she saw he wasn't blue. She took the baby's head in her hands the way she had taken Adolphe's hair. Adolphe was caught up in other things—using the time to film Marat's scenes and realizing that he'd shot all he could in Wyndeaux, that the big scenes would have to be filmed in Paris. Adolphe needed to get back to a studio—either Avril's or, ideally, Pathé's, and construct a Bastille for the section of the picture that involved its siege. But Paris was problematical: Adolphe knew there were new rumblings there, and interference he wouldn't be able to tolerate; he knew Janine would adamantly, for reasons she still hadn't told him and which he'd never asked, refuse to return to the city; and there was Wyndeaux itself, which Adolphe was loath to leave, for reasons he asked himself continually, never receiving an answer.

Coordinates of crisis and conflict crisscrossed the landscape. Almost immediately Janine became pregnant again, to Adolphe's astonishment and rage; he railed at her in the bedroom, stricken with resentment and frustration, even as the other child cried in the night. Then the following week, he found Janine and Jacques gone, the lamp burning by her bedside and everything in disarray; and assuming she was leaving him, he summoned two stagehands in the hotel and they ran across town for the station. They could see the train huffing in rattled repose, smoke billowing from its front and the ground quaking from pending departure; the cries of the baby would be heard from the platform where Adolphe had waited patiently for her that first day. They caught up with two men forcibly putting mother and child aboard, and the scuffle resulted in Janine breaking loose and running to Adolphe with Jacques in her arms, while the two abductors lay beaten and dazed in the doorway of the train's second car as the engine pulled out heading back to Paris. But relieved as she was by the rescue, back in her room she would not tell Adolphe who the men were or why they were trying to take her back; and Adolphe wound up storming from the room, slamming the door behind him, while Janine sobbed on the bed. From the next room he listened to her all night.

Adolphe placed two guards by the actress's door. But when the strangers who had tried to take her showed up again six days later, still a little bruised and bandaged from the fracas, it was Adolphe they came to see. This time there was no fracas. Contritely they took off their hats when he answered the door, and presented him with a card that read *Varnette*. They said Monsieur Varnette requested a meeting with Monsieur Sarre for the purpose of discussing a business proposition. They led Adolphe to the station where the Paris train was waiting once more, gleaming and wreathed in blank white smoke, with a single private car where the shades of the windows were drawn—all but one. When Adolphe was ushered into the car this Monsieur Varnette was standing at the window staring out; over his shoulder Adolphe could see the still blue night of the empty station, as though it had been vacated just for this meeting. The car was adorned in dark maroon silks and velvet, immaculately trimmed with ivory and gold; a small lamp shrouded by a cover of etched glass burned on the desk, where a crystal brandy decanter stood waiting between two snifters. Monsieur Varnette's head turned slightly at Adolphe's entrance; he watched back out the window another moment before approaching. When Monsieur Varnette stepped from the corner shadow of the car, Adolphe thought he felt his whole self rush up from the pit of him, leaving him and looking back down on his own flabbergasted panic.

The two talked. Adolphe could barely concentrate on what the other was saying; at first he couldn't even bring the brandy to his mouth, then found himself gulping it down, all the while studying Monsieur Varnette's face. Varnette did not look much different from some years before. Part of the side of his jaw seemed slightly misshapen, and he carried one side of his body a bit stiffly; perhaps those were the results of the fall. At no time did he seem to recognize Adolphe. He spoke calmly, charmingly, while Adolphe just sat staring into his eyes, trying to determine what exactly Varnette remembered, and whether the memory was obscured by the circumstances of the event—the crazed way he looked when he took her, the way Adolphe had pushed him out the window without allowing for a second glance—or the trauma of the event, or the fact that Adolphe simply didn't look much like Adolphe anymore; everyone told him that, that he always looked different. Finally beginning to relax, Adolphe mused awhile over his ability to change appearance, which he decided was directly related to his power over light and shadow, before finally turning his attention to what his host was saying.

Essentially, Varnette was explaining that his father had brought Janine's mother from Tunisia, having bought her in an auction; and that since the mother was property of the father, the daughter was as well. And that since the father was now dead and had left everything to the son, both women belonged to him. The mother, Varnette said, was still in the private brothel on the rue de Sacrifice. The daughter he had come for now.

You're talking about slavery, Adolphe said to Varnette. Nobody has slaves anymore.

Everybody, answered Varnette, has at least one slave.

Varnette completed his proposition. He went on to say that he wasn't interested in physically trying to wrest the girl from Adolphe; it would be much easier for Adolphe to deliver the girl over to him. He conceded that going to the police wouldn't do; this left Varnette to deal with the situation in the way that suited him best, which was to buy back what was already his. Sometimes, he smiled almost sheepishly, one simply has to buy back what one already owns; after all, Adolphe had the upper hand since he had the girl. Adolphe asked if Janine was Varnette's wife. Of course not, said Varnette. She's my sister.

He went on with his plan. He knew Adolphe was filming a picture, and Varnette was ready to place a great sum of francs at Adolphe's disposal. Adolphe was mortified. Sitting there listening to Varnette brought back to him all the things he felt when he lived on the rue de Sacrifice; he wanted to tell Varnette that he was sorry the fall from the third floor window hadn't killed him. He quietly got up to walk out. Varnette also stood, still charming and deferential, said he understood Adolphe's reluctance, he could easily believe a man would want to keep a girl like Janine (how many faces light the trees of the Champs-Elysées?), but would Adolphe at least do himself the favor of taking Varnette's card—upon which Varnette wrote where he could be reached in Paris—and let him know just in case, by some chance, he should change his mind. Adolphe stuffed the card in his pocket and left, out the cabin, from the car, past the two who had escorted him.

When he had gotten beyond the station, Adolphe believed then that his victory over Jean-Thomas was now complete. Moreover, this was a triumph for everyone who had despised Jean-Thomas at Number Seventeen. On the way back to his hotel his thoughts turned to the picture, and he imagined wonderful scenes, saw them across the streets and walls and in the windows before him as if they were projected through his eyes.

Two days later he received a wire from Avril: "Pathé withdrawing completely. Stop production."

A letter from Avril followed the next day. It enclosed a press clipping from *Le Figaro* announcing the halting of production on *La Mort de Marat*. Avril made no attempt to mask his bitterness toward Adolphe. He wrote that the young director had "arrogantly squandered the opportunity of a lifetime," convincing the studio, through Adolphe's own "clandestine and egocentric" manner in making the movie, that in fact the movie would never be finished. Adolphe's first decision was to not let his company know. But when rumors spread throughout the village, he was forced to go before them, amassing them in the old theater where they had shot the assembly footage. He implored them to stay with him and help him finish the picture. He implored them for ideas on how to raise the money to finish the picture. His company was dedicated to him and to the movie; but they had questions as to how much more there was to shoot, how long it would take, how much it would cost—exactly where he still planned to go and how far he wanted to take them. When he evaded these questions, someone pointed out that the big scenes, ones that would have to be shot either on a studio lot or in Paris, had not even begun to be filmed.

He felt it all unraveling; he saw himself losing everything. He knew only one thing and that was he couldn't lose his picture, he would do anything to save it. He told all of them he would raise the money, and then he wired Pathé begging for another six months and the money for the big scenes: he offered to let them see what he had so far if that would placate them. He received no answer from Pathé. He wrote Avril. He received no answer from Avril. He wired every other studio in Paris, and failing to receive answers from them he wired studios in Berlin and Rome. He received wires from them expressing interest in *Marat* and wishing Adolphe the best; but alas, no money. He wired Griffith in America. Griffith wired back that he remembered Adolphe's picture vividly, that he had awakened many mornings after seeing it with the picture's faces in his mind; he hoped Adolphe would finish the picture, he hoped Adolphe didn't mind *Orphans of the Storm*, Griffith's own film of the French Revolution; but, said Griffith, he was having his own problems, making a picture now about the American Revolution, and Griffith could offer only the observation (meant, perhaps, to be ironic) that since he had had such success with the French Revolution, perhaps the French director would have better luck with the American Revolution than the American director was having now.

And in the course of this, Adolphe avoided Janine, looking at her longingly and with resentment, which she took to be his frustration over her new pregnancy.

One long black night Adolphe took the train to Paris.

Nothing about Jean-Thomas' manner had changed at all; still courteous and charming, he was not smug or gloating. There were things Varnette had to understand, said Adolphe; and Varnette listened calmly. I need Janine in order to finish this picture, said Adolphe. Without her there is no picture; without the picture there is no agreement to be made. So you would have to give me the money now, with the understanding that I would turn her over to you when her role is finished. I cannot be held accountable should she leave you again, Adolphe went on; you'll have to be responsible for keeping her once you've gotten her. Finally, she's pregnant. It's my child. We already have a son. I would like the boy sent to me when he's fifteen years old.

Varnette listened intently and then pulled from the drawer his checkbook. You'll have to finish filming Janine's part immediately, he said. How soon can you do it? It's hard to say, Adolphe answered. I'll give you funds for the next six months, said Varnette, as well as arrange for a studio lot in Paris. We can begin work constructing the sets for the scenes you need to do here. I have to build a Bastille, said Adolphe. A huge Bastille, bigger than life, one that towers over the people in the streets, one that seems larger than it actually is. It must have very long spires, and very deep cells, and it must remind a person how trapped he can feel.

The following day the Paris newspapers announced that a private French corporation had agreed to finance the completion of the picture, and that in exactly one year and one day, the Paris Opéra would premiere *La Mort de Marat vue par Adolphe Sarre*. Two days after that story appeared, appeared another, reporting that the uncompleted film had screened to an artists' club in Montparnasse attended by the cream of Paris's cultural vanguard, and the reception had been astounding; film makers and writers and visualists of various media were quoted as saying Adolphe was making the greatest film ever, one that would catapult film decades forward much as Griffith's *The Birth of a Nation* had done. Sarre, the newspapers stated, returned to Wyndeaux in triumph.

In triumph, he sat on the train like a dead man, staring out the window into the dark. From the station he walked back to the hotel alone, in the early hours of the morning, to find Janine waiting up for him. She threw her arms around him when he arrived. She curled herself up next to him and pressed her face against his chest. They went to bed and later in the night he got up to sit in the window, in the corner of the room, pulling his coat around him. He stared at the walls, watching in his mind the images he'd shown the artists of Montparnasse; and when those images ran out he watched the ones he knew he would film next. The siege of the Bastille, the execution of Louis the king and his Austrian queen, Marie Antoinette, dogs licking the faces that dropped from the guillotine to the ground below. When he saw the hanging bodies of the September Massacre, he knew every body would have to be Charlotte Corday's; from the window of the hotel he saw the small dangling bodies in all the other windows of the village. There in the room he concocted more elaborate techniques for his picture. He split the frames in two, three parts, then nine, then twelve; he considered altering the entire film to give it a three-dimensional effect, which he knew he could do, since he had discovered long before that dimension was only another illusion, that everything was flat after all. As the film progressed toward an end, it would swing farther and farther in its shifts between extreme close-ups of faces and epic vistas of history, until the rhythm was intolerable.

As the days went by he began adding to the script more scenes for Charlotte, to the confusion of his cast and crew; the joke circulating the company was that the film would be renamed *La Mort de Charlotte*. A month went by and then two, and he began receiving wires from Varnette. I need her a while longer, Adolphe would reply; and when another two months passed the wires became more impatient, threatening. The company began to have the feeling Adolphe was stalling. Meanwhile, her pregnancy notwithstanding, he took to making love to Janine more violently; and one night she realized a camera was running just inches from her face as they did it. I trust you, Adolphe, she kept saying, clinging to him; and he said to her, looking at the ecstasy of her expression, That is the look I want, for the moment when you murder Marat.

That was the scene they shot over and over. Two more months passed, and now there was no more time: the wires from Varnette were ominous: the Bastille set was ready and he wouldn't commit any more money without the return of the girl: he accused Adolphe, accurately, of prolonging the completion of the deal. Moreover, Janine was now visibly pregnant at six months; the murder scene would have to be shot in extreme darks and lights, and another week or two it would be impossible to hide her condition without shooting everything from the neck up, which just wouldn't do, since murder is an act of the body, or at least the hands. All day Touraine sat in the bathtub, head wrapped in a towel. Repeatedly Adolphe called his stagehands to bring more hot water, since he wanted to catch the steam rising from the bath. Repeatedly Adolphe ran Janine through the scene, demanding more of her, turning the scene more and more violent until by the twentieth take she was beginning to break down. You murder so gracefully, Adolphe hissed at her; I know you're not really so meek. Repeatedly she poised herself above Touraine and raised the knife; repeatedly Adolphe called upon her to invest in the act something strange and more twisted. Finally he decided Charlotte should kiss Marat first; he even considered having Charlotte make love to him in the bath. Someone suggested to Adolphe that it probably didn't happen that way; Adolphe replied he wasn't concerned with the "accepted view" of history. History was his and it was what Adolphe said it was; and if he determined that Charlotte raped Marat in the bathtub before murdering him, then that was how it happened. When someone else on the set said perhaps this would seem a bit melodramatic, Adolphe exploded, screaming that, all right, Charlotte would not rape Marat, Charlotte would not kiss Marat, but Charlotte must kill Marat with more passion than Janine was giving the scene; and he showed her as she began to cry: he placed the knife in her hands and brought it high above her head, and brought it down aimed for his own chest. And only at the last moment did she pull back the knife, her wide eyes fixed on him, all the crew fixed on him—there was an audible gasp when he brought the knife in her hands toward his own chest, like the gasp that greets a man who has wavered and nearly fallen from a tightrope, very high up.

They finished the scene and he stumbled out like the dead man who had ridden the train from Paris; that night the crew celebrated the end of its work in Wyndeaux, while Adolphe sat saying nothing, talking to no one. Janine sat by him, watching his face. Finally, after she had asked what was wrong too many times for him to bear, he took her hand and they walked down the wharf up to the hotel where he told her to pack. We'll go to Venice tonight, he said, together; we'll spend a few days by ourselves and then you can remain there while I finish the picture in Paris, and I'll return to you. Excitedly she packed her things and dressed Jacques. It was only when he was pulling her and their son down the street that she realized he hadn't packed anything; he kept looking for a light. A light off a window, or by a street, or from the moon. One light close at hand through which the two of them could run and never come back. But there was no light, only the blue, and then the train station. Varnette was waiting.

She didn't see him there with his henchmen until they were only feet away; and then her mouth opened and she caught a small cry with her hand. She looked at Adolphe, incredulous, and then back at Varnette, in his long beige coat, staring at her. Adolphe, she said. She took her hand from her mouth and put it on his neck. Adolphe, she begged.

He stopped. His face was convulsed and hot. He was breathing heavily, never looking at her but looking ahead. "You laughed," he finally said. "You laughed that night."

She looked in his eyes, trying to get him to look at her. "What night," she murmured.

"The night he had you. That night in Number Seventeen."

For the life of her, she could not remember. She could only remember being in a kind of shock, and if she laughed it was hysteria; but she could not remember.

"It doesn't matter," he said. "What does it matter. Whether you're with this brother or that brother."

She narrowed her eyes, searching his. "Brother?" she said. She looked over her shoulder at Varnette, and then back at him. "Brother?" Adolphe stared at her blankly. She said, "You're not my brother. Did you think she was your mother? She wasn't your mother. Your mother left you by the Seine. No one ever knew your mother."

He just looked at her. He began to form a question on his lips, his eyes began to register what she'd said, when the two men came and took her and the child. They pulled them away from him, and then Adolphe looked past them to Varnette and the private car behind him. Varnette barely glanced at Janine. Janine continued to watch Adolphe, beseeching him. Varnette smiled a small smile and licked his lips. "I will finalize our financial arrangement tomorrow, monsieur," he said. He turned slightly, and then added, "For a man who doesn't believe in slaves, you've done rather well. Particularly considering that, when was it, five years ago? You nearly killed me for her." The two men pulled Janine aboard and then Varnette followed; and as the train pulled out of Wyndeaux, Adolphe Sarre heard her calling him from far down the tracks.

He continued to stand there long after the train was gone. At dawn he left the station. He walked back the same streets he had come. He couldn't be sure whether what he saw was the same blue light or the break of day. All the windows where he had looked before were black and dull, and he couldn't bring himself to look in the faces of those who were already out and about. Nobody called to him as he walked past, though everyone in the village knew him; in a stupor he seemed to stumble into things on his way to the water, past the gates of the city, the vines of the walls hanging in the archways and brushing his forehead as he rushed forward. He passed the cafés and bars. Finally, when the sun should have been breaking over the woods behind him, when the wind brought the smell of the vineyards kilometers away mixing with the smell of the ocean salt, he came to the wharf's edge, amidst the houseboats docked in rows and the bridges that linked with the land. He stopped and stared to the west and the overcast sky that had the flat tone of metal. At that moment he was thinking of when he was a boy living in Number Seventeen, and the early hours like these when he would prowl the house, lurking around the slumbering courtesans, and how by the doorway he always heard the sound of the falling blocks from the ice truck in the street. He waited for the light of the sun to blister the water. Staring at the water, he waited for one splash of blinding light on the surface. At that moment, when he saw that light, then he would dive through once and for all. If, at the close of the war, he had decided there was no point in going beyond what he saw, if he'd decided what was behind the screen was no different from what was before it, he nevertheless believed now that it couldn't be more terrible, it couldn't make him feel more detestable, because at least the barbarism would not be his own; and perhaps, in leaping from the dock, his arms pointed sharply in front of him, and in slowly gliding through to the other side, he would emerge as nothing, as though he never existed—which was all that he wanted right now. He stood there waiting for it to open up to him but it did not. There was no light on the water. There was only, curiously, his own reflection; he saw himself standing on the deck of one of the houseboats. When he looked up he saw himself, in a blue and white striped sailor's shirt, open the door of the boat's cabin, and disappear inside.

One morning in Montreal, a small boy named Fletcher Grahame was staring at the Saint Lawrence River from the study window when his father accidentally fired the flintlock. The antique gun went off right behind his head. As the sound rose in his ears to become the sound he would hear off and on the rest of his life, the roar of the river matched that sound and the two became inseparable for him; long after that he would hear the crack of the flintlock whenever he gazed too long at the water's ongoing flow. At that particular moment Fletcher turned to see himself in the mirrored panel of the room's corner, and the way his face formed a series of anguished concentric circles that became more constricted as the sound grew more unbearable. He was not to forget the way he looked then. Moreover, all the expressions of all the people in his father's paintings, propped in easels around the room, transformed with the boy's own expression, until it was clear to the boy (he was a serious boy, not fanciful or irrational) that the flintlock's report had seared all of them; all the faces in all the paintings looked as though they couldn't stand the ringing in their ears. His father just stood there in the red coat he always wore when he painted or thought of himself as a painter, staring at the hot gun in his hand as though a ghost had spoken to him. A huge hole smoked in the upper wall, torn by the blast of a pistol that had not been fired in a hundred years. Fletcher's father set the gun back on the shelf and backed away from it, expecting the epiphany to simply vanish; and when he saw the expression on his son's face he began to sob with the child, out of horror as plaster fell from the wall's wound.

Indeed it was for his most famous painting that Mr. Grahame had received the gun when he himself was quite young. This had come in the painter's one true moment of glory, at the age of thirteen. He had completed an epic titled *Convention Hall During the Reign of Terror* to accompany a film premiere in the early twenties. The painting was quite large, amply filling the wall of the study now, and it brought the prodigy real fame. The young painter was even brought to Paris to see his painting hanging in the Opéra where the film was to debut. When, inexplicably, the movie was withdrawn the day of its scheduled opening, an opportunity was quashed for the painter as well: the boy took his painting back to the village where he grew up, and later to Canada when he left France. He changed his name to the decidedly English Franklin Grahame, and married an English girl fifteen years younger and lived among the English half of segregated Montreal, all of this reflecting some sense of having been betrayed. Nevertheless he kept the flintlock which had been presented to him for the painting, and which had been used in the film itself, and which as far as anyone knew had remained unloaded and unfired since revolutionary days. Now in the smell of gunpowder and continuing echo of the gun's resurrection, to Fletcher Grahame the people in his father's *Convention Hall During the Reign of Terror* looked as though they were holding back not only the deluge of blood but this same explosion, even Danton and Robespierre and Marat themselves—as though the entire assembly was driven to frenzy by a sound they couldn't shake from their heads.

Reasonably, Fletcher didn't blame his father for the gun's death throes; inexplicably, he blamed himself. His affection for his father was so overpowering that the boy could only hold himself accountable for his father's grief, which he assumed, because he was so young, had everything to do with the accident. Later, as he grew older, neither his dedication nor his guilt were shaken by potentially disillusioning realizations about his father's so-called genius. In fact, Franklin Grahame was not a good painter at all, and became an increasingly disturbed one after the incident with the gun; neither his style nor technique nor vision progressed beyond his one big masterpiece done at the age of thirteen, and finally the study became filled with portraits of children peering in the window—the Saint Lawrence behind them—screaming through the glass at the flash of a weapon stupidly detonated. Later, the painter began rendering pictures of little bodies actually shot down, some falling through the glass, some lying just beyond the walkway. After Mr. Grahame died, Fletcher's mother continued to maintain her husband was a great and overlooked painter and turned the house into a museum of his work, explaining the paintings' power and the details of the artist's life to her guests, habitually subtracting ten years from Grahame's age—this to convince people he died a young tragic prodigy rather than a middle-aged failure. Still later, when Fletcher corrected his mother on the age, she denied it vehemently, though the arithmetic would have seemed irrefutable. But by this time the young Grahame had already known the truth awhile, ever since he bought through a retailer a one-reel silent movie with no credits titled *The French Revolution* and saw his father's masterpiece in celluloid. Then it became clear that this was the same movie which *Convention Hall* was painted for, and that his father was not even really a talented young prodigy but rather a talented young copier, who expertly derived this epic from a single frame of film.

One night when he was fifteen he took the film to the Montreal Cinema Archives to show its curators. These men found the picture a source of some amusement and fascination; the head of the archives, a man old enough to have seen *The Great Train Robbery* as a youth, was impressed with Fletcher's interest and promised him he would pursue it. He also offered to let Fletcher keep the film in the archives vault; they signed an agreement to this effect, establishing that the film belonged to the boy. I would think the film belongs to whomever made it, said Fletcher, and the archives director liked that. In the meantime he caught the boy's enthusiasm, which was difficult to analyze; Fletcher hadn't told anybody about his father's painting, and at this point Fletcher wasn't sure why the film was so important to him: he knew its passion and recklessness captivated him, though he was not a passionate person. The archives director, whose name was Aggie, called the boy about a week after the film's showing and invited him to come over and talk about it.

Dr. Aggie was genuinely excited when Fletcher showed up that night. He led Fletcher into his study and they talked awhile about mundane things like Fletcher's schooling and Fletcher's interest in movies. Fletcher explained to the old man that he'd begun collecting pictures as a hobby, his father was a painter and the notion of paintings that moved impressed him, and he'd send away for a number of films through advertisements and journals. This particular one he ordered with several others through an ad, almost as an afterthought. It had become his favorite, like history peering back at him through a white window. "Well, I have made an exciting discovery," said Aggie, pulling a reference book from his shelf; he reseated himself in a reclining chair. "I have reason to think this is a lost reel from *The Death of Marat.* Do you know that picture?"

"No," said Fletcher.

"It was made by a young director named Adolphe Sarre a few years after World War I, then was never shown to the public. Supposedly this Sarre, who wasn't all that much older than you when he began the film, continued working on it for decades. Those who *have* seen it," said Aggie, "say it's the greatest film to come out of the French cinema in the silent era. Some say it's the greatest silent picture ever, presaging other film makers by years. Thirty years ago this film was a real legend."

"Why didn't he finish it?" said the boy.

"Some say he did finish it. But he insisted it was never done, so he went on with it, long after the actors and most of the crew were gone. The actor who played Marat succumbed in a mental institution a couple of years after the film was to have premiered in Paris. The woman who played Charlotte Corday is believed to have died after World War II, also in Paris. The only one who stayed with him was his Danish cameraman, by the name of Rode."

"So what happened to the movie?"

Aggie shrugged. "Hollywood bought him out. He didn't know that of course; he thought they were going to help him finish his masterpiece. They brought him over in the late thirties, with his son Jacques, and Erik Rode. But they really had no interest in finishing the picture, they only wanted to invest enough money in it so they could take it away from him."

"But why?"

"It terrified them," said Aggie. "The man was expanding the screen and dividing it up, shuffling it like a deck of cards. Hollywood found it trying enough adjusting to sound, they didn't want to go through all that again. Ironically, sound was a concept Sarre never went for. So fifteen or twenty years later when Sarre's own son was made head of the studio, Jacques himself sabotaged the picture. Tried to burn it."

"Is Sarre still alive?"

"I have no idea. The last anyone heard, apparently, he was

still living in Los Angeles." Aggie put the book aside.

"And the movie?" said the boy.

There was no ready answer to that one either. By the time Fletcher was a student at the university, he had read everything written on the subject of Adolphe Sarre and *La Mort de Marat*, all of it from before the second world war. Fletcher's dreams became filled with scenes of *Marat*, each freezing at a given moment, celluloid transforming to tapestry, blacks and whites taking on the muted tones of oils. At that same moment each character looked the same, faces constructed in concentric designs; and Fletcher Grahame was always awakened by the sound. He would sit up in bed and wait in the night, his hands on his head, waiting for it all to stop.

It was not that Fletcher visualized his father every time he thought of Adolphe Sarre, because he had seen pictures of Sarre as a younger man; it was that, years later, every time Fletcher thought of his father he visualized Adolphe. He saw Adolphe Sarre in his mind, painting those awful paintings in the studio, only they were wonderful paintings once Sarre finished with them. *Convention Hall During the Reign of Terror* looked like it did in the movie—more real and lifelike than anything Franklin Grahame actually painted. This was because Sarre was more than an expert copier: he *was* a genius, an extraordinary prodigy; he was the things the older Grahame had professed to be, and which Fletcher's mother continued insisting he had been.

Sometimes Fletcher even saw Adolphe Sarre firing the flintlock behind his own head; sometimes it was Sarre's face that appeared so anguished to him, and remorseful.

By the time he finished his university work he had collected well over half the picture. It was about this time Fletcher began trying to locate Sarre in Los Angeles. Bit by bit he gleaned all the essential footage of the movie except for the film's editing. He still hadn't found a scene with the flintlock. During the following years he traveled all over the world in search of the ending, with the financial support of the archives who, though Aggie was now dead, persisted in the old curator's commitment to helping Fletcher recover what was considered a lost masterpiece.

When his efforts to track down Sarre failed, when he was unable to ascertain that Sarre was even still alive, Fletcher tried Sarre's son, Jacques, who was producing films in Los Angeles under the name of Jack Sarasan. The conflict between Sarasan and his father was a matter of record at this point; but Fletcher assumed that if someone else wanted to save *La Mort de Marat*, Sarasan could no longer have a reason to object. Moreover, Sarasan would at least be able to tell Fletcher where Adolphe Sarre was, whether the director was dead or alive. But nothing came back to Fletcher from Los Angeles; telephone calls were not answered; a flight out to the coast produced not even a cursory interview. People in the studio came to know exactly who Fletcher was, what he was doing, and just how much of a nuisance he had become doing it.

He finally found Jack Sarasan due south of Montreal in Manhattan. Sarasan was sitting with a starlet in a French restaurant on East 57th Street, when Fletcher appeared at their table. At first Sarasan professed not to know Fletcher or what he was talking about, and the restaurant's maître d' was prepared to escort the intruder out. Fletcher told Sarasan he was thinking of eventually writing a book about his efforts to restore the film, that he was certain Sarasan would be interested in clarifying the history involved. "I couldn't care less," Sarasan told him, looking up from the table as he wiped his mustache with the napkin. Still, when the maître d' placed his hand around Fletcher's elbow, Sarasan indicated to let him be. "Yes, all right, I know who you are, Grahame." He looked at the chair across from him. "Sit down. Listen," he said. "My nephew's in with you on this, right?"

Fletcher stared at Sarasan blankly.

Sarasan drank some wine. He didn't offer Fletcher a glass. "You would've thought the old man was *his* father. He didn't know Adolphe existed until someone told him he was living in Hollywood." The starlet stared between the two men at a spot of velvet on the opposite wall.

"Is he alive?"

Sarasan never looked at Fletcher, always directing his attention toward the meal. "You tell me about my nephew, I'll tell you about my father."

"Still in Hollywood?"

"Adolphe? Paris."

"I had heard—"

"He's in Paris, Grahame." Sarasan now stared straight at him. "I sent him back to Paris years ago. What is it with you and this movie? Is it art?"

"Yes," said Fletcher, "it's art."

"So why are you talking to me about it? I have nothing to do with art."

Fletcher pursed his lips. "I realize that at one point in time the industry may have been frightened of this picture—"

"Frightened!" said Sarasan. "What are you talking about?"

"So ahead of its time. But films have caught up, there can't be anything about it that's threatening anymore."

"I don't know what you're talking about." The starlet focused more intently on the spot. "You know, you *do* sound like my nephew. Except it doesn't take you all day to get one word out. In *my* boardroom, in front of *my* directors, he stood there screaming at me when he found out I sent *my* father back to Paris, do you know that? I think you're obsessed with this movie."

"I was about to say the same of you," said Fletcher.

Sarasan called the mâitre d'. "Publish your fucking book," he snarled. The maître d' approached and Fletcher was escorted out.

Fletcher Grahame arrived in Paris one autumn afternoon via the Gare du Nord (via Dunkerque, Dover, London, Shannon, Montreal), bringing with him a large trunk. At his hotel he negotiated with the concierge to keep the trunk in the hotel cellar; he paid the concierge fifteen francs a day simply that he might have a key to the cellar where he could check on the trunk whenever he liked. It was clear to the concierge that there was something about the trunk of the utmost importance, because Fletcher checked often.

Fletcher was making arrangements. By now he was a man of about thirty—tall and thin and taciturn, with wire-rimmed glasses and thinning hair of moderate length, always dressed in businesslike fashion, suit and tie, carrying a briefcase. He spent a lot of time going to newspaper offices, film academies, libraries. On his fourth day at the hotel he told the concierge he thought he'd be leaving soon, and the concierge could have his cellar back. He said it with a slight smile, making a joke.

That day Fletcher wore a different suit, cleaned and pressed, dark gray; he spoke to the concierge on his way out. He was a bit nervous this morning. Forty minutes later he was standing before another hotel, on the other side of the city, near Montparnasse. Fletcher looked at the buzzers by the door and, not finding the name he wanted, rang the concierge. A woman answered a moment later. Like most Parisian concierges, she stared at him suspiciously.

Fletcher asked if she spoke English. Of course not, she said. He nodded and asked in a stilted French if there was an older gentleman living in the hotel, "he must be in his eighties," Fletcher said. "His name is Adolphe Sarre."

No, she told him. There was nobody staying in her hotel by that name.

He said he'd been led to believe that somebody by that name was in fact living in the hotel. He stepped back into the street to check the address. Seventeen rue de Sacrifice.

Nobody by that name, she said. Then she closed the door.

He went back to the hotel and told the concierge he couldn't have his cellar yet.

Several weeks passed. Fletcher reinvestigated every lead. He couldn't go on paying the concierge fifteen francs a day to store a trunk he had hoped to deliver within his first week. The concierge asked Fletcher what it was he had come to Paris for. Fletcher looked at the concierge —a man in his early fifties— and asked him if he knew the name Adolphe Sarre. The concierge had never heard of Adolphe Sarre. Fletcher asked if the concierge ever went to the movies. Not often, said the concierge; few movies he much liked anymore. Adolphe Sarre, said Fletcher Grahame, made the greatest movie of all time. It was never finished, and it was never shown. Fletcher told the concierge he had come to Paris to finish Adolphe Sarre's movie.

After exploring several more leads, and coming to several dead ends, Fletcher went back to seventeen rue de Sacrifice. He gave the concierge his card, and told the concierge he was sure there was no Adolphe Sarre in her hotel if she said so; but if perhaps the concierge was mistaken, to give Monsieur Sarre the card, on the back of which Fletcher wrote: *Marat*. Fletcher returned to his hotel and sat in his room, on the bed, without the lights on, in his dark gray suit. Some hours later he was still sitting there when, at a few minutes past five in the afternoon, he heard the phone ring in the lobby. It continued ringing, and after four or five rings there was triggered in his brain a gunshot, ascending in shrill intensity. As usual he put his hands to his ears in a futile attempt to stop the sound; and since sometimes it blocked out all other sound and left him partially deaf for a while, he could not hear the concierge's voice when the phone was answered, and he could not hear the concierge's steps all the way up the stairs—though he could feel the series of small vibratory thuds. In this way he did not hear but felt the concierge outside the door, and presumed that there was a knock. Still Fletcher didn't move, only sitting on the bed in his dark gray suit, now rumpled, with his hands clamped firmly over his ears. "Oui?" he called out, and barely discerned the concierge's reply: "Monsieur, there is a call." After a pause: "Are you resting?"

"I'll take the call," Fletcher said, swinging his legs over the side of the bed. The concierge seemed to jump with a start when the door opened. He stared at Fletcher a moment and then turned and led him down the steps to the phone. When Fletcher took the receiver the hum in his head seemed to come and go. "Hello."

There was silence on the other side; Fletcher knew he was there, and maybe he was talking to him right now, and Fletcher wasn't hearing him because of the sound. The hum had seemed to die, but Fletcher felt a flash of panic and couldn't decide whether to speak presumptuously. "Monsieur Grahame?"

"Yes," he answered, with relief.

"Do you speak French?"

"Not very well. Perhaps if you speak slowly..."

"I will. I'm afraid my English is poor." Fletcher thought he heard him laugh. "Almost forty years in the States, and I never really got the language."

"Yes, well," Fletcher said, "I grew up in Montreal. I had the opportunity to learn French, but my father was absolutely opposed. Considering he was French, it was rather unreasonable, on his part."

"Rather."

"As a young boy he painted a mural for your film."

"Really? Yes, I think I do remember . . . I think. It's, uh, been many—"

"We are men who speak our own language, monsieur," Fletcher blurted. He thought it sounded silly then.

He heard him laugh again. "Is that to our credit or detriment?" There was another pause. "What is it, Monsieur Grahame?"

"The film—"

"No one cares, Monsieur Grahame. No one cares about that. I never finished it. I don't know where most of it is, actually. My son may well have destroyed it."

"Some of it," Fletcher said, slowly, catching his breath, "some of it was in Los Angeles. Some of it has been in New York. Some of it was in London. In fact, I first stumbled on a reel of it in Montreal."

"Well, it would take years to get it all in one place, I would think."

"I have taken the years, Monsieur Sarre. I've been all over North America, and I spent seven months in London before I arrived a few weeks ago. I spent four months in Ireland before coming away empty-handed."

After a pause the old man said, "Where is the film now?"

"In the cellar of this hotel." He waited for him to say something. "I'd like to meet with you. I can bring the picture."

Silence again.

"Monsieur Sarre—"

"Nobody cares, monsieur." Quietly and bitterly he heard him say it. "I'm old. I'm eighty-something. That's old. I never finished it."

"I've come a long, long way," Fletcher said, and felt all the years rush forward to this moment.

Silence again. "Come tomorrow morning at ten, then."

"I'll bring the picture."

"Don't bring the picture. Just come yourself. We'll talk." There was the final pause, as though he was about to say something else, or perhaps change his mind. Then he hung up.

Ten o'clock at seventeen rue de Sacrifice, Fletcher Grahame was led into a private chamber hidden from the rest of the hotel, occupied by a tiny man the top of whose head was bare, his long wispy white hair falling nearly to his shoulders. For a man who insisted he no longer concerned himself with the past, Adolphe Sarre surrounded himself with memories. On the walls were two enlarged frames: Thierry Touraine in the bath, two crossed flint-locks mounted above him, scattered editions of *L'Ami du peuple* around him, his head wrapped in a towel and tilted back, his eyes open and fixed on the ceiling and in his chest above his heart in a splash of black blood stood erect a dagger. Next to that was a smaller picture taken in the late twenties of Griffith with his hand on Adolphe's shoulder; Griffith was already washed up by then and Adolphe was a legend, the cinematic visionary who never finished the greatest picture of all time. There was a clipping of Lillian Gish. On the shelf next to those pictures were the collected works of Eisenstein, Buster Keaton's book, and *Les grands auteurs du cinéma*. Next to the shelf was a chest nearly as large as the one brought from Montreal. Next to the chest was a bed and a chair. On the wall next to the bed were still more old photographs: a gallery of directors: Griffith the colossus, Josef von Sternberg, the Russians Eisenstein and Pudovkin. Next to Pudovkin was the second enlargement. It was huge, nearly filling the wall; and one saw her eyes first, and then her mouth, in a swirl of dirty blond hair which came out gray and charcoal in the print—and it was the ineffable sadness that was so unbearable to look at. It was the trace of betrayal, and the way she appeared wounded, as though to open her up one would fall in forever; and the sound of her face was the freefall of her plummeting soul. Next to this picture was nothing.

Fletcher looked all the way around the little room, staring a long time at the frame of Marat dead in the bath, and at the two guns above Marat's body; he turned to the old man. "It is an honor for me, monsieur," he said, his voice passionless.

Adolphe gestured. He didn't look any younger than he was. He glanced around the room himself, and shook his head with mock disgust. "Old people," said Adolphe. "Old pictures. It's nonsense, really."

"Not at all."

"Of course." He looked up at Fletcher. "Listen," he began, then stopped. "Sit down," he said. "Do you mind sitting on the bed?"

"No."

"I like the chair." He sat in the chair. "Listen," he started again. "I'm moved, really, by your concern. But the film is a dead issue."

"I don't believe so." Fletcher leaned forward, intently. "I believe I have all the film but the end."

"There is no end. That's why you don't have the end."

"I've read you filmed the end. The murder of Marat."

"That wasn't the end," said Adolphe. "The execution of Charlotte Corday was the end. I never shot that."

"I believe—" Fletcher stopped a moment. "Forgive the presumption, Monsieur Sarre. You could as easily end it with the death of Marat."

"Perhaps. But . . ." He shrugged, as though he was indifferent. "I doubt very much you could have all of it. Some of it must be in terrible condition. This is a relic, after all."

"There are things in that film," Fletcher said, "that are still astounding today."

"People will only laugh at it."

"They won't." Adolphe just shrugged again. Fletcher couldn't decide if it was simply that Adolphe didn't allow himself to hope any longer, after all these years; Fletcher's father had come to that point. The two continued to talk but the old director seemed entrenched, insisting that the business of completing a film he'd begun almost seventy years before, and had given up some thirty years before, was the pursuit of a very lost cause. Fletcher insisted in turn that the picture would still capture the imagination of people who cared about the cinema, and the fact that it had never been released added to its mystique. Fletcher wondered aloud if that was what Adolphe was afraid of, that perhaps the film would not live up to its legend; and then he insisted the film would surpass its legend, creating a new impact.

It was all put forth so earnestly that Adolphe could only relent. The next morning the trunk was delivered, early; and Fletcher turned in the cellar key for the final time. Over the next couple of days Adolphe looked at what Fletcher had done. He was mildly astonished. Fletcher had located material that Adolphe had forgotten entirely, that he'd assumed was lost forever. Moreover, Fletcher had reassembled all the pieces into a whole, very close to what Adolphe himself might have done: even the culminating rhythms of the montage, the nerve-touching breaks between close-ups and wide-angles, between the intimate madness of Marat and Charlotte and the boggling turmoil of the peasants in the Paris streets. Adolphe could not, after all these years, help but be exhilarated that here was someone who understood what the director was trying to do all along. But, he continued telling Fletcher, it was too late.

"Is it possible," Fletcher said, when the old director talked like this, "that no one else came along before me?"

"Oh, someone came," said Adolphe. "Only one. There were many inquiries, but only one came, like you, to finish the film." Fletcher waited as Adolphe looked at the wall and gazed around and then shook his head. Fletcher waited; and Adolphe's eyes drifted to another place, and something was sorted out. "Do you know who she is?" he said, to the picture on the wall.

"The actress who played Charlotte Corday."

"The mother of my daughter, and the grandmother of my grandson." He said nothing of his son. "The last time I saw her, she was walking with our four-year-old daughter in the Tuileries. I was standing on the other side of the gardens. The child looked exactly like her mother, and I know, because I remember when her mother was four years old. She turned and looked, and I walked away quickly, before her mother might turn and see me too."

"Did you see them again?"

"Not ever," he said. "I never saw either one of them again. I received letters from my daughter much later on, after she had grown, and knew who I was. I outlived them both."

Still, Fletcher waited. "I don't understand," he finally said. "Then it was your daughter who wanted to finish—"

"My grandson," said Adolphe. "My grandson was the one. My grandson whom she sent to the States—" He stopped.

"Yes?"

"The first time I saw him, it was from far away," said Adolphe thoughtfully, "much like I had seen his mother from far away. But he never saw me, and he was only a young boy. He never knew anything of me until later. That was when he came to Paris to finish the picture."

"Why didn't he?"

"Why didn't he what?"

"Finish the picture."

"He went to see his mother, who was dying."

"He never returned?"

"No."

"You never heard from him again?"

"No."

"He deserted you rather easily then," Fletcher said in his monotone.

Adolphe was silent a moment, then he shrugged. "A strange young man. One way one moment, another way the next. But people always thought I was a strange young man. I think he was more my son than my son was, if you know what I mean."

Fletcher didn't think about why, but when he heard that, he didn't want to talk about it anymore. In fact, he decided there were some answers he didn't want to know at all. He had found Sarre, he told himself, and all he wanted now was to finish the picture. From that point on the two men gave all their time to viewing over and over the footage Fletcher had collected around the world. Thirty hours of it, all of it projected on the blank wall. Over and over, as the nights and days went by, they watched the thirty hours. No use, said Adolphe. No use contemplating a completed film without the end; and the end, he said, is gone forever.

When the archives in Montreal notified Fletcher they no longer had the funds to finance his work, then he had no choice but to make his quest public. He took out advertisements in newspapers, interviewed film scholars and historians, pored over the reference material of cinema libraries. He double-checked the sources he'd spent all the preceding years checking. He spoke to gatherings of students and artists, and always brought with him part of the film. Repeatedly he was astonished and depressed how many in his audiences had never heard of Sarre; the years in Hollywood had blotted out his importance in French cinema history. Because Sarre was regarded by many of the class instructors as something of a crackpot, it was Fletcher's task to make his case: that he was attempting to restore to an original form a picture that never really had an original form, or at least anything that could be considered definitive. The reactions to Fletcher and the film were always the same—a bemused fascination—until he actually showed the segment of footage. Then they were electrified. The responses and questions were always the same as well, asked so many countless times that Fletcher understood them even when the sound of a gunshot in his head left him reading the lips of those who asked. Soon magazines and journals "rediscovered" the director. The Paris Opéra invited Adolphe to show Marat— "the masterpiece that could not be finished"—some sixty years after it was first scheduled to premiere. Adolphe refused: how could one have a picture called La Mort de Marat without la mort, he asked, it was ridiculous, like a novel without a final chapter; it was unthinkable; it could not be shown unfinished.

Fletcher had about come to the conclusion that the ending of the film did not exist. He had no doubt that Adolphe once shot it, he had no doubt it existed once upon a time. But given what was now a virtual dragnet throughout the world film community, given that the film had become a cause célèbre among film makers and students alike, and given that an enormous amount of publicity had not produced the ending or any trace of it, it seemed clear that the conclusion of the film had been destroyed, probably by Jack Sarasan, or buried so deeply beneath layers of indifference and ignorance and anonymity that it was unlikely ever to surface. So Fletcher thought perhaps the film should be shown without the ending; perhaps that was as complete as La Mort de Marat was ever to be. Yet he couldn't help but admire that for Sarre the artist it wasn't enough, that nothing less than the complete realization of his vision would suffice—there would be no *Marat* unless it was Sarre's *Marat*. Fletcher recognized such a commitment as the madness it possibly was, but he couldn't help admiring, if not the madness, then the commitment itself.

This went on nearly a year when one afternoon Fletcher was in Adolphe's room alone, waiting for the old man who had gone on one of his rare excursions outside the hotel: he was looking at the photographs on the walls again, studying each one with fascination. He looked at the books and then picked up more clippings and photographs from the trunk. He had never looked in the trunk before. Adolphe had never opened it. Fletcher shuffled through a few mementos, turned over a few old journals, and caught, in the peculiar light of this room that seemed to come from nowhere, the glint of metal; and reaching down through the debris of the old man's memories, he pulled it up: round, silver, dusty, and written across the edge of the can on a bit of tape: *Marat. Finis*

He heard the door of the house open and close, and he just stood there looking at the film. He just stood there with the film in his hand and turned as Adolphe came into the room. He looked at Adolphe and Adolphe looked back at him and at the film in his hands, and his small eyes seemed to bulge. For a moment neither said anything; the old man was white and the protégé was gripping the film so hard the metal almost bent beneath his fingers. He was shaking. The old man leaped forward, his hands flying for the film, but Fletcher yanked it out of reach. Adolphe looked at the opened chest and back at Fletcher's hands. "How dare you," he muttered.

"How dare I?" Fletcher whispered hoarsely. He looked around incredulously; the room became a vision of mortification to him. "How dare I," he said again, almost to himself, and looked at Adolphe, who sank onto the bed. Fletcher slowly sat on the edge of the trunk with the film still in his hands. He closed his eyes. The old man seemed smaller, whiter in the corner on the bed. He wasn't looking at Fletcher at all but seemed to be curling up, burying his eyes away from the room's light. "You had it all along," Fletcher said finally, after several moments. He spoke evenly, like it was rational, like it was one of those things he always understood.

Adolphe said nothing, burying himself beneath his arms at the far region of the bed. When enough time passed that he might have understood some explanation was awaited, then he looked up, but not at the other man.

"You finished it a long long time ago, didn't you," Fletcher went on. "It was always really finished, but you always found reasons for it not to be finished. Greedy producers, changing times, your son, all of it. Everyone gave you a great many reasons for the film to never be finished." He thought. "Was it that you were frightened the film could not be as good as—"

"No." Adolphe laid his head back against the wall.

"It was," said Fletcher, "so much a part of your life that you couldn't let it go—"

"No."

He looked at the old man and stood up from the trunk, sputtering, "Then why? Then you tell me why."

And Adolphe didn't look at him at all. "I was never worthy of it," he finally declared. He sat listening to the sound of it, considering what it meant, determining how long he had known it was so.

Fletcher began shaking his head. He kept shaking his head, standing before the old man. No, he answered. He kept shaking his head. No, he said again, and walked from the spot where he stood and walked back, shaking his head all the while. His knuckles were still white from holding on to the film. What is it that you're telling me? he said. That this has been penance? Adolphe said nothing. Fletcher turned from him and pulled from the side of a cupboard the projector. He set it up and began threading the film through. "It doesn't matter," he said. He was no longer red; he was speaking at a level that could barely be heard from across the room. "The film isn't yours anymore." He nodded at Adolphe. "I've inherited the conviction you once had for it, however long ago it was. You forfeited your right to it when you forfeited your belief in it, when you used it to pay off your conscience for... whatever." He closed the door of the room and looked with exasperation at the light that never went away; then turned on the projector.

The first and last minutes had been spliced or lost; what was here was only the core of the footage. Charlotte Corday was sitting in a house. Right away something seemed wrong, it didn't fit. The house didn't appear furnished in the period; and the woman was quite a bit older than she had been in the rest of the film. She looked to be around fifty. The camera followed her from room to room; and the more the camera revealed of the house, the less right it looked. There was no sound, but there were subtitles in English, not French, which the old man could not read. But Fletcher could read them, and when the old woman talked about the night she discovered her twin sons drowned on the beach, he began to realize this was not Charlotte at all, and certainly not *Marat*. The footage ran out and left the two men staring at the blank wall, stunned. Fletcher turned to Adolphe. "Where is it?" he said.

Adolphe looked back slowly. He focused on Fletcher. "Where is what?"

"The ending. The murder of Marat."

Adolphe shook his head, befuddled. Fletcher walked around the projector and stood there, looking down at him. Adolphe kept pursing his lips, like he was about to ask a question. He stared back at the wall, and then at his hands. "I don't know," he finally said. He gestured toward the wall. "I don't remember." He stopped a moment, almost lost. "She looked so much older," he said.

Fletcher pivoted away from the old man. He sat on the bed next to him but didn't seem aware any longer that Adolphe was there. He placed his face in his hands. "So I," he finally said, "continue looking, I suppose." Adolphe was lost in a memory.

Fletcher was lost in despair. Now he was unsure, for the first time, that Adolphe had even filmed an ending, though Adolphe claimed to. He distrusted everything Adolphe remembered or did not remember. The film in the can had nothing to do with *Marat*. He rewound the film and put it back in the metal box and put the box in the trunk.

And yet, and yet. There was that picture on the wall of Thierry Touraine in the bathtub, dagger in his heart. And there was simply no real way to make the film a coherent whole without the murder; the entire film was structured, both narratively and stylistically, to lead up to the scene where the girl killed the revolutionary. Without that scene the two characters in the film remained isolated forever, paths never crossing; to show the film to the public without the murder would be to leave it forever unfinished. Fletcher simply wasn't ready to do that yet: not after coming this far, he told himself.

So Fletcher continued looking, and the search, despite the publicity, became more difficult, not less. If all the speeches and magazines and newspapers had ignited interest in the subject of Adolphe and *Marat*, those same forums became impatient and snide when the mystery appeared to be without solution. Now almost everyone seriously questioned that there was an ending to the film; and, as had happened decades before, the worth of the film became suspect, the film and its art were as good as nonexistent if they remained unrevealed to the world.

Days passed. Responses came floating back to Fletcher from unseen places outside seventeen rue de Sacrifice: dark phone calls in the middle of the night, and letters that always led to nothing. Adolphe was a prisoner of and resistant factor in the film's destiny. Another autumn came and then the second of two embalming winters; and one day the telephone rang. It was a man asking about an ad he had seen in *Le Figaro*, which had run so long now Fletcher had forgotten it but for the moments he had considered and then declined to cancel it. But this call, Fletcher realized immediately, was different, because the man on the other end was describing the scene of Marat's murder in some detail, down to the crossed flintlocks above the bath. "What kind of condition is the film in?" Fletcher asked.

"It seems to be in good condition," said the other man.

"I'd be interested in seeing it."

"Well, would you want me to come there?"

"No. I'll come to you."

"All right. The electricity is off more than on in the hotel where I'm staying."

"It's been like that in Paris for a while now."

"Yes, in the States too."

Fletcher said, "If it is the film, what's your price for it?"

"I'm not selling it," came the answer. The voice on the other end waited for Fletcher to respond, and when he didn't, went on: "I think there's been a mix-up."

"What do you mean?" Fletcher said.

There was more silence. "Well," he said, "if this is the film you're looking for, and if I'm right, then you ought to know what I mean. I mean there's been a switch. If I have your film, then you have my film."

Fletcher said nothing.

"Maybe this is a mistake," said the voice.

"No," Fletcher said quickly. Then, "Tell me about the film you're looking for."

"It's been some time since I saw it. Several years. There's a woman in a house." Still another pause. "Maybe this is a mistake," he said again.

"I don't understand how this switch took place," Fletcher said.

"I don't either."

"You must have some idea."

"Why should I, if you don't?"

"I'm representing another party."

The other voice finally said, "I don't know how the switch was made. I don't remember. But I'd like the film back."

"But perhaps it isn't your film," Fletcher started.

The man said, "It is. Obviously, obviously you have it."

"Can we discuss this in person?"

"That's fine, but the trade is the deal. I'm not negotiating. I won't sell it. If you want to meet, I'll see you underground at the Métro at Saint-Germain-des-Prés. You'll have to bring the other film with you. Is three o'clock all right?"

At two-thirty Fletcher Grahame left seventeen rue de Sacrifice. It was a long way to Saint-Germain-des-Prés; though some of the underground stations and pedestrian passages were open, the trains themselves hadn't run in over a year. Fletcher walked down the boulevard Saint-Michel hoping to flag a taxi, with no luck. Then he walked up the boulevard Saint-Germain. The streets were filled with smoke from all the fires. Some people wore handker-chiefs to keep soot out of their mouths and noses. It was mag-nificently cold, like Montreal, and everything was slick, so the walk was that much slower. When Fletcher got to the main entrance of the Métro at Saint-Germain-des-Prés, a huge bonfire was roaring there, with a crowd of people gathered around; there was no getting through the gateway. Fletcher crossed the street to the other entrance, and gingerly made his way down. Under-ground, he stood waiting in the designated place for his rendez-vous.

Five minutes later, he saw him approaching from the far end of the tunnel. He had black hair and wore a long, old blue coat, and there was a film can under his arm. He looked younger than Fletcher had expected, but what was startling was how much he looked like old photographs of Adolphe Sarre. When he walked up, there was no exchange of names, only a perfunctory hand-shake, and a nod of recognition. "The hotel's electricity seems to be on in the afternoon," explained the other man.

They went to the hotel and walked up the two, three, four levels. The room was very cold but there was a small heater which would go fifteen or twenty minutes for a franc when the electricity was on. Indeed, there now seemed to be power. Once again, though, Fletcher protested. "I don't see," he said, "that I should have to bargain with you to get returned what is mine."

"You're only returning to me what's mine," said the other man.

"I don't know that it's yours."

"No more or less certainly than I know this picture"—he tapped the reel in the projector—"is yours."

Fletcher gazed at him sullenly. "Let's see what you have," he finally said. The other man began the film; and within the first several seconds, Fletcher's heart stopped. Faded as the images were in the afternoon light, they were nonetheless what he'd always imagined they would be, and that was what so astounded him—the lack of surprise, the manifestation of his own imagi-nation; and he had a difficult time believing it was real, the woman on Adolphe's wall coming into Marat's private bath, and in ecstatic frenzy killing him. His body lurched at the knife, and every detail was vivid: the steam rising from the bath, the way the muscles in her legs tensed when she committed the act, the splash of water from the tub, the passion with which she backed away from the blood. The stills in Adolphe's room had come into motion like the paintings of Franklin Grahame's study taking on life, with a resounding clarity. Fletcher realized he had been reconciling himself to the idea that the film, like his father's "genius," was a hoax of some sort after all. But now it did exist, before him, and with it a new certainty: there were the guns above the bath, and no one in the scene was aware of them at all, or supposed that at least one of them was loaded and ready to fire, and that thirty years later someone would hear that report for the first time, and that sixty years later he would still be hearing it. The film ran out and Fletcher just watched the wall. He finally looked up at the other man, who was winding the film back and packing it in its can. Neither of them said anything.

When he finished, the man said, "I'd like to see the other picture," and he pointed at the film in Fletcher's lap. Fletcher stared at him.

He didn't understand why he was so reluctant to hand over the other film. Somehow he didn't seem to feel he should have to give anything for what he'd just seen; he had already given enough and he was entitled to it. Moreover, for some reason giving something to this man in particular was worst of all. But he held out the film, and watched as it ran through the projector; and it had been on the wall of the room less than a minute before it was shut off. "What's wrong?" Fletcher said, now suddenly alarmed.

The other man just leaned against the wall next to two shuttered doors that led to a balcony. He stared at the floor, breathing deeply.

"What is it?" Fletcher said again. "Are you all right?"

"Yes."

"You look like you're sick."

"No."

"Is it the film you were looking for?"

The other man nodded. Fletcher licked his lips, and waited. Finally the man raised his head and looked back at the wall, and then at Fletcher. "Well, then it's settled."

"Yes."

"The two women in our pictures, they look very similar." He handed Fletcher the film.

"Like mother and daughter," Fletcher agreed.

"Do you think so?" the other man said.

"It's not likely."

"No. I suppose it's not."

Fletcher licked his lips and said, "Well." He tapped the film under his arm. "Then it's settled." He licked his lips again and nodded again, resentfully. He pulled his coat closer to him. "Don't understand how the two got mixed up but it's straightened out now."

"Yes it is," said the other one, waiting for him to leave.

And Fletcher Grahame left, somewhat quickly.

When he awoke, in the middle of the night, he believed she was there. Ever since seeing the film, Adolphe was racked with the memory he couldn't locate; he felt himself lost in a remembrance warp. Over and over he scanned his past, for that day or week or month when he found her again, walking the halls of that old house. He sat up in bed and shook his head. Why had he blocked it out? he kept asking himself. Why had he allowed himself to go on thinking the last time he saw her was that day in the Tuileries Gardens, when there she was, on his celluloid, years later, lonely and sad? If she had allowed him to film her that way, she must have forgiven him, he decided. Or perhaps she simply no longer remembered him at all.

He wished he had understood what she was saying in the film. In the muted, ever-present light of this room, he didn't remember anything. I'm so damned old, he told himself.

And then he wondered the obvious; he approached, not too cautiously, the inescapable—that she was in fact still there, behind the screen. That she had, of course, never left, but was there behind the walls now. Janine, he said, and he looked around him. Somehow she had gotten back there, she had done what he could not do: rush through the first opportune door into the light on the other side. It occurred to him that to have taken such a chance, and to have found such courage, she must have felt very defeated and betrayed, and without much reason to be alive. To have gone over there like that, not knowing what it would be like, she would have had to come to the conclusion that nothing could be worse than this, that nothing could make her feel more desolate or unhappy. And he knew he had done that to her, he had made her that way; he knew he was no human being—just a projection, another shadow of somebody else's form. He remembered lying on the battlefields of war amused and fascinated by the lights in the sky while men agonized and expired around him; and he realized that growing up as a child in this very room, where he had now retired to die (he looked around him; he ran his fingernails along the wall and pressed his lips close to it. *Janine*, he whispered), was perfect in its perversion, in the twisted wholeness with which the fact surrounded him. He realized he was meant to be abandoned from the first; and from the first he had abandoned the world he lived in. He wished to be abandoned now by life.

He got up and opened the chest before him. He took out the film. He wanted to look at her again, to watch her move. He wanted to try and understand the words. He didn't care if she was old, he didn't care if her dirty yellow hair was gray. He didn't care if her sad mouth had grown small, and her sad face had grown small; he thought it was possible he could project the film on the wall and, in the glare of light when the film ran out, get through. He fumbled with the projector and film; but then he got it started, and he watched.

Before him, he saw not an older woman in a house but a young girl raising her knife in the air, and the close-up of her eyes those last days in Wyndeaux when he made love to her. Astonished, he went to the chest again.

"What are you doing?"

Adolphe whirled around. The sound of the projector clicked and fluttered; he hadn't heard the other man approach.

"What are you doing?" Fletcher said in the doorway.

"Where is it?" said Adolphe.

"Where is what?"

"Janine in the house."

"This is the film," Fletcher said, indicating the projector.

"This is *Marat*."

"That's right. The picture is now complete. We open at the Opéra in three months. It doesn't give us a lot of time. We're moving tomorrow."

"Moving?"

"To a larger studio. We have a lot of work ahead of us, getting the film into shape. I'll be hiring a staff."

Adolphe shook his head. "What are you talking about?" He looked dazed.

"Go back to bed," Fletcher said.

"Wait a minute," said the old man. He grabbed Fletcher by the shoulder. "Where's the other film?"

Fletcher stared at him, expressionless. "What other film?" he said flatly.

"Janine, as an older woman. You know." He motioned with his hands. "In the house . . . we—"

"There is no other film."

"But there is. You remember."

"No."

"Janine—"

"That was not Janine."

Adolphe looked up at Fletcher. "What do you mean?" he said.

"That was your daughter," Fletcher said. "Janine is gone, remember?"

"But—"

"Go to bed, Adolphe," Fletcher said. "*Marat* is finished. We play the Opéra in March." He added, just to make sure it was understood, "This is your big moment."

Adolphe sat in his chair, the one he liked, long after Fletcher had left, staring at the light of the projector, not hearing its whir. Occasionally he would lean back in his chair and press his ear to the wall, listening.

Twice, he mistook the lights. Because he was so old—somewhere past eighty, he never knew exactly—it wasn't unreasonable to assume that perhaps his eyes were going, that he was seeing things. But even at this point in life his eyes were still good, remarkable in fact. A scan across the Paris facades from his houseboat on the Seine revealed nearly everything to him. And drifting into Paris that October, when it was already becoming bitterly cold, he only assumed that what he saw were more fires in the windows along the river. Fires on the street corners, fires on the bridges, fires in the buildings themselves: Parisians setting their furniture on fire, diaries and family portraits, stale food, up in smoke. Drifting into Paris on the Seine that October, one small inferno after another passed him by, while great hunks of ice scraped the hull of the old houseboat, the vessel resoundingly rocked by every collision.

The first mistake was a light on the rock beneath Pont-Neuf; he thought at the time it was an odd place for a fire. As the boat approached the rock he realized it wasn't a fire at all, but rather a glowing fragment of ice perched precariously in its place and poised for the taking. He took it, leaning dangerously over the edge of the boat and, rather nimbly for a man of his age, snatching it up as it glided within reach. Mystified, he put the glowing ice in the cabin of his boat some distance from the stove, wondering if it would melt down to its source of light, or if the light would simply melt with it. He sat in the cabin staring at the ice until he became drowsy, and then fell asleep; he woke with a start, with the horrified expectation that he would find nothing but a pool of glistening water where the ice had been set. Rather, he found an old cognac bottle, with a long curved neck. In the flickering light of the lantern, he held the bottle close to his face, and there blinked up at him, from within the bottle, two blue eyes.

The old man looked at the eyes, then looked up from the bottle. That night he lay staring at the ceiling of the cabin, baffled—and it was not until he woke, at three in the morning, and glanced over quickly at the bottle again, that there unlodged from the gravity of his deep-gone past a memory. Not all of it he could catch. He got up again, held the bottle before him again, and remembered the eyes again: was it Crete? Or Naples. Or the coast of Morocco. Or the beach off San Sebastian?

The Seine froze overnight; he woke to find the boat wedged fast in the middle of the river. He realized he was going to be here awhile. In the mornings he would rise and walk across the ice to the quays, up the steps to the boulevards along the Seine, to the boulangeries to buy bread. At night he would listen to the sound of the ice against the boat's body, pressing its wooden fiber. He missed the way the boat usually rocked, and found it hard to sleep.

The second mistake was another light on the river. He saw it first from far away, one evening as the dark flaming red of the sun crossed the black sky. This light on the river moved like a torch, from far past the cathedral and bookstands, gliding over the boulevard Saint-Michel, then to the island. The torch seemed to flicker wildly as a gust came up from the frozen river. He continued watching the light for a quarter of an hour until it reached the Pont-Neuf, very close to where he'd found the bottle, until it was so close that, like the bottle, he saw it wasn't a flame at all but rather her yellow hair.

Slowly he walked across the river, its silver gleam rising around him. She came down the steps. When he asked why she was walking in the cold, and when he told her he'd thought she was another bonfire, loose and tumbling along the riverbanks, she said something back in a halting and broken French. He spoke a halting and broken English. He asked if she'd like something hot to drink; and she, happy to make an acquaintance, accepted the invitation. She explained she had a rendezvous to keep in an hour there at the Pont-Neuf.

On his boat, he made the thick coffee in a pan over the small stove in his cabin. She huddled close to the fire, she did not visibly shiver. "Coldest winter ever," he said, stirring the coffee with a large spoon. "I've been alive over eighty years."

"In Paris all that time?" These questions took a while to get out, since she had to grope for the words.

"Here and there." He wanted to put his hands by the fire but he couldn't stop stirring the coffee or it would cool. "Got like this last winter."

"Is that when people started burning everything?"

"That started this winter. Everything but the walls themselves and their beds and the food that could still be eaten."

"I've never been so cold," she admitted.

"It must get cold where you're from. Aren't you English?"

"No."

"Dutch."

"No." She laughed.

He pondered. "American?"

She laughed again.

"American," he reasserted.

"Yes."

"Hollywood."

"Yes."

"Really?" His face lit up in the glow of the stove.

"Do all French people believe all Americans are from Hollywood?"

"Yes, they do," he answered solemnly. "Or New York." He took the coffee from the stove and poured it into cups. He had a small carton of milk sitting on the shelf. "The milk is cold. If you have milk in your coffee it won't be as hot."

"I don't want milk."

"But it never gets this cold in Hollywood, right?" he said, pouring himself some milk anyway. He watched the steam rise off the coffee. She drank hers, and blanched a bit. "Strong, right? Americans cannot drink really strong coffee. I thought you were all cowboys who could drink strong coffee." She laughed.

"No, it never gets this cold in Hollywood." She added, "But it gets cold where I grew up, in Kansas."

"What is Kansas?"

"Kansas," she said. "*The Wizard of Oz.*"

"What is the Wizard of Oz?"

"*The Wizard of Oz* was a movie. Maybe it never got to France."

"I saw a movie once," he burst out. "An American movie, with cowboys. Broncho Billy."

"That sounds like a very old movie," she said, sipping her coffee.

"Very old. I was... very young." He shrugged.

"That's the only movie you've ever seen?"

He announced, matter-of-factly, "I took my name from it."

"Broncho Billy?"

"Bateau Billy. Know what bateau is?"

"Boat," she said.

"That's it. Boat Billy."

"Billyboat." She laughed, and he laughed too, though he didn't understand the joke. "But that," she said a while later, "can't be your actual name."

"No," he only agreed, "it cannot."

Then they said nothing, and then talked a bit more about living on a houseboat. She asked if he always lived on the river, and he said no, sometimes he would sail down the coast of France and Spain and Portugal, had even sailed into the Mediterranean several times in his life; if one knew the currents and stayed close to land, the voyage wasn't difficult. Fishing villages dotted the way south, and he had seen different lights all the way to Athens. Curiously, he'd never been moved to sail north of the Seine; and curiously, he'd come north the many winters, if only to be in Paris when the season was loneliest.

He left after a while, to get some groceries: fewer and fewer of the markets were operating as the winter progressed, and it worried him that it was barely November and already so hard. January and February loomed deathlike. He told her she could wait in the boat, by the stove, if she chose to. She lay back on the small bed and watched the ceiling of the cabin; like him, though she hadn't been conditioned by experience, she nonetheless missed the rocking of the boat. So lying there she closed her eyes, turned on her side, pulled the blanket up to her face; and after a bit, staring at the insides of her lids, she could feel the boat rocking and could feel herself sinking deeper. It was much like the sensation she'd always had in her room on Pauline Boulevard, sinking into the bed, that large gray fleshy rose closing its petals around her. Now she submerged into the boat, floating down through its stern, suspended in silver ice on the bottom of the river. Nothing moved, there was no sound, she was not cold.

For once, her dream wasn't torn between her husband and her lover. That was the form her dreams usually took. This time, she dreamed of her dead child. In her dream, she understood he was dead and accepted this without dread. As in the past when she dreamed of him, or thought she was dreaming of him, he never manifested himself fully; he never appeared to her completely embodied. As in the past, when she had only heard his stuttering voice, this time it was his eyes that appeared before her—intense, glistening blue eyes. The eyes registered no physical pain, but were heartbreakingly sad and lonely; embedded there with her in the frozen river, the ice seemed to melt in tears, trickling down the jagged bergs. Once more, she felt she'd let him down; and the sense was so overpowering—the sense of him being there, with her, so close—that it woke her.

She emerged from this dream to see his eyes still watching her from some feet away.

Her immediate reaction was to turn away, to lie with her head on the pillow staring at the wall by the bunk. She waited a bit and then looked back. The eyes were still there, perched on the shelf much like the carton of milk, caught in their glass vessel and continuing to watch her. She sat up with her hands in her lap, and then walked to the bottle and picked it up. She turned the eyes upward and looked down to see them; she tilted the bottle back and forth, expecting to see the lids of the eyes slip shut like pink doors—or perhaps a flurry of glitter, like those glass balls with small scenes inside. But the eyes seemed to blink when they wanted to, and if she held the bottle off to her side, they continued peering at her from their corners.

She put the bottle on a table, and sat beside it in a chair. Now that she had found him again she wasn't sure what to do. The eyes blinked at her almost inquisitively; it occurred to her that his eyes had always looked this forlorn. She thought of how best she should apologize. Somehow it seemed unnecessary; it was clear he understood she was sorry, it was clear that didn't matter so much. Of course she wondered how this had happened, of course she was aware how unusual it was; but that it was him was irrefutable to her, and all she could do was ask herself, over and over, what to do now. The only thing of which she was certain was she wouldn't leave him again.

Not again. Minutes ticked by until her rendezvous at the Pont-

Neuf drew near. Darkness had fallen. When the hour struck, she picked the bottle up in her hands, wrapped it in the blanket from the bed and stood out on the deck of the boat. It was cold to her beyond comprehension or experience. The wind was ripping down the river; and from the deck, in the light of a streetlamp on the bridge, she could see him waiting. She looked at the bottle and then at the bridge; she called to him, but her voice was sent scattering back to her by the wind. She didn't feel she could just walk off the boat with the bottle without telling the old man first, and she wouldn't leave the child for a moment. She had done that before, she knew; and she somehow understood that she had lived with it the rest of her life, that somehow it had changed everything. So she clung to the bottle as though it was her life; and then, when she saw him turn in the light of the streetlamp as though he would leave, she gingerly skittered across the ice from the boat stationed mid-Seine, to the quay, from which she ran to the steps and up to the bridge, only for her heart to fall when she reached the light and he was gone.

Still clutching the bottle to her chest, she stood waiting for him to return; she started back when he did not. Above her the deep blue night separated to form a perfect white lunar hole, and the light glittered across the Seine and over the houseboat that was frozen in the river like an island. When she got to the cabin, she collapsed on its bed and opened the porthole at eye level to look out on the ice in the moon. She was so thoroughly cold she no longer felt it. Almost immediately she drifted into another dream, hypnotized in part by the moon shining off the bottle she held before her, and the eyes that glistened as they watched her. I must be a fool, she said to the bottle, to believe it's you; and then she wasn't watching anymore. Her lids fell heavily and she looked up from time to time to the night sky outside the window — it was almost bright and gleaming. She bit her lower lip, when she drifted awhile: she saw him coming for her, walking naked on the ice; he was erect and huge. She opened her eyes and the terrain was blank and blue. She bit her lower lip again, clutching the bottle, when she heard the footsteps outside the door.

The quays were studded with bonfires; one by one the bridges before her seemed to float off and sink. Some people walked along the riverside. Occasionally someone, not wanting to go all the way to the next bridge, would try to traverse the river by foot; she could see their forms move in and out of the smoke. At first she thought the footsteps would be the old man's, but they weren't an old man's footsteps—too authoritative and belligerent. She could barely open her eyes at all in the cold and she wondered if she was freezing; she was quite comfortable. The bottle kept watching her. When she heard the door open, she understood it wasn't the old man but an intruder. She heard him approach behind her and felt him standing over her. The bottle continued to watch her, and she let her hand drop to the floor and the bottle slipped away. Inside the cabin was no light at all but for the moon. She spoke, in a dream. There was no answer.

She shifted a bit, still lying on her front, her face to the window.

She remembered something like this before. She was in the sand, then. The one behind her dropped to his knees on the bed. That had happened before too. She was drowsy now, drugged by the moon, when his hands reached in front of her and unbuttoned everything, from her breasts to her thighs, every seam ripped away; and in the stark cold she knew—she could see by the light of her arms through the haze—that she glimmered like the ice on the river.

She moaned in the window when she felt him come into her. She reached up lazily to the edge of the window and gripped it. She felt his fingers brush the distance of her hips and pull her closer till he was far up inside. The cabin was now filled with the smoke from the ice and the fires; in the extraordinary cold she was hot and sleek. She held fast to the window while he took her. She watched his hands on her wrists, the deep rendered lines and blue veins and long white fingers like maps. I want to swim in this river, she said, and touched a vein, I want to be your blue Moorish slave. She writhed a little this way, a little that. He raised his long white fingers to her lips and took her hair in his hand. The moon filled her eyes, and when he touched her a bit more deeply with each thrust, the orb's placement seemed threatened, as though it would rush past its own edges.

Michel, she said. He did not answer. If it wasn't Michel, it didn't matter; she now had nowhere to go. She could hear him breathing. When she turned just enough to look up, she couldn't see his face in the smoke, or his chest; she could only see his forearms coming out of the fog to hold her and his waist rolling up out of the fog toward the center of her. She only saw his fingers emerge to touch her face. He caressed her and held her immobile while he finished. Her hair caught on the wood of the cabin, she heard the sounds of the river beneath the ice while his sounds grew louder, hushed in the same sort of flow until she couldn't tell one from the other. One last time she stared at the moon, and it turned to a blaze the wet of her body and the ravishing subjugation of the moment; and she felt herself go: she felt him go: she thought she was falling, the yolk of the moon breaking and a long line of white light running to the horizon beyond the farthest bridge.

And then when he was still, his face buried in her neck, she raised his eyes to her and kissed them. He was unconscious, his black hair was wet. She ran her fingers across his brow, and cupped his face in her palm. She kissed him again. She pulled him to her and buried her profile in his hair. The moon was in the cabin; she inhaled the languid smoke. She listened to the sounds of the river through the wood. She wrapped her legs around him, and wondered what she was going to do. "I love you, Adrien-Michel," she whispered, and supposed he never heard her. "But I don't want to. I don't want to."

He heard the river when she heard the river. He pressed his ear against her breast, listening, and through her body heard the sound of ice and water below them. By the same token, he had come to see the visions she saw: having discarded the patch, he could now look into the gold tempest of hair around her face and see whatever it was she was watching. On the plane, flying into Paris, circling over the city, he stared at her as she sat watching out the window and he saw, on her brow, the fires in the streets, in the shops, on the river, before the Métro gates. There streamed across her temple a hundred billows of black smoke rising over the ice: the spires of the city were in the shadows of her eyes, and the bridges on the Seine lay on her lips. He could lower his eyes to her breasts, and place his hands around them and catch in the slope of her curves the glimpse of a particular alley in Montparnasse, or the Quartier Latin, or the garment district east of Châtelet; he could hear the bells of cathedrals.

They had been in love in Paris less than an hour when he had her on the hotel stairs; the key had slipped from his fingers and he pulled apart the buttons of her skirt, slipped her panties down to her ankles as she clutched the railing alongside her. That night they did it in the brush outside the Orangery Museum, when he looked in the small of her back and saw the lights of the Place de la Concorde coming through the smoke, indistinct and diaphanous. Across Paris he ravaged her: in a private courtyard near Pigalle, when he saw in her thighs the translucent form of a face behind a stained-glass window; in the Bois de Boulogne, when he caught in the corner of his eye the dark black foliage of the trees rustling across the back of her neck. On her shoulders he saw the cafés, and he took her in the farthest and deepest corner just before an underground grotto closed and lapsed into black completely; as a jazz band played to one side, she felt the heat of the stone walls through her sweater and against her face as he was inside her. In her hands he saw the headlights of a taxi dim and die, and he entered her as the glass of the shop window behind her turned slick from the heat of her legs; when they came to a halt, the taxi turned its lights on for them again, and they got in.

It was months later, on a train moving through France when he was without her, that he realized he had expected they would one day stumble on one of those places in Paris and both remember where and how they had met before. Having come to Paris in pursuit of the past, it seemed logical to him that their pasts would coincide somewhere on a street corner or a bridge: he would suddenly regain everything, all of it would come back to him; and she would just as suddenly, in the same rush, give up what was waiting for her in Venice, understanding she no longer wanted or could use it. This did not happen. Waiting for her at American Express was a telegram from her husband saying the Venice bicycle rally was postponed till early spring; and nothing came back to Michel at all other than the memories he had of that morning he woke in his room, his life a blank. So they decided to stay in Paris until he could relocate something, which was the film he had expected to play across the wall of his apartment that afternoon on Pauline Boulevard, only to find instead some silent historic artifact depicting murder.

He understood and accepted that she would have to see Jason again. As much as he wanted her, he understood that coercion on his part was out of the question—that she had to decide to leave Jason fully on her own, and that she had to resolve her own doubts. He couldn't understand the doubts, actually. He couldn't understand why there was any question in her mind at all; he resented that he had to compete with Jason, who both Michel and Lauren understood did not deserve another chance. But somehow, understanding that was not enough. It wasn't enough for Lauren that Jason didn't deserve the chance: the situation still required that Lauren actively deny Jason that chance.

She thought she was ready to do it. She could sit and count the ways he had wronged her. She could add up his love affairs on the fingers of both hands, but the women he had merely fucked required more digits than she possessed. She could forget those women, she could accept that he'd only placed his penis inside them and left nothing more than a white discharged puddle. But the phone calls were something else, the women who had called begging her, his wife, for only a moment to speak to him again. And so in her head were all the words, the ones she said on her wedding day—that damned oath—and the ones she heard on the telephone; and she was just sick of them. She was sick of hearing them. She wondered if she loved Michel for how few words he spoke.

Why? she said to herself when she looked at him. Why you? When he made love to her the first time, she cried for him because she was afraid: still more words then—the doctors telling her to be careful; and she figured the long thin line of sutures in her belly would burst and out something would fall. But she did not burst, and nothing fell out, and soon she was only ravenous for him to be inside her; she found herself clawing at his backside, and pulling at his hair. The idea of giving him up was abominable to her. She forgot Jason altogether; she felt not a shred of guilt when she took Michel into her. Why you? she said to herself again, and bit his ear; and she supposed it was his eyes, and she noted how he looked so young but for his eyes, which were sad and touched by the wounds even he could no longer remember.

Michel, she said, and never knew what to say next. When he was inside her, there was no one else in the world who belonged there. When he took her, she was never sure whether she was his slave, or in fact he was hers. It felt like both to him. He determined, sometime between that late hour he kissed her on the stairs outside her apartment that night, when all the power had gone, and that afternoon he saw her in the hospital asleep, that he would win her. He realized, of course he was smart enough to realize, that his first glimpse of her before he woke that morning in Paris could have been anywhere, anytime: passing on the street, sighting her in a cruising car, envisioning her in a dream. It might have been the slightest, most apparently trivial of moments when he first saw her; but she was the one he remembered because she was the one he was meant to remember. And yet despite this, despite knowing she was *meant* to be his, he always approached her with a fear that nearly cast him into stasis: he wasn't reassured by destiny. He saw himself, rather, as destiny's outsider, the one destiny had no use for; he traveled outside the blueprint. Neither Michel nor fate had any faith in the other. And so when he came to the Pont-Neuf, after exchanging the film with Fletcher Grahame, and she wasn't there to meet him, he was cold in a way that had nothing to do with ice or wind off the river. He waited, and angry after a while, turned to leave, walked to the boulevard Saint-Michel and stared blankly at the lights. Then he walked back and saw her returning from the bridge across the ice to the boat frozen midway. Then he followed her and, as he always did, claimed her.

He found out about the bottle later that night when the old man who called himself Bateau Billy returned. Billy didn't seem alarmed or angry or even surprised to see the young man there; he shook Michel's hand—once—with a French formality. Michel spoke in French and the old man responded. Lauren said little, standing off in the shadows of the cabin, still holding the bottle to her. "You found the eyes," Billy noted, pointing at the bottle; and she only stared at him in silence. He looked at her, then at Michel; both men were watching her and then looking at each other. "Well," said the old man, "it's an amazing effect, isn't it? I think it always means something different to each person." There was a memory of another blonde holding the same bottle, once, but he'd given up on the placement of memories, realizing it wasn't important. "If you would like, you may have the bottle," he said. "I make a gift of it to you. But in return you must visit me as long as you're here in Paris. It appears from the river that I'll be here the winter."

"I'll be happy to visit you," said Lauren.

"Will you come tomorrow?"

"I'll come each day if you like." They left, making their way across the river in the dark, and then walking the distance to their hotel, forsaking a cab so as to save a few francs for the heater. All the way Michel watched her hold the bottle. He didn't ask any questions other than, "What's in the bottle?" Had the old man said ice? You found the ice, he had said. Lauren said, "It's just a bottle," almost so inaudibly he didn't hear it at all; he sensed something private, so pursued it no further. The days passed, and she went everywhere with the bottle whenever she left their room, carrying it against her breast.

He had, if anything, learned too well not to ask questions. He regretted, for instance, not asking the stranger with the film questions. That there lay, in the switch of films, answers to his past, seemed maddeningly obvious to the point of now making him feel stupid. And the similarity of the women in the films seemed rather too coincidental, though they could not have been the same—Michel dated the other film around the early twenties, and his film was made almost fifty years later: an age discrepancy, he calculated, of twenty or so years.

He put off making the call. He thought of many excuses for not making the call. When he did make the call, he asked for the gentleman who had placed the ad in *Le Figaro*.

"Monsieur Grahame is gone," said the concierge.

"Gone?"

"Moved."

"I don't understand."

"Moved. Both of them."

"Both of whom."

"Monsieur Grahame and Monsieur Sarre."

He hung up. In fact, he slammed the phone down on the receiver as quickly as he could. He walked back to the hotel. He walked up the four flights of stairs and into the room; Lauren was there. He lay down on the bed beside her and stared at the ceiling; and as she lowered her head to the side of his, to study his profile, he understood what he had just done, and had been doing all along. What is it? she said.

He had, of course, come in pursuit of something; but there was another man, the one he didn't know, who was running away from the object of pursuit. This other man was the one Michel had been before he woke that morning, here in this city, some years before. And each time Michel came close to what he was pursuing, the other man took off, taking Michel with him. Wrenched back and forth in this way, Michel could only become physically sick at the sight of his own past; given the choices, Michel didn't ask the pertinent questions when he had the chance because he didn't really want to know. And now, on the phone, face to face or, one might say, voice to voice with an answer, he had immediately severed that opportunity as well, and did so quickly, panicked that someone might tell him too much. "I'm a fraud," he said to Lauren, while still watching the ceiling. She raised her fingers to his mouth but he moved her hand. "I've always been a fraud. I'm still wearing a patch, trying to appear as though I'm far above the things I don't want to see." He went back to the café and telephoned again. He apologized to the concierge for disconnecting the call so quickly, and asked if there was a forwarding number for either Monsieur Grahame or Monsieur Sarre. She warily replied that there was not. He asked if there was an address. There was no address, she said. He asked if he could leave a message for Monsieur Sarre with her. She didn't expect to see him again, she answered. He asked if she could tell him about Monsieur Sarre—who he was, what he did, was he a Parisian or a visitor, had he lived at this number a long time, was he a young man or old, did he have any living

relatives. The concierge told Michel she didn't like these questions, she was uncomfortable with the conversation in general,
and she wished to end it. She hung up, and when he dialed back
he heard the phone ring many times; no one answered.

She held to that winter that everyone else wished would pass.
She watched from the balcony of their hotel as November shifted
to December and December to the next year. She watched the
ice on the city thicken and the fires grow more frantic. When
the sun appeared in the sky, usually about three-thirty in the
afternoon, it was always a blue ball without glow; it changed the
clouds to strange shades of magenta and silver. The streets would
turn dark, slivers of light off the ice consumed by shadow, until
the moon rose and the sky succumbed to deep blue; then the ice
glimmered in the lunarcast of the night. All across the city, as
seen from her balcony, structures jutted up before her like jagged
canyon peaks, honeycombed with caverns where the fires burned.
Fires burned in the streets; every once in a while she would catch
the sight of flames flickering from around some corner or from
beyond some rooftop. Primordial Paris: empty, frozen, infernal,
undetermined inhabitants scurrying through its subterranean passages, the increasingly panicked sounds of more furniture broken
to feed the fires, the crackling of more pages igniting, more
incinerated mementos. From her balcony Lauren could see, in
window after window, families huddled around their televisions—screens shattered, small fires flickering in the hollowed
sets. Around Christmas there was a moan; she heard it begin at
the river, the direction her balcony faced, and move toward her,
until within three nights it had reached her. All the city moaned,
at first like the cry of cats, then old and deathly, then overwhelming in unison and power. By the last night of the year,
when there was no more the sound of the cars or the pedestrians
in the street or, certainly, the river rushing by or, certainly, the
radios or televisions, that moan was the only sound of the city;
it was then she believed Paris belonged to them, her and Michel.
She would give herself to him on the balcony, no longer cold at
all; she would call to him to enter her as the panorama of their
ice world, with its array of eruptions, stretched out before her.

She would feel the gauzy pallor of the flames in her eyes, and tilt back her head to the stars through the clouds, while he held her breasts and her nipples became erect. She would reach back and hold him, pull him to her, and feel the gust from Brittany across her face as he exploded in her middle. Dropping his forehead to her shoulder, he seemed to drift: and she recognized in her own moans the cacophony from the skyline.

She had to decide. She had to decide by spring, and the winter seemed perfect for it. Michel continued to appear to her as he appeared in her apartment on Pauline Boulevard—the time his presence made itself known on the stairs in the dark, or when he carried her into the hospital, which she did not remember, and carried her out, which she did. She loved him for the fact that something had cut so deeply into him, something had so shaken his sense of himself, that the self vacated and he created himself anew. Jason had never been cut, not really ever; he had gone through his life and his crises blithely unaware that he was mortal, let alone vulnerable. Jason was a god of sorts, while Michel was inescapably knowing of his mortality, which made his manifestations all the more profound. For this reason, Jason took Lauren's love as though he was entitled. Michel never assumed he was entitled to anything.

In the face of such a massive set of denials, Lauren had no choice but to choose her affirmations carefully; she couldn't make mistakes, she couldn't afford to fool herself. When spring arrived she would go to Venice to meet Jason, and then she would be enveloped by nothing but affirmations, which only would confuse the issue. As for Michel, he didn't ask questions, or demand the resolution of choices. What disturbed her most deeply was that she loved him limitlessly, without reason, the way she had loved Jason. She distrusted the feeling altogether.

Now she watched him try to piece his past together in little celluloid boxes. She saw that he could hardly bear to watch the film himself, but the two of them watched it together, the old woman in the house who spoke, according to the subtitles, of living in the window. What does she mean, living in the window, said Lauren. Michel shook his head. They watched the film over and over, trying to figure it out. This went on for a number of days, until one afternoon a woman with a child clinging to her leg stood on the balcony across the street screaming at them; through their open window she had seen Michel and Lauren running the projector. She called to the people in the streets below and told them that two people were using electricity to watch a movie while her child was freezing. People in the street were actually stopping to listen to the woman, and somebody shouted that perhaps a pleasant bonfire could be made of the hotel. The concierge was banging on the door desperately, and Michel shut the projector off. After a while, the power was allotted to each room in more miserly quantities. Then Lauren and Michel used their electricity like everyone else, to keep working the small heater which at least served to warm their hands and feet. At night they walked to the Luxembourg Gardens, where every evening a huge fire was built in the empty fountain, and hundreds of people would gather to try and keep warm.

Michel took to looking at the film frame by frame, sitting in the room by the balcony and holding the strips up to the gray light of the sky. She wondered what he was looking for; she supposed he wondered the same. All she knew was that when she found Jules again, there on the houseboat, it suddenly made her decisions easier; and she hoped relocating this movie would do the same for Michel. She wasn't exactly sure what decisions Michel had to make, but she was certain he had to make at least one or two; it was unbearable to her to think she was the only one with momentous choices confronting her. She was always a bit afraid he would find something, in one of those frames he scrutinized so carefully, that would take him away from her; she watched his expression anxiously, waiting for him to stumble upon some lost love huddled in a back corner who had slipped by unnoticed on previous examination. But she assumed the best. She assumed that, just as rediscovering Jules had somehow eliminated a responsibility she had to Jason, just as finding again the child Jason had all but abandoned convinced her she no longer owed Jason anything or needed him, just as the dissipation of guilt in this discovery lessened her sense of a price to pay, then too the illumination of Michel's past would unknot the obsession that drove and split him; he would be something unified again;

she knew of the two people within him, and how they were running opposite ways. When his own past once again belonged to him, all of him would be going the same way, and in that way she and Jules could go with him.

By late January the cold was at its zenith. That week several whole buildings were set afire; there had been general mutterings of this sort of action since before Christmas. Then one night the Odéon Théatre was ablaze, and the next morning Lauren and Michel found the streets filled with cops and soldiers, with barricades from Saint-Germain-des-Prés all the way past the boulevard Saint-Michel. This did not stop the arson (it seemed unreasonable, given the cold, to call it arson). Certain structures were deemed expendable and unnecessary, including theaters, monuments, museums, certain very fashionable shops, synagogues and, for some, the homes of the rich. There were even a couple of army tanks stationed by the Louvre, off the rue de Rivoli; the trees were scorched black and flocked with snow. Several people were arrested three nights after the Odéon incident when they tried to burn the cathedral of Sacré-Coeur. To many people in Paris, the vision of Sacré-Coeur burning above the city like a torch sounded exquisite—a pyre that could keep them warm a long time, perhaps even into the hours of the following morning.

Lauren was getting one telegram after another from Jason; in fact, her trips across the river to the American Express, limited to once a week because of the long freezing walk and the curtailment of office hours, usually found two or three wires waiting for her. Each one seemed more urgent than the one preceding; they reminded her a bit of the letters she used to write him in the early days of their marriage, though of course these were more terse, economical. He'd never sounded like this before, and she remembered the strange uncharacteristic concern he'd shown on Pauline Boulevard before he left for Europe. She was astounded by the immediately recognizable truth: that Jason was afraid; and when she confirmed to him that Michel was with her—"I know," she wrote him, with an unconsciously malicious irony, "that you'll be relieved I am not living in a strange city alone"—the telegrams stopped for a while, then began arriving in droves. She answered that she couldn't leave Paris, all the rails and airlines were shut down; this wasn't completely true, as Jason himself confirmed with a little checking. There was, in fact, one train a day out of Paris, from the Gare de l'Est, on the only railway the bulldozers and steam shovels had managed to keep clear; it was long and circuitous, making its way to Tours and then south along the French coast to La Rochelle, Wyndeaux, Bordeaux, Biarritz, then inland to Toulouse, edging along the Pyrenees to the Côte d'Azur, Marseilles, Nice, Monaco, across the Italian border to Genoa, Milan, finally Venice. A three-day journey at best, longer given unforeseen weather conditions; but it did get to Venice, Jason pointed out, and he saw no reason why Lauren couldn't have come to him long ago. He saw no reason. Finally she telephoned him from the post office on the Ile de la Cité, as he had so often requested, and over the kilometers he said to her, "You like Michel."

"Yes," she said.

"You're involved."

"Yes."

She could almost hear him over the telephone nodding his head the way he did, that way that never conceded panic, that intended a perseverant cool at all costs. "May I," he said, "see you once, before you come to any decisions?"

"I think you're entitled to that." She regretted that it sounded officious. "I have to go to Venice," she told Michel the following day, in their room, when they were in bed, afterward.

"I know."

"I have to see him."

"I know, I know." He didn't look at her.

"Are you angry?" she finally asked.

"No. I'm afraid," he said matter-of-factly.

Afraid, he went on. She watched him poring over the film day after day; and after they'd talked of her departure his search became more intense, as if to rescue himself from his fear. One day he called her to come look at something. Peering through a magnifying glass, she studied the frame. "I don't see."

"There, on the wall by the bed."

The frame showed his mother walking through a room, toward another doorway.

"There's a date."

"I see now. A.D. nineteen-something."

"You can make out a nine? I wasn't sure."

"Well, I'm assuming it's a nine. That seems likely, doesn't it?"

"Yes."

"Nineteen fifty-seven."

"You're sure?" he said. "I couldn't see that."

"I'm guessing. Is that an important date?"

"I don't know." He shook his head. "Maybe I came to the States about then."

Finally one day he put down the film and came and sat by her. He could see she was reluctant to say it, so he said it for her. "You'll need to get to the station early. Trains are packed these says. They're not taking reservations and everyone wants to get out of Paris."

"It's almost spring," she said. "Maybe it won't be so crowded."

"Maybe not."

She waited.

"Well," he said. "Then I'll leave a message for you at American Express in Venice, and you can let me know when you're ready."

"Adrien-Michel . . ."

"I know."

"Venice, then," she said.

He looked at the film in his hands, absently; he wrapped the film around his hand the way a fighter tapes his knuckles before a bout. She touched his leg and wanted to make him a promise. He realized she was about to make him a promise so he spoke first. This isn't important anymore, he said of the film. No? she said. No, he said, shaking his head. He strung out the film to show his disdain for it. What is the importance of placing a memory? he said. Why spend that much time trying to find the exact geographic and temporal latitudes and longitudes of the things we remember, when what's urgent about a memory is its essence? Are you giving up on the past? she said. I gave up on it long ago, he answered. I cast it away one night and was rid of it the following dawn, but never accepted the fact. I gave up on the here-and-now, thinking the here-and-now couldn't be any good without the past. But the past has determined the here-and-now, hasn't it? she said. Sure it has, he said. Sure it has.

He pushed her back on the bed and pulled her hands above her head. He took the film and bound her wrists together. It doesn't hurt you, does it? he said. No, she said. You can't get away though, can you? he said. No, she said, I can't get away. He opened her coat and then her clothes; when he pulled her clothes from her legs he bound her ankles. She stared up at him while he unbuttoned his own clothes and dropped them to the floor. He fell to his knees beside the bed and bit her back. He wrapped the strips of film around her body till they crisscrossed her from neck to thighs; she could hear the second of two francs drop in the small heater and the hum of the coils as they grew hot. She couldn't see the heater's glow slip over the room around her, throwing the corners into dark. She felt him take her and separate her; she felt a spasm when he slipped his tongue into her. When she felt his teeth sink into her thighs, she tried to pull away and heard the film reel fall from the edge of the bed and hit and roll across the floor. She strained against the knotted celluloid around her wrists and feet, and he took her by the breasts as she began to move desperately. Nothing around her made an impact, not the sounds from the boulevards below or the cold through the window or the voices from other rooms— nothing until she smelled the burning of the chestnut trees: and that took her back somewhere: the sensation of his tongue inside her felt like a wisp of smoke winding up through her, and she remembered once long before in Kansas waking in the middle of the night and smelling the fires outside her window, and the patter of her brothers running in the hallway outside her door; and terrified she had gotten from bed, a small girl, and stumbled sleepily out into the hall, and then out to the porch to see the commotion in the night: people running back and forth in the dark, figures outlined by the huge bonfires on the flat landscape and the fall leaves crackling from the heat, the long full skirts of women sweeping by, the wide spinning umbrellas they held to shield themselves from the raining soot, and more and more leaves fed to the fires. The terror of the autumn night burnings thrilled her; she turned and saw him standing in the distance, his hair black like the soot. Michel, she said. She tried to push him away but his tongue slid further up. Michel, she cried, Adrien. He gripped her hips and pulled her closer. Do you feel my tongue there? he said. She nodded speechlessly. Can you feel it in the chambers of your heart? Michel! she said, please I can't stand it; but no sound came from her when she saw the tip of his tongue wind up through the aorta, along her throat and dart before her eyes. There was that heart-stopping ascension from the fork of her body upward, and she thought she was falling from the bed only to look up and see his eyes looking into hers as he drove himself into her. She held her hands to her chest and collapsed before him, her own eyes stark and wide and her mouth parted and frozen, and she languished beneath him while he had her. He pulled her hands away from her breasts and took those; he pulled her hair from her mouth and took that. I knew from the first, he told her. I know, she said. I knew in the dark on the stairs, he said, when I kissed you. She said, I know that. I had taken off my clothes for you, he said, there in the dark— did you know that? Yes, she answered; were you this big for me then? He buried his forehead in the shadow of her neck. She said, You could have not have been; and she lowered her arms and pressed the celluloid and flesh into the small of his back. You could not have been this big, she said; and he told her, muttering in her ear, I was, I was this big, and I was there on the stairs for you waiting in the dark. And I heard your footsteps on the stairs and I grew erect for you in the dark, with the lights all over the city gone out; I thought when I crossed the floor to you and kissed you I would fill the world. Lauren, he said, and he laid his hand on her face and began to thrust furiously, I was a dead man before you; and then he was released, in a tremor that seemed to catch and suspend him upright: he gave a small scream. She watched his face pass from stricken to dazed; he folded into her. With the long hard breath he seemed to expel, he only said, You. His fingers slid away. His body slipped from hers.

• • •

Winter broke. For several days the sun even shone, white and wintry, and after the light one could feel its heat: the roofs of houses ran in the streets, and the ice cracked readily on the sidewalks. Walking to the river, Lauren felt among the people palpable twin senses of relief and debasement. Crossing the river to American Express, she passed one charred hovel after another; the mix of ice and ash covered her shoes, snow and soot settled on her coat. Doorways were blackened, windows were gone, debris littered the distance, all the way up the avenue de l'Opéra to rue Scribe.

Another wire from Jason was waiting for her when she got to American Express just before it closed. She didn't have time to send a reply. She could send one the next day, she thought, after she said goodbye to Billy. She left the office and went into a café, laying her coat on the accompanying chair and setting the cognac bottle on the table before her. She ordered hot tea. She asked the waiter for the time, and though she still had an hour and a half before meeting Michel, she decided to drink the tea quickly and be on her way. She watched the crowds in the streets and then saw the streetlights come on for the first time in weeks, and dreaded everything.

She picked up the bottle and left in the dark, and realized how novel the partly lit streets seemed; for months, the only light had been the fires, and army searchlights sliding across the city in pursuit of arsonists. Even now not all the lights were on, but rather every two or three; people hurried from one light to the next through alternating pockets of darkness. They seemed to resent the light; they had learned to do that.

She was, then, amazed by what she came upon just a block from American Express. It was a premiere, with limousines in front and huge generators in the street hooked up to klieg lights sweeping over the cold white facade of the Opéra. People were dressed in gowns and formal evening wear, even top hats, parading in to see a movie. It was as though the winter had never happened. A crowd was gathering outside, held back from the arriving elite by velvet ropes and gilded posts, and several very serious cops; Lauren could already hear the muttering. The people in the crowd all had the hard look of the winter in their faces, and the people exiting their limousines were soft and shining and obviously hadn't been cold for a handful of moments between them.

It was when the last of the limousines pulled up that the commotion began. Out of the back came a tall, serious-looking younger man with glasses, and behind him a small, very old man; he gave Lauren a start because for one ludicrous moment she thought it was Billy. He seemed in a daze, not really a part of what was happening; the younger man took him by the arm and led him up the steps. The guests of the premiere applauded; and when the celebration had become intolerable, the applause was answered by a cobblestone hurled from somewhere behind Lauren. The stone struck the wall of the Opéra, tearing a gash in what appeared to be an old mural depicting a scene from the film. The young man stopped and stared at the hole in the painting. Another cobblestone went into one of the kliegs, shattering the glass that fronted the light but not the light itself. Voices rose from the crowd, obscenities were shouted; and those who had arrived for the showing rushed anxiously inside. Another cobblestone was hurled and the police began pushing the crowd back, moving the gilded posts in an attempt to extend the borders of the velvet ropes. On the steps before the Opéra, both the young man and old man stood without stirring, the former just looking at the painting and the latter just looking at the klieg. Lauren saw the old man's face light for the first time with an almost odd anticipation; as the shouting around her rose to a howl, the younger man closed his eyes and his face turned in color, until finally he grabbed his head with his hands as though trying to hold something back. The sound of the crowd seemed to become unbearable for him. He pivoted wildly in his place and stepped forward on the steps facing the crowd. "Don't you know this is the greatest picture ever," he called, his eyes wide and his hands still holding his head, "don't you know I've spent my life—" He did not finish. She saw the stone rise and fall almost so slowly she would wonder later why she didn't scream. In a moment everything stopped, and in the next moment everything shifted; she was to remember vividly the gold frames of the young man's glasses skipping across the steps to the bottom; the expressions around her froze as though winter had returned. She looked back to the young man and watched his face explode in red.

He dropped. The old man stood looking down at him, stunned. Outnumbered police found themselves falling back before the rampage. People were rushing into each other, some trying to get into the Opéra, others—including Lauren—trying to get away. In the jostling she kept looking at the old man, horrified that he was going to be struck down too. "What about the old man?" she cried, to no one, really; to which someone else shouted, "Yes, get the old man!" She shook her head, kept glancing back at him; he just stood there as though fixed on something, entranced and drawn. To what she didn't understand, until he finally began to run, or at least move as quickly as he could move, not toward any sort of safety, not toward the crowds: he ran for the klieg. He was held by its blinding brilliant light, and he ran for it as though he would hurl himself into it. He had gotten from the steps, the broken glass of the klieg crunching beneath his feet, and he was almost at the light when a cop pulled him back. Literally dragged away, the old man continued to reach for the light; it was clear to Lauren he saw something in the light no one else could see. She clutched the cognac bottle closer to her.

She felt what seemed like a dozen pairs of hands holding her; she kept trying to free herself, becoming more immobilized. It was when she couldn't move at all, and she thought her legs were about to be pulled from beneath her, that suddenly she was alone, the tide suddenly changed, and she was loosed from the rest. She ran, blindly, to the other side of the avenue. She stopped, looked back at the melee, and ran on; blocks away, she could still hear the shouting and sense the ground trembling below her.

The old man walked to the river. The dawn receded before him; as though in a trance, he was thinking nothing. He wasn't thinking of lights, he wasn't thinking of *La Morte de Marat*, he wasn't thinking of Fletcher Grahame's faceless body, he wasn't thinking of her. Had someone stopped him on his way to the river and said, Adolphe, have you heard from Janine? he wouldn't have known who Janine was. Had someone stopped him and asked of the night before, and what had happened, and why, he wouldn't have remembered it. Had someone stopped him and asked where he was going, he would have said, The river, and had they asked him why he was going to the river, he wouldn't have been able to answer. So he walked along the streets that morning, and occasionally someone looked strangely after him as he passed; when he reached the river, he walked to the Pont-Neuf, and stopped and stared, for no reason he understood, at the bottom of the steps that led from the bridge to the quay.

The young woman walked to the river. She was going to say goodbye to an old man on a boat. Her lover had said he would meet her after getting some bread at the boulangerie. When she got to the river she saw that much of the ice had broken up; in some places rushing water could be seen, and the ice was floating in small bergs. There was still a thin sheet between the quay and the boat, which hadn't yet broken free. The old man on the boat saw her and waved, and she waved back. Can I cross the ice? she called to him.

He shrugged, and called something back. She couldn't make out the French. She held on to the cognac bottle tightly and tested her footing on the ice. Halfway to the boat, she heard the ice crackling beneath her, and as she moved on frantically, it began breaking in her wake. The old man helped pull her aboard the boat as her last step gave way. They both looked back. "I think you have freed the river," he said to her. "Until next winter, at least."

"Will next winter be like this too?" she said.

"I don't worry about coming winters."

"Did you hear about last night?"

"The riot at the Opéra," he said. She felt the tremor through the deck of the boat beneath her. "Be careful. The river's really breaking loose now. The boat will jolt sharply in a moment, when it's free."

She looked at the quay. "Michel won't be able to cross."

He sat down to wait. "Were you there?"

"Where?"

"The Opéra."

"No. Yes, I mean." She looked at him a moment. "Were you?"

"No," he said. She looked back at the quay. "Isn't that your friend?" The old man pointed.

"Yes." She waved to him. He held up the bread. She gestured at the ice and water, shrugged her shoulders, and her eyes wandered from him a bit. She sighed and said to the river, "I have to leave Paris."

"For Hollywood?" said Billy.

"Venice."

He didn't ask her to explain.

"I don't know what I want anymore," she said, looking over her shoulder to the quay where Michel stood. She waved again, and there was a resounding explosion heard from one side of the river to the other, almost as though she herself had caused it. "Be careful," said Billy, grabbing her by the elbow; but it was too late, the jolt came, and she was jarred by the spasm of the boat, barely catching her footing.

The bottle flew from her arms.

It hit the ice, it did not break. But more ice gave way beneath it; the current of the river caught the bottle, juggled it between and past the ice, pulling it under and then surfacing with it. It was already beyond the reach of Billy's net. Lauren just stood with her hands over her mouth.

The old man watched the bottle, then looked at Lauren. She looked back at him, over to Michel who stood watching everything, and now was walking down the quay trying to follow the bottle's course. He looked up at Lauren and pointed out the bottle drifting past. For a moment the bottle seemed to come toward him, and he fell to his knees on the quay, and then flat on his stomach, waiting for it to approach within his reach. Instead, the river took it farther away.

Lauren realized then that both Michel and Billy must have thought she was mad. Yet it didn't seem to matter to them; they accepted that, for one reason or another, the bottle mattered to her and they respected the madness. Billy was pushing the rest of the ice away with a long pole. "Do you want to go after it?" he said.

The boat started downriver. Lauren looked at Billy, looked at Michel, looked at the bottle in the distance. The boat moved past Michel toward the Pont-Neuf.

She saw Michel smile sadly at her, and nod. "See you in Venice," he said, when she was in earshot.

"I wanted to kiss you," she said.

He nodded.

She had wanted to kiss him. She didn't know under what circumstances she would kiss him again; she didn't know if she would ever kiss him the way she had before.

It was at the Pont-Neuf, by the steps, that Billy looked into the cold black water and saw his own reflection, standing, curiously, not on the boat but rather above him, on the bridge. He looked up just as the boat passed under; and on the other side of the bridge he saw himself, walking across the river.

By the time he took the train, the dreams had stopped.

Something had replaced his passion for the past; something had shut off the flow of memorial fragments that drifted up to him at dawn before he woke. The flashing glimpses of twins and Paris, of uncles and California, found their own level of saturation, until mind and consciousness seemed blind to them; and then he forgot them. That left his nights blank and undisturbed; he could not, offhand, remember the last dream. He could not remember the last returning memory. He could not remember the feeling of being at loose ends; the ends he pursued were clear enough to him now. They led to a train, they led to Italy; and three weeks to the day he waited, since that morning he watched her sail down the Seine with the old man; and five days before the scheduled start of the Venice rally, as the Seine began to mysteriously disappear, he left Paris on the only train still departing the city.

He didn't miss the past anymore. He cast it from him the way he ripped the patch from his eye, and for the same reason. He wondered if the train would near the beach on its way south; he wondered if he might catch the sight of a boat on the edge of the sea.

He met an American playwright named Carl who had lived in Paris off and on for a decade. They ran into each other at a bookshop and got to talking. Carl was staying with some Trotskyites he knew on the other side of the river; he had been there most of the winter. The Trotskyites lived in rather high style but they were loyal to Trotsky in their hearts, and were not deterred by the philosophical inconvenience of so many bourgeois luxuries surrounding them. All the Trotskyite women were named Christine. They invited Michel to stay at their apartment. At night when he tried to sleep he could hear the Trotskyite Christines fighting in the next room.

Carl was planning to leave Paris and go to Toulouse. The Christines told him that Toulouse was the place to go and hear hot jazz; after hearing hot jazz in Toulouse he could investigate the odds at getting a train across the frontier and traveling on to Barcelona. The afternoon Michel and Carl decided to leave Paris the Christines gave them a ride to the Gare de l'Est, where they stood in the station bar and drank until the moment of departure. Michel and Carl got seats on the train, which was full but not packed; the exodus out of Paris had abated with spring, though there was still only the single train running daily out of the city— a situation Carl didn't think would change before summer, if ever. In their compartment the two men sat across from each other and watched out the window, where the Christines periodically waved to them between shaking their fists at each other. Carl read a French newspaper. People bustled up and down the aisles. Michel sank back in his seat and fell asleep before the train pulled from the station.

When he woke, the suburbs of the city were rolling past him. Carl was twisted against the window asleep, his mouth pressed to the glass. The newspaper was crumpled in his lap, turned to the obituary page. Michel blinked slowly at the newspaper, then sat up and stared at it awhile longer before reaching over and taking it.

He looked at the listing that caught his eye. "M. Adolphe Sarre, pioneer of the French cinema" was the way he translated it.

The obit identified Sarre as the director of a film called *The Death of Marat*, begun shortly after the first world war and finally assembled in a completed version only this year. The article quoted several critics and historians who spoke of Sarre in admiring but strangely ambivalent terms. He had died in his sleep; since a "disturbance" at the film's opening some weeks before, which resulted in one death and several serious injuries, his physical and mental health had declined precipitously. His exact age was unknown, as were the details of his early years.

Very carefully Michel folded the newspaper again and replaced it on Carl's lap. Then he sat back in his seat and watched the passing suburbs again, which were gradually disappearing altogether. The sun bore down on him through the glass, and when he returned to sleep, the dreams began all over again, one after another.

In the first of the dreams, flitting across his eyes before he even shut them, he saw Lauren on a boat.

• • •

They sighted the bottle on the coast three days after leaving Paris. It was dusk and they sailed into a forest. Only the tops of the dead trees were exposed, bare and twisted; small fine branches brushed across their faces. The fog was thick and the light of the fallen sun glowed beneath the sea, so the tops of the trees appeared red. The branches waved back and forth before the boat like bloody arms above the water, and in the wind from the west they seemed to moan like lost sailors. Billy didn't understand where the forest had come from. He'd never seen it before, and now, gazing at the coast, that didn't look quite the same either. He was afraid Lauren would think perhaps he was becoming confused like any other very old man. The ocean turned dark, the old man and the woman continuing to maneuver the boat through the thicket of treetops with their long poles; and then they saw, in the light of the moon, the glint of the cognac bottle bobbing in the water just beyond the edge of the forest. More frantically they worked their way through the trees; each time they hacked at the branches with their poles, the trees seemed to shudder, the blow to the bark seemed to blacken, the moan from the forest sounded lonelier. By the time they freed themselves the bottle was farther away, barely visible to the south in the moonlight. Darkness fell utterly, and Lauren took to standing at the boat's edge holding the lantern before her, casting what light she could on the waves. Finally out of exhaustion from navigating through the sea forest they dropped anchor and slept. In the morning, of course, no bottle was anywhere to be seen.

All the way down the coast they witnessed the rituals of winter's end. In the woods that lined the beaches, Lauren could see the people dancing at night, the women in long burgundy dresses and men in long coats, weaving through the orchards in each other's arms, each man carrying a flaming torch so that the entire shore was a nocturnal pattern of crisscrossing light and smoke. At the water the men would hand the torches to their partners and the women would cast the torches to the sea, the waves exploding one after the other. Lauren could still hear the singing after the boat had left the dancing far behind. Five days out of Paris Lauren and Billy came to a seaport circled by high fortress walls on the one side and another forest on the other, where the trees were blue and hung like teardrops against the landscape. A row of docks and bars stretched past the fortress walls, far behind the water's edge. All the boats were immobile in the sand. Billy stood watching the shore, and took his pole and drove it down into the water alongside the hull. He seemed startled when the pole stopped. "Where are we?" said Lauren.

"We are in too shallow water," said the old man. "Take a pole and help me push the boat farther out."

When they had moved the boat, the old man decided they would drop anchor. The water was still not very deep, and strangely tepid; the two waded to the docks. On the beach they passed dead fish and seaweed that lay dried in the sun. Half a kilometer down from the city walls, the land curved upward; the terrain became hilly and difficult. An old house overlooked the rocks, its windows naked of glass and doors banging open and shut in the wind; a path led from its front beams down to the sand, and not far from the path, standing alone in the middle of the beach, was a huge stone, perfectly black and almost perfectly round, and nearly Lauren's height. To have gotten to this place on the beach the stone had to have been moved by many men or some very violent sort of upheaval. In the sun against the white sand the black stone could be seen from a good distance away; Lauren and Billy had in fact sighted it from the boat.

The two walked down along the docks and through the old city gates. In town they bought enough bread and cheese and fruit for several days. The old man calculated that by then they would be off the northern coast of Spain. On the way back Billy stopped outside a bar and stood awhile staring. "What is it?" said Lauren. Billy looked struck. He went in and Lauren followed him. Inside he stood staring at the curvature of the café's interior, as though he expected something else. "Have you been here before?" she said.

He turned to her as she peered around the room. "Yes," he said. "Have you?"

"No," she answered, with some surprise.

He nodded. A few sailors sitting at tables looked at them. All the bottles were gone, and the room did not glow like a lantern. They bought three bottles of wine, opening one. There at the bar Billy got into a conversation with a fisherman sitting at the closest table. Lauren sat drinking her wine and after a while the conversation stopped and Billy said to Lauren, "The shoreline began receding about ten days ago, he says. People came out one morning and found dead fish and animals all over the beach, as though the sea moved so quickly even the fish hadn't time to move with it. The boats were all aground. The men in the village plan to push the boats out tomorrow."

Lauren nodded.

"Everyone's in shock," Billy went on, "because usually nothing happens here. Wars, plagues and disasters have always passed this village by, he says. I told him about the forest we sailed through up north. He said he'd heard of a couple of villages flooded south of here, and other villages suddenly finding kilometers of new beach."

Lauren nodded again. "Has he seen the bottle?"

Billy spoke to the sailor. The sailor listened, his features registering nothing. He shook his head once. Billy answered, "Nothing astonishes them anymore."

When they returned to the black stone on the beach, Billy looked to the boat out in the water. They'd have to leave the next day if the sea continued to retreat; he didn't want to chance the boat sinking into the sand. While Billy gathered wood for a fire, Lauren walked up the path that led to the old house. The wind had died and in her approach she caught the house standing very still, none of the doors moving, none of the dead blue shrubbery stirring. No sign of a human life was to be seen, and in the open doorway, when Lauren called out, no one answered.

Twilight swirled before her as she moved first through the lower level and then upstairs, where she found the bedrooms and a tiny sitting room. There was one large bed in one bedroom and two tiny beds in another bedroom, and a third small bed in the sitting room. She recognized the view from one of the windows. From another window she could see the large black stone where Billy had a fire burning on the beach. She recognized the hallways from certain vantage points. For a while, perhaps half an hour, she sat in the small room on the third tiny bed and thought how appropriate it would be to find the bottle here, to walk out the door and see it there at her feet, or catch the glint of it on the beach. She thought how appropriate it would be to open a cupboard in the kitchen and find the bottle looking at her, or to see it on the windowsill of this very room. That she should rediscover Jules where Michel had been a child seemed ludicrously perfect, and she sat studying the room carefully, to make sure she was missing nothing.

The old man was standing at the base of the path when she exited the house; he'd been watching the front door expectantly. She was unsure how long he'd stood there, or how long he'd refrained from calling her. They slept on the beach. They woke in the morning to scores of sailors pushing the boats toward the water. The tide was now farther out than the previous evening, and Billy's own boat appeared to be tottering precariously, scraping the ocean bottom. Better go, he said to her, and the two of them gathered up their food and started for the boat, the voices of the sailors and fishermen rising around them as they exhorted each other to pull faster and push harder. When she was submerged to her knees, Lauren glanced back over her shoulder at the old house in the distance and it occurred to her, maddeningly, that she had neglected to check the date that was carved in the wall over the bed. She wasn't convinced it meant anything but Michel had thought so, and now she thought to herself, When I see him again and tell him I have found the very house, he'll want to know the date. I won't be able to tell him because I was so busy thinking of the bottle.

As Billy had predicted, they were off the northern coast of Spain within three days. He was stunned to find the beach of San Sebastian stretching far from the city's edge; the sand was covered with townspeople walking up and down in a daze. Lauren and the old man got food in San Sebastian and sailed on. The sea was calm all the way down the coast of Portugal, and the beaches grew larger and larger until, suddenly, one afternoon past Lisbon, the two found themselves face to face with a new range of cliffs that Billy had never seen. He sat at the front of the boat on an old empty wine crate, the palms of his hands flat on his knees, gazing at everything around him in wonder. After a long, long lifetime of navigating these coasts, everything had become strange. It didn't seem quite fair that after struggling against the regressions of old age, everything should now conspire to cheat him of the things he knew well, and upon which he'd come to count. Along the cliffs of Portugal were a row of bells, suspended in erected wooden squares that could be seen framing the sky in a series of blue windows. Within the windows, surrounding the bells, were round iron cages where wild cats were kept and fed by the peasants nearby; when the cats tore at the cages attempting to escape, as they did constantly, the bells rang and could be heard from a far distance. In this way boats would not sail into the new cliffs at night, or in the fog. Though deaf to the bells by this time, the cats were no less sensitive to the thundering rhythms. When Lauren and Billy sailed by, the cats turned to her as they had always done; the sight of her on deck was enough to strike them motionless; it wasn't even necessary that they hear her calling them, it wasn't necessary that she attempt to call them. She sailed past standing silently on deck. The cats held themselves to their cages watching the woman on the passing boat; and for kilometers around, the people noticed the bells had stopped ringing.

One morning she woke to a shadow across her eyes. Then she saw it, glowing and hot-blue, a towering rock that shone like a huge looking glass in the sea. Sitting on the deck of the boat, she caught the reflection of her yellow hair off one of the jagged peaks; and she could see him sitting, as he always did, on the empty crate staring straight before him, the palms of his hands on his knees. What is it? she said, and turned when the massive mirror flooded her eyes with a flash of sunlight. He didn't move at all, or answer, not stirring from the box or moving his fingers or his legs; and when she asked again, it seemed like several moments before he said, Gibraltar. She lifted her head to the rock again; she could see the heat wriggling skyward from the surface. Billy turned and pointed the other direction. Africa, he said, to the far coast. Farther south is Casablanca. This direction is Algiers.

And Italy? she said, and when he pointed across the Mediterranean, she slid into something like despair, because she knew her quest had nearly run its course.

They drifted eastward along the northern Moroccan coast; Gibraltar dropped far behind them, a huge cave into which the sea and sky disappeared. The wild groves of Africa streamed by, and at dusk the dunes trembled and young brown men emerged from beneath, shaking the sand from their shoulders and running along shore, waving to her. At night pinpoint lights glimmered deep within the trees.

They drifted this way several days, never exceeding the current, altering the natural course only when the water became dangerously shallow. As with the coasts of France, Spain and Portugal, the beaches of Africa had grown enormously, to the best of Billy's recollection; he hadn't sailed these waters in a lot of years. They docked in Algiers for food, then set sail for Sicily. Heat intensified; food spoiled quickly. The old man's watches from the crate grew longer and more still.

They had been at sea nearly three weeks, and were half a day out of Tunis, when they saw the boats on the far edge of the water, a series of dots moving south: Scandinavian yachts and large Dutch houseboats, ancient Arab dhows and Indian baghlas, Chinese junks and Somalian sambuks. As Lauren and Billy approached, the activity on board the vessels became more apparent; varying in size and crew, all vessels were intent on a like destination, and it wasn't long before the new boat seemed to fall into place. Each boat was carrying a different cargo: fruits and vegetables, carpets and chests, tusks and skins, guns and daggers, opium and cannabis, figurines and miniatures and statues and art objects. Some carried livestock—chickens and pigs—and one transported a white horse, still and magnificent in the sun, its gaze fixed on some point along the horizon. There was a boat carrying three black female nudes, statuesque and gleaming; they were bound at their wrists, bright gold rings shone from their ankles, and they stood facing Lauren and staring at her hands. She put her arms behind her back. For as far as she could see, both before her and behind her, the line of boats glittered various colors in the afternoon, gliding soundlessly to Tunis.

By early evening the city could be seen on the coast; she could make out the strange round spires and a thundering black human flow between the buildings. On the beaches stood erect huge sails of blue and gold, hovering over the white sand as though to navigate the entire city south; there was the rustling and hubbub of carts on the docks, to which the sea rushed on collision course. Domes of silver and shaded glass shimmered in the twilight, and houses perched precariously on poles, as though impaled above the other rooftops. The people in the streets rushed to the sight of the boats, but no one waved or cried to the marketeers; they watched in silence, without expression. The boats surfaced like a caravan from the ocean bottom, with their agents and brigands, merchants and dark priests in robes and tunics, cloaks and head-dresses and jewelry. The entire city went quiet. As dark fell the lights of the city shifted in color, first in orchestration and then individually, chaotically, popping and bubbling in different hues: the whole of Tunis seemed to be exploding in concise, hushed detonations. The black flow of the avenues stopped, all the faces turned seaward.

That the boats, as Lauren and Billy had been doing since passing the last Portuguese latitude, were moving with a natural current seemed to alter Lauren's own rhythms and intoxicate her; the sea itself seemed to be funneling into Tunis—not the center of town but just beyond, around the corner of Africa, on the edge of the Carthage rubble. Her sense of failure left her—all the failure that the years compounded as the boats wound and rushed along, like the nights and days that had brought her this far. She found herself languishing on the deck of the boat and given to its unshakable passage, watching the three women on the other boat who studied her in return, never moving, never struggling. The channel of water became so narrow as to barely accommodate the hulls; the ruins of the ancient ghetto loomed, a huge sunken harbor in the distance and walls and pillars buried and blackened by the Punic Wars. Doorways were filled with earth and the halls were rivers lined by the hardened stone galleries in which Phoenician marshals once sat. As the boats descended further, the ceiling of the city rose above her until it was far from view; at times she could catch in the light of the torches the last remnants of the gold-leaf frescoes that overlooked the stairways; sometimes, in the light of the torches, she could see the rotted statuary in the palace corners. Brown faces darted among the black windows and archways. Echoing from some unseen hall Lauren heard a fugue of flutes, ominous and looping, so ceaseless she couldn't be sure if the continuing somersaults of sound were a melody or in her own mind. Occasionally in the dark she caught the glimpses of a lurid red and heard sharp cries from beyond each turn in the waterway, which itself rumbled forward with greater speed.

The music looped through her mind, the glint of the gold rings around the ankles of the nudes on the boat before her flickered across her eyes, the glow of the torches and the lapping of the water and the rippling heat of the moment captured her, and she stared ahead through a series of arches, one within the other, arch within arch, perfectly in line, continually multiplying as the boats sailed on. She thought of her child and began to cry. She dreamed of Michel: he was in motion too, and surrounded by the whisper of small spiraling voices.

He was somewhere in France. He heard them call his name. Michel, said one. Adrien, said the other.

He froze, listening to the patterned thud of his heart. He blinked in the dark and waited: the train was frightening in its rush. Just when he decided he was hearing only the echoes of a dream, he heard them again.

Michel, Adrien, they said, and he sat straight up in the dark, his back to the window. They began whispering to him, and he realized they were in the very next compartment. Sometimes they laughed. Little brother, they whispered, in unison through the wall, are you listening?

Michel did not answer. He's not answering, said one. He's asleep, said the other.

He's not asleep, he's just not—

Little brother, are you asleep?

Michel looked over to the doorway, and for one reason or another wasn't at all surprised to see his uncle standing there.

Jack Sarasan was bracing himself against the rattling of the tracks beneath his feet. Michel sat waiting for some sort of explanation, only to realize his uncle was waiting too. Instinctively Michel understood. He cleared his throat. He blinked at his uncle once, the verses flashed through his head—and with the first word on his lips he tried to begin. He couldn't say it. It caught not in his throat but rather on his tongue, entangled, building in pressure until it felt like it would blow up in his face. His uncle continued waiting, leaning in the doorway; and when Michel forced the word in a long clattering stammer, a cacophony of sound, more sound and sputtering, Jack's face became contorted and purple. He stepped forward, raised his arm, and brought his hand crashing across Michel's mouth.

Michel shook himself and woke.

He looked at the compartment doorway, empty, the door sliding back and forth in its slot with the rhythm of the train. He listened for the sound of voices in the next compartment and heard none. It was early evening outside the window; the train was stopped in an unknown village. Carl's seat was empty, though his coat and newspaper remained. Two other passengers were in the cabin with him—a man in his mid-fifties, somewhat stout and staid, dressed like a banker; and, presumably, his daughter, appearing no more than twelve or thirteen years old, in a hot pink dress with little gold buttons shaped like tiny menagerie creatures, and a hot pink bow in her blond hair.

Soon they were traveling through the woods, and the foliage was thick and the dark glistening color of the cold sea.

Michel watched out the window, his face turned from the other passengers, so they could see only in the reflection of the window and the light over the trees that his face was damp. He wanted to say something to himself to prove he didn't stutter. He might have said something to his traveling companions, asked the time perhaps, but the prospect of failing was too humiliating to risk. Now he remembered quite clearly his first truly incandescent memory since he'd met Lauren, and that was of talking to himself as a child. He talked to himself in his room, walking in circles, and on the stairs to his aunt's and uncle's house, and on the way to and from school, and in the back of the limousine. When he talked to himself he was fully aware that it looked foolish to others, but this was the trade-off: that he never stuttered, that in conversation with himself he was always eloquent and lucid, articulate and impressive in ways he never was in dialogue with anyone else. So now Michel understood that when he forgot who he was that morning in Paris he forgot how to stutter, and now he sat in his seat terrified to make a sound, verbally paralyzed, struck dumb. He struggled to take hold of himself. I cannot have come to this, he thought: I've taken so many chances already, I have to take one more. He made himself turn to the banker and his daughter to ask the hour, but they were gone.

He got up from his seat and stepped into the aisle. No one was to be seen. The father's and daughter's luggage was still in the rack. Michel walked up the aisle and back down, looking for somebody to ask the time, but he saw no one. He was confused. Before the last stop, the train had been full of people. Now he returned to his seat and waited. Through the window the woods went on and on, and though the sun was gone completely the sky was still a grainy blue. Michel leaned back into the seat, afraid to sleep again.

Finally Carl returned with bread, yogurt and pudding. Michel watched him as he sat down. When Carl began to say something Michel leaned forward and raised his hand. What is it? said Carl. Michel opened his mouth and watched Carl as though waiting to hear what he should say. Are you all right? said Carl.

Michel said, "I don't know." He stopped, listening to himself. "Do I sound all right?"

"You look a little off, if you want to know the truth."

"Do I sound all right?"

"You sound all right to me."

Michel eased back very slowly. He was still listening, though the cabin was silent.

"We have other passengers?" said Carl, looking at the luggage.

"Father and daughter."

"Too bad. We had the cabin to ourselves for a while, when you were asleep. A lot of people had gotten off."

"Where are we now?"

"Not far from the coast. Last stop was Wyndeaux. I've been talking to some people on the train. I met several from Toulouse."

Michel nodded.

"You remember," said Carl. "Jazz capital of the world, right? According to the Christines?"

"No jazz in Toulouse?"

"They have never fucking heard of jazz in Toulouse." He shook his head in disgust. "Have some yogurt." He produced a spoon.

Into the night the train crept south across France, through the vineyards of Bourdeaux, then to Biarritz where the train turned sharply east. There a new throng of people got aboard, so the compartment was filled by dark, the banker and the girl having returned to their seats, followed by two young Frenchmen and two very old Frenchwomen. Halfway down the coast the temperature had risen sharply. Carl was talking with the girl, who was sketching in a pad. She had full pink lips approximately the color of her dress and bow, and large round green eyes; as the cabin became warmer the girl's eyes seemed to turn flushed, and the bow drooped slightly to brush her face. She was fascinated by Carl, who appeared too barbaric to be French but who spoke the language without the trace of a foreign influence. The five men in the cabin were watching the young girl. As the train pressed farther on and the climate became lugubriously hot, the girl's father glanced nervously around the cabin from one man to the next. The old women noticed nothing: one of them turned off the light overhead, throwing the cabin and the faces of the passengers into fluctuations of shadow and moonlight; the other old woman got up and shut the window. Everyone looked at the closed window in disbelief. The train continued on, the night stretched longer before them; the girl's pink bow slipped to her shoulder, the shoulder straps of her dress slipped to her arms in the heat: she turned in her sleep so that she was twisted in her seat facing Carl, the tips of her fingers barely touching her lips, her eyelids fluttering in the glimmer cast by the window. Carl looked at the girl and looked at Michel and looked at the other men, all of whom sat staring wide-eyed in the dark while the women slumbered away. Carl finally got up and opened the window. As soon as he sat back down, the old woman immediately woke and got up and shut the window. The girl slumped forward in her seat, pressed against Carl; and the father reached over and pulled the girl away, waking her with a jolt as she gazed around sleepily wondering what was going on. The men readjusted themselves uncomfortably. Michel opened the window.

The old woman got up and shut it. The train smoldered.

Finally Michel and Carl pulled themselves from the cabin and went out into the aisle of the car. Shutting the door, they stood leaning in the opened windows of the train, joining a line of men smoking cigarettes and murmuring in low voices or watching the countryside pass in the dark. Carl rested his arms in the window. The wind was relief from the heat but it was a hot wind, and as they moved farther south the night didn't cool. After half an hour Carl said, I think I can sleep now, and stumbled back into the cabin. The aisle emptied until only Michel was left. The train came to another stop in another station; there were no great flurry of passengers getting on or off. He rested his head against the glass and thought of her, probably in Venice by now, with her husband. It was an unbearable vision. He closed his eyes to it. Now in the middle of a hot and infinite night, in the middle of an undetermined and eternal territory, he felt more alone than he ever remembered with the exception of the one night he found her on the floor of her apartment and believed she was going to die. In the window of the train, with his eyes closed, he began to talk to himself and said to himself her name, over and over, to hear for himself that it sounded all right each time he said it, and that it never tripped him up, that the sound of it never defied his will to speak it.

There was the jolt of the train starting, and Michel looked up in time to catch the sign hanging above the station's platform as it fell away from sight. It was an old sign and its peeling green letters read WYNDEAUX.

We left Wyndeaux hours ago, thought Michel. That was when he turned and saw them at the end of the aisle.

They were standing behind the glass door at the end of the car, watching him in a casual, unsurprised way. He lifted his head and stared at them, even shook his head to be sure he was awake this time—at which they laughed. They looked exactly the way they always had, blond and fair and very young, and of course they were exactly identical. They wore proper blue suits, with proper blue ties, like little French children; one of them pulled at his tie to loosen his collar, as though he too was very warm. The other one waved.

Michel started walking toward them. They laughed and ran the other way, disappearing from the door.

Michel reached the end of the car, and was moving through the passageway to the next car when he bumped into the conductor. He peered over the conductor's shoulder into an empty, shadowy aisle like the one he'd just left. The conductor looked at him a bit disapprovingly. Monsieur? he said, and then something else; but Michel was watching the end of the next car, for the slightest movement of something, for a light going on or off, for the last glimpse of a door closing. The conductor repeated himself, and Michel finally broke his concentration to stare at him in confusion, and then realized he was being asked to produce a ticket. The conductor studied the ticket and gave it back with an abrupt nod, noting the passenger was not in his cabin. Michel glanced once more down the aisle, then turned back for his cabin. When he got there, he found it was empty.

They were all gone: the banker, his daughter, the old women, the young men. Carl was gone too. Perhaps I was mistaken, thought Michel. Perhaps that last stop was Toulouse, not Wyndeaux. He was disappointed that Carl didn't say goodbye.

As he stood there rattling to the motion of the train, the compartment doors and closed window shutters rattling with him, there was something Michel couldn't fail to notice. Streaming into the compartment beneath the shutter of the window was a searing daylight.

Michel stepped to the window, and raised the shutter.

Outside the sun was shining on a passing field and the sea beyond; the light was muted and slightly opaque. The grass of the field was high and green, and off to one side Michel could see the village surrounded by what looked to be a series of high fortress walls. A rippling across the water's surface and the bending of the grass told him there was a light wind, and a houseboat was anchored not far out.

Then the train broke its speed and began to slow. The tracks gradually turned, revealing a curve in the terrain. As the train steadily rounded the last part of the bend, Michel saw a man and woman in the grass making love. The woman was oddly familiar, and it was only after a moment that he recognized her.

She was in her mid to late twenties, still a young woman, and the man on top of her was quite a bit older, around fifty, wearing a blue and white striped sailor's shirt even as he made love to her. For some reason Michel couldn't decide if he looked familiar too. For some reason, two resounding, ineluctable ideas occurred to Michel as he was watching this. The first was that he was witnessing the twins' conception. The second was that he was witnessing his own. There was no way, particularly in this moment of astonishment and shock, that he could reconcile these two ideas: he knew his logic had to choose between them. This was after all not some once-buried but now uncovered memory to question and ponder, since either way this was nothing he could ever have actually witnessed before. He understood it was something else, and he slammed down the shutter of the window.

Irrationally, all Michel could think was, I must be in the wrong cabin. He stumbled back into the aisle and went to the next compartment. Once again, he found only empty seats, empty racks above. Once again, there was beneath the rattling shutter the light of day. He stood there with the glare sputtering at him from outside the train; and then in one quick motion he stepped across the floor to the window and yanked the shutter up. On the glass was the print of a small hand. Beyond the outline of the hand was the beach. The sea. A house on a cliff overlooking the cove, and his mother now standing at the foot of a path that led to the shore. In the sand was a pit. In the pit lay the bodies of the twins; they were not bloodied in any way, or marked by violence, but their eyes and mouths were wide open and their faces were blue and lifeless. They lay in disheveled configurations along the edge of the hole, and from far down the shore Michel watched a large, almost perfectly round black stone roll forward. It continued moving steadily along the water until it reached the pit, where it fit perfectly into place covering the bodies.

Michel ran from the window. The train was once again stopped; only when it once again started did Michel realize he hadn't felt the motion beneath him. Steam rose from the floor, the train pulled from the station, and as the nocturnal flow of the countryside rolled past Michel could now see, looking out the window of the aisle into the night, not a single other face peering from the cars either before him or behind him, the windows forming a checkered stream of gold boxes with no sight of another human being. Far off down the tracks the engine vanished in a silver huff. Michel began running down the dimly lit corridors looking for someone. Every compartment was empty. The same dazzling light from beneath the shutters of every compartment window blurted across the opposite walls. He ran to the next car, and the one after, looking for one cabin window in which was not trapped the daylight. He realized, instead, that *he* was the one trapped— on a train where the deepest night was on one side and the brightest day was on the other, from which unconscious, unrecalled scenes of his past gasped into each compartment. At the last car he ran into the conductor; he half expected the man to dissolve when he touched him. The conductor stared at him unmoved. Monsieur, said Michel, struggling to catch his breath, not really believing he would get an answer, Where are we? We are in France, monsieur, said the conductor. Yes, I know, said Michel, but that last stop, what was that? That was Wyndeaux, monsieur, said the conductor. Still trying to breathe, Michel managed to say, How many times, monsieur, do we have to leave Wyndeaux? The conductor tried to draw him to the window. You need air, monsieur, said the conductor. But Michel wasn't listening to him. Michel was listening to something else, coming not from any one compartment, or the end of the aisle, or the next car. It was coming from outside the train, just beyond the closed windows. It was a furious tapping on the glass, and their high frantic little voices calling to him to come and open the shutters. Michel looked all around, and when he turned back the conductor was gone, without a sign he had been there, without a sign of his departure. No other motion stirred the train, no other soul indicated a presence. So Michel ran on, weaving among the narrow walls, from compartment to compartment and car to car.

One morning she woke to a shadow across her eyes. Then when she saw him, he was sitting as he always sat, hands at rest on his legs, gazing straight ahead. She blinked and saw that everything was on a slant. It was indicative of how deeply she had slept that it took her several moments to look around and realize the sea had abandoned them, and was now two or three hundred meters in the distance. The boat was run aground in the wet sand. In the other direction were the morning hills. They did not look like Tunisia. Lauren put her hands to Bateau Billy's face, and called to him, and saw his open eyes and open mouth were not going to answer. She pulled away when he began to topple from the wine crate. Oh, Billy, she just said.

Because it was so hot, she didn't have much time. She had nothing with which to dig but her fingers. The sand was wet enough that she could dig a deep hole in the course of an hour. She was parched and famished. When she dragged him from the boat, the sand got in his white hair and all over his old face; she shut his eyes but could not close his mouth, it was too late, and so sand got in his mouth. She tried to clean him a bit, but she had nothing to wrap him in; and there was no time, not for him, maybe not for her. So she rolled him into the hole and then moved back the sand she had displaced; and hoped the Mediterranean would return someday to cover him.

It was three weeks to the day since they had sailed from Paris. Now she walked to the sea. She took off her dress and held it tight as the waves came and cooled her. In her mind she said goodbye to her child. She walked back from the sea naked and continued awhile before pulling the dress on over her head. Planes roared by; she realized how long it had been since she'd seen a plane. These were headed her direction. They passed the Sicilian shore and turned south, where the horizon was always engulfed in smoke.

Jason had waited the winter. He hadn't planned on being in Venice this long; he had expected his wife to join him when she reached the continent, and from there they would travel together south. They would spend Christmas in Naples, and they would move to Rome and then to Florence as the winter waned. They would capitalize on the delay of the race; this would give them time together after the separation and Lauren's surgery in Los Angeles. At first Jason anticipated all this with only mild enthusiasm. He felt as he had often felt before, which was constrained, immediately less free. This feeling meant even more than in the past, because Jason had finally realized he was over thirty years old and that certain things had to slip away: the girls he had in Italy suddenly seemed very young. He came face to face with the fact that he was never going to win a medal in the Olympics. His peak had come three years earlier, when he raced in the Tour de France and was the only American in history to place as high as second, beating even the favored Soviet rider.

Left in Venice, he had no other choice but to look at these things. Lauren arrived in Paris, and Jason sent a telegram and waited, expecting to see her within the week. He was in no hurry: young German women walked past his window on their way from the train station. The bicycle sat in his room, upside down, perched on its seat and handlebars as he fussed with gear ratios and the pressure of the silk tires that brushed past his fingers. At night he went with his teammates to the trattorias. He tired of Venice.

She did not come. Not after a week, or two weeks, or a month. He was irritated; he wanted to get out of the city and go to Naples. He wanted to get a room overlooking its bay before the influx of Christmas tourists. As winter fell, all Jason's teammates left for the south of Italy. Jason sent more telegrams. He didn't leave his room much; that was because it was cold, of course, not because he was waiting for a phone call. He found himself working on the bicycle less and less, only spinning the front wheel and watching the room through the passing spokes. Christmas arrived.

• • •

He began walking to the train station every afternoon. The train was always due at four. Sometimes it wasn't too late, arriving five-thirty or six. But he was always there at four in case it came on time for once: the hours would tick by. Then he would see the train's one white light from far across the water, coming from the mainland. The train would empty, a throng of people flooding the platform, and then just a trickle; many had gotten off at Milan and caught other trains going south. When the trickle was over, he would still sit waiting, in case she was the very last one. Then he would go back to the hotel and check his box very carefully to see if he had gotten any messages. If anyone else in the hotel got any messages, he would read these too, to make sure they hadn't been for him and put in the wrong box by mistake.

He realized she wouldn't come before spring when he learned she was with Michel.

He couldn't imagine she thought Michel was more beautiful than he was; he couldn't imagine Michel made love to her the way he did. Yet he always had a feeling about Michel, since the night he first saw him in the apartment down below, standing there in the middle of the room alone. To be going through this now, Jason thought as he lay in bed at night, while the one front wheel of the bicycle continued spinning in the dark, makes no sense at all. It's as though I had come back from Vietnam un-wounded, only to be shot: I've weathered this already, she has never left me before, when I was seeing a lot more women than I've seen lately. It never mattered before what I did; she loved me too much to leave. Now that he was beginning to realize a certain part of his life was over, now that he was ready to settle down, she was challenging his preeminence in her life: that was how he saw it. It simply didn't occur to him, he simply was incapable of entertaining the possibility that she really considered leaving him; and yet in the midst of all his other new doubts about himself, the incredulity with which he first confronted this one gave way to an ominous sense of inevitability he had felt from the first, and which now grew each day that she didn't come to him.

• • •

That winter the canal froze over, and snow fell on the city for several weeks. Then the winter broke early. Jason began to notice some of the back waterways were very low, gondolas and boats stranded against the sides of the buildings. One day he left his hotel to walk to the station and saw people milling alongside the Grand Canal and talking. The canal, he then saw, was virtually disappearing. At the station he saw the Adriatic was gone: the large strand of water which the trains crossed from the mainland had begun moving east.

By the following week, Jason's teammates began returning from their vacations to find a barren city. The Grand Canal was virtually dry, and the back canals were empty, except for pockets where the flow wasn't as free and the water stood stagnant and still. The other riders told Jason that in Naples the beach had tripled virtually overnight. The garbage that had lined the bottom of Venice's canals for decades was everywhere to be seen, and in the sudden heat wave that descended almost immediately thereafter, the reek became unbearable, along with the insects and rats hovering over and scrambling among the refuse. Tourists began leaving in droves, bicycle rally or no. Traversing every small bridge meant confronting herds of rodents; every dock where the town fishermen usually brought their catch was swarming with gulls mauling the dead fish. Finally the military came in and began cleaning up; but the smell didn't go away, having permeated each house, each room, every doorway, the pores of the village.

The weather was sweltering, to the chagrin of the officials who had originally scheduled the rally for autumn to avoid the summer heat, then had rescheduled it for spring to avoid the winter cold—only now to be caught in premature heat. Still, the rally would either take place this time or not at all; most of the racers were loath to cancel it. For his part, Jason would have welcomed a cancellation. He wanted to leave right now; he also wanted to stay as long as he had to in order to wait for her. He was in the crossfire of two divergent impulses, neither of which had anything to do with the rally. He had always anticipated these competitions with relish, even a sense of compulsion; there was once a time when the idea of not riding in a race would have been abhorrent, particularly this race, which he knew would be his last. He did not feel this way anymore. Other things were collapsing, his own priorities were scrambled, and he so dreaded the prospect that the race would arrive before her that he could hardly think of it.

Two more weeks went by, and then a third. He took short practices, exercised lethargically. He felt tight; his legs itched from not shaving. His teammates, who depended on Jason for a good showing, became angry at the possibility that he would let them down. He didn't join them in the trattorias, and he sat listlessly through the team sessions in which the course of the race was discussed at length. He understood he had to concentrate on the details of the rally because this rally was unlike any other he had raced in: it was less a test of speed or power than of mental and physical agility and cunning. But Jason sat facing the direction of the station, or the American Express, trying to understand why three weeks had passed and he'd heard nothing from her: she had said she was coming, and that she would notify him when she left Paris.

He telephoned the American Express in Paris and they told him nothing, impatient with his requests and hanging up on his demands.

He was also surprised to find himself thinking often of his dead son. He had never thought much of the son he had by Lauren, though it wouldn't have been fair to assume this was indifference. It occurred to him now that his son had terrified him, from the moment Lauren told him she was pregnant, followed by that moment in San Francisco she had brought Jules in and set him on the bed at Jason's feet. The two had stared at each other wordlessly then, and the most meaningful communication they ever shared was exchanged in that moment. Later it was Jules' stutter that terrified Jason; it indicated the new gap between Jason and Lauren, for they had always shared a common and desperate love of physical beauty, beginning first with their taking of each other. The gap was, apparently, that Jason regarded Jules' impediment as hideous, and Lauren heard it as a thing of wonder. Lauren acted as though the stammer was indicative of something bottomless in the child, a revelation so awesome and terrible it simply couldn't be uttered, and consequently rendered everything else unspeakable as well. Jason figured Jules was broken, like a spring that was loose or a mechanism that was flawed. So he avoided the truth of his own fatherhood, even as he acknowledged the fatherhood of another child who was less personally threatening: no matter how beautiful Jules grew to be, he wouldn't be beautiful when he opened his mouth, and the idea of a gold-medal stutterer seemed incongruous. Simply put, that Jules stuttered this way reminded Jason he was a failure; and that judgment of himself had pursued Jason too long and he was losing the energy to run from it.

So they never talked. When Jules was a small boy and Jason was there on one of his infrequent visits home, they sat and watched each other just like that first time on the bed in San Francisco. Now, having come to a standstill and with his own sense of failure bearing down on him, and the impending loss of the woman he thought he owned showing up his perfect beauty for the useless business it was, he started seeing Jules all the time in Venice—a small boy on this bridge or that, just standing waiting for his father. Jason never called to him; he would simply walk past the bridge and look at the boy, whose eyes never left him. Far past the bridge Jason would turn and glance over his shoulder, and Jules would still be there with his hands in his pockets just like any kid, and his blue eyes visible from many meters away. He realized suddenly that Jules had something to tell him about Lauren. He went back to the bridge and the boy was gone.

But he showed up later, in San Marco Square, where Jason was sitting at one of the outside cafés getting quietly drunk. The other members of the team were watching the beautiful girls who passed back and forth across the plaza; Jason was staring off into space and then there was Jules, sitting in the chair right before him, his small arms at his side and his small hands in his lap. He had something to say, that was apparent; and Jason wanted to beg him to tell him what it was, but he somehow couldn't. He just couldn't bring himself to beg the son that he'd never before brought himself to acknowledge. They sat there staring at each other, Jules wanting to talk but unable to bear the shame of stuttering for his father. Jason wanted to tell Jules he didn't care anymore that Jules stuttered, it was all right, he knew certain things now and he could stand it, and he had to hear news of Lauren, whatever way Jules could tell him; and then his head was filled with a thousand things: he could sense the boy's wrath, he could sense the boy thinking Now he wants to talk to me, he never wanted to listen to me before but now he wants to, but it's too late. This, thought Jason, was the boy's revenge.

The team found some girls from Geneva. But when a doe-eyed brunette nestled close to Jason, he shook her off, and went off alone.

He went back to his room and sat in the dark. He sat before the window drinking until he was heavily drunk. Several of his teammates came by and banged on his door, calling for him to come out, then insulting him. Jason you wheelsucker, they shouted. The next time someone knocked on the door he surfaced slowly from sleep, assuming it was another of his mates trying to rouse him. The knocking continued and he heard a woman's voice, and with great hope he jumped up, thinking it was the landlady with a message from Lauren. He got to the door and flung it open only to see Lauren herself, in a faded and tattered dress, an old Italian sweater she had gotten somewhere, bare-footed, a gold ring riding the top of her ankle.

The embrace, the kiss were perfunctory. They slept saying nothing. Lauren was exhausted. The next day they went to buy her shoes, and something to eat.

They spent their time together in desolate silence. At San Marco Square they had a drink and watched the people wading across the lagoon from the Lido. "It's different now that most of the water's gone," said Jason, and Lauren nodded, distracted. "We haven't been together much lately," he said finally.

"We've never been together much," she answered.

He said, "Where did you get that thing on your foot?"

"Tunis," she said.

"Why?"

"I don't remember."

He thought a moment. "Where is Tunis?"

"Africa. I came by boat. From Sicily I got a ride up through Italy. In Rome I got a train. After I left Rome the station blew up. Did you hear they blew up the train station?"

Why did you come by boat? he thought. He said, "Who blew up the train station?"

She shrugged. "I don't know," she said, "politicians. It was nerve-racking coming through Florence." She said, "I think I made good time, three days all the way from Sicily. Considering how terrible the trains are, how terrible everything is."

"Is it all terrible?" he said, at the Rialto Bridge.

"Of course," she said, staring into the empty Grand Canal. "The sea has left, and there are no lights anymore."

"They still light the square till nine or ten o'clock. We'll see it tonight." That night a billowing fog, first visible to the east, blew into Venice within an hour. The two of them sat alone except for a few people drifting in and out around them. The cathedral was nothing but a huge hot shadow over to the side. Neither of them said anything. He knew she was thinking of Michel. Now that she was here, he wanted to be someplace far away from everything he remembered. "When is your race?" she said, after a while.

"Is he coming?" he only answered.

"Yes."

He nodded. "Soon?"

"Yes."

He nodded again. He stood up. "Tomorrow," he said, "the race is tomorrow. I have to sleep."

They returned to the hotel and prepared for bed. None of the things Jason had expected to be said were said on this first day together after almost ten months. She seemed in no hurry to talk. Sitting naked on the bed she watched him a moment, but glanced away when he looked at her too long. She pulled the sheets over her, and he turned off the light and got into bed; race or no race, he pressed himself up against her. He ran his hand down her side; she turned and sat up. He sat up beside her, angry at how everything was so humiliating. He sat back against the wall, waiting; she pulled her knees to her chest and rested her chin. He didn't touch her; he wanted her to sense his low-burning wrath. He wanted her to come to him afraid she had made him angry, the way she used to come to him. He wanted to be in command, the way he used to be in command. "We have to talk," he heard her say. He just lay back down and turned his back to her. When he felt her lie back too, and when he was sure she was asleep, he said, in a low voice, "It tore me up, the nights I knew you were making love to him." When he finally fell asleep, she looked over at him and then to the window. She was awake long into the night, thinking about Michel, and wondering where he was.

It was a complicated race to begin with. It started at the station and ended at San Marco Square, a distance that could be walked in half an hour. In between those two points were exactly twenty-three other points spread out over the town, with which each rider had to make contact at least once. Every participant in the race had an assigned code letter and seventy-five numbered tags on the bars of his bicycle: at each contact point, the rider would rip off the next number from his bars and drop it in his team's box. It didn't matter what route the rider followed; he could chart any course he chose, but he couldn't leave more than three of his numbers at a given point, he couldn't leave any two consecutive numbers at a given point, and he had to leave at least one number at every point. Every time he left a number at a contact point that precise moment was logged in a book by referees stationed there, to assure that every rider had torn off his numbers in order. Number seventy-five had to be dropped in the box at San Marco Square.

These complications had multiplied by the morning of the race. While ramps had been constructed over the steps of the bridges so they could be crossed by bicycle, the canals were now empty—which raised the possibility of a rider actually using the canals themselves. There was nothing explicit in the rules that prevented this. Yet it threw all previously formulated strategies into chaos, since hundreds of new courses for getting around the city were now existent. Since everyone was thrown into identical chaos, the judges decided to let the rules stand as they were, though it did seem to give an added advantage to those Italian riders who knew Venice well—an advantage they had at any rate. No one was going to disqualify the Italians, since this was Italy and Italian racers were so highly regarded. The newest complication, evident this particular morning, was the fog that Jason and Lauren had watched cross the Adriatic basin the night before; the lagoon was throttled with it, making Venice's labyrinthine passages all the more baffling and dangerous.

In the fog that morning the bicycles did not glisten the way Lauren remembered Jason's bike glistening on the Kansan road the first time he rode past her father's farm. It was as though the sea itself had billowed and risen and moved back to where it belonged, in the city; everything was hot and steamy even as the canals were dry and barren. Standing there on the steps of the station waiting with all the rest of the onlookers for the race to begin, Lauren listened so intently to the sound of a piano from someone's room that she didn't notice how Jason kept looking at her, as though he was waiting for one glance of reassurance to tell him she would still be there when it was over. Where is the music coming from? she asked several people, but none of them seemed to hear it. She asked one old Italian gentleman standing nearby. "Pardon me, signora," he said, sympathetically, "but I'm afraid I don't hear music." Then, across the canal, as though the notes of the piano had parted the way, she could see an open window behind a balcony, and a white curtain blew behind the glass as the fog drifted by. Look, she said to the Italian gentleman, it's coming from there; and the old man nodded kindly. At exactly ten o'clock, Jason looked at her one last time; and now in an almost desperate attempt to get her acknowledgment, he even waved to her. She barely saw him from the corner of her eye; she'd been watching the window with the curtain, and she'd been listening to the piano which came to her somberly and hauntingly through the fog. She looked to him, and he waved again, and she lifted her hand to him, and replaced it in her pocket. She felt utterly alone. She wished the race would begin. At a signal, there was the whir of wheels and the slight blush of the wind as all of them passed, some crossing the Scalzi Bridge heading deep into the thick of the village, many of the others moving up the Lista di Spagna along the Grand Canal's periphery. In no time, every one of them was gone, and the crowd was left to look at nothing but the officials' main table, crackling with walkie-talkies and bulletins from the twenty-three contact points and San Marco Square. Other than that there was only the music. The crowd dispersed and Lauren stood by herself, listening to someone she couldn't see playing music no one else could hear.

All that day she felt someone behind her, quite old; she would catch a glimpse of his white hair as he stepped back behind a corner every time she looked. She wondered if it was the old Italian gentleman who stood beside her in the crowd at the beginning of the race; there were times she was sure it was Billy, who had clawed his way up out of the Mediterranean sand. She felt he was waiting for her to lead him somewhere, and she wondered if he was impatient. After getting something to eat and walking around several hours, she found her way back to the station to wait for the train. Today it arrived on time, and she waited until it emptied completely and no other soul could be seen. She had been certain he would arrive today; she was thrown into confusion by his failure to do so. It was awful to think, as she thought now for the first time, he might not come at all; yet she didn't believe that, she was sure he would come, he had to come. She set off for the American Express near San Marco Square, hoping to get there before it closed. The footsteps behind her were never hurried or frantic, simply keeping pace with her, and after a while she forgot them.

She arrived at American Express a few minutes too late. Dejected, she returned to San Marco Square, where she could see the porticos of the plaza through the mists, and the tower which shot up vanishing into the fog. Lauren thought about taking the elevator up anyway. Not a single rider had come in; a small group was at the officials' table, where there was a lot of rushing around and static from the walkie-talkies. When Lauren got to the top of the tower, she was above the fog; nothing of the city could be seen, though the casinos of the Lido were visible to the south, dark and dead; the sea was far away, shuddering on the eastern horizon. She was up in the tower about half an hour and decided to come back down. She looked around to see if her follower was nearby; but there was only one other couple, with a small child. At the bottom it was as though she had fallen back to another world altogether. She decided to see if Jason had come in yet; she routinely expected him to finish among the first.

There was still a great deal of concerned activity among the officials, and not a bicycle to be seen. Everyone was talking in a number of languages. She stood and watched the scene listlessly, lost in her own thoughts, until the excitement of the officials and several onlookers pulled her attention back. She looked to see if a rider was finishing. There was still no sign of a bicycle. Lauren walked up to one of the American officials. Excuse me, she said.

He said something into his radio.

"Excuse me," she said, "do you know when they'll be finishing?"

He looked at her blankly. "Who are you?" A voice came in on the walkie-talkie and he turned from her. There was a splatter of conversation.

"What's going on?" Lauren said, to nobody. Italians were gesturing at the fog. She waited for the American to finish with the radio. "What's going on?" she said again, this time to him.

"Jason's wife," he said, pointing at her.

"Yes," she said.

With an expression both annoyed and befuddled, he listened once again to the radio, determined there was nothing of importance, and said to her, "They're trying to find the riders."

"What do you mean?"

"Not a single rider has come in at any of the contact points."

"What?"

"None of the contact points has reported seeing any of the riders since the race began."

"That seems odd," Lauren said.

It was now eight hours since the race had begun, and only a couple of hours before nightfall. In the fog, in a city like Venice, the prospect of locating anyone was unlikely. Everyone kept telling each other how improbable it was that anything could have happened to fifty riders; but the officials organized search parties anyway and sent them out. After two hours each of the search parties returned without one rider to be shown for the effort.

By now the entire city knew about the bicyclers, and everyone was advised to keep an eye out for them. There were scattered reports of glimpses of riders here and there; people heard the mechanical locking and shifting of gears just behind them, or around a corner, or in the next corridor. In the dark the whirring of wheels was heard by everyone, echoing from some place several bridges away. Torch-bearing volunteers returned all night to San Marco Square (which this evening was kept at least dimly lit past the usual hour) claiming to have caught a fleeting glance of someone down an abandoned canal; but the cries of the searchers went unanswered, as though the riders themselves were dashing around the city unaware they were lost. By midnight the square was packed with people, all standing around waiting, while the canals and passageways were streaming with search parties led by those townspeople who had spent their lives in Venice and understood its secrets. The officials decided on a new strategy, based on the idea that trying to track down anyone who was constantly in motion, as a bicycler would be, in a place like Venice was impossible: they would attempt to limit the means of motion. There were four hundred bridges in Venice, almost all of them with ramps for the bicycles; the ramps would be taken away. This would at least slow the bicyclers down. Secondly, men with torches would be placed along the Grand Canal, the Rio Nuovo, the Rio di Cà Foscari, and two or three other major waterways of Venice, all of which crossed the city; the riders couldn't get anywhere very long without using the bridges or coming into contact with these main channels, or coming to a dead standstill, in which case the search parties would find them. The only flaw to this plan, someone suggested, was if the fifty riders each happened to be riding in fifty very small, confined circles.

That raised in everyone's mind an ominous possibility no one wanted to consider, let alone give voice to: that at this point the riders had driven themselves utterly mad. The mainland airport outside Venice Mestre was now contacted to send a helicopter over the lagoon; it arrived an hour later. Whirling over the fog, perilously avoiding the tower, the helicopter boomed out to the entire city a message for the bicycle riders. The message explained to the riders, in a very matter-of-fact tone of voice, that they were lost. They had been lost for hours, the message said. The race was not supposed to take this long, the contact points they had been searching for were not supposed to be this difficult to find. The message explained to the riders that they should be quite exhausted by this point. The message explained that they could stop racing, because the race was over. In Italian, the voice explained that the Italian team had been declared the winners; in French, the voice explained that the French team were the winners. In German, the Germans had won; in Russian, the Soviets were victorious; in English, the Americans, Britons and Australians had emerged in a stunning three-way tie. At any rate the race was quite finished, and each rider should get off his bicycle at once and sit down wherever he was and relish his victory. Someone would be along shortly to escort him to the winner's box in the square, where a large enthusiastic crowd was waiting to cheer him.

Through it all Lauren waited at the base of the tower, where she finally fell asleep. About four in the morning, a man woke her. Signora, go back to your hotel, he said; you will hear if there's any news. He gently pulled her to her feet. She thanked him and trudged on, across the square, disappearing through one of its porticos into the back passages of the city. Every second or third turn was lit by a lantern hanging from one of the archways; she had no idea exactly where she was going, and she tried to pursue a straight line from the square, figuring that going in one direction would at least get her somewhere. She was most conscious of trying not to backtrack on herself. The lights were only blurs in the fog, and at times she had to extend one arm lazily before her in case a wall suddenly sprang up in her path. It was still very hot, and she removed her sweater and wiped her hair from her eyes. Everything inside her that she was thinking and feeling ran together like the corridors of the city. The anxious gut-wrenching fear of something having happened to Jason ran head-on into the anxious gut-wrenching fear of something having happened to Michel: they both ought to be here, she said. She asked herself whether, down deep, she was most afraid she would wind up without either one and therefore alone; she considered this fear with contempt. The sheer terror of being alone was something she could no longer justify to herself. It represented to her a sort of capitulation to the fear of taking chances: it was the kind of resignation she had made long before, from which meeting Michel had set her free. Because of this she had an instant compulsion to get the gold ring off her ankle any way possible, though she was not at all clear how it got there. Because she was not at all clear how it got there, she had an instant resentment toward her long-prevalent lack of clarity as to when and how she had really first met Michel. She no longer liked at all the things that weren't clear to her, though Michel had argued in Paris that it didn't matter, the clarity of details, if the sense of things was clear. The compulsion to remove the ring passed—it was only a ring—but it left certain resolutions, and certain possibilities, one of which was that she might be best off without either Michel or Jason. She asked herself now if she loved either of them. She answered that she certainly loved Michel. She answered that she no longer knew if she loved Jason.

She was becoming more confused in her direction and she was determined not to get lost. When she came to one of the empty canals she decided to leave the walkway and follow it, on the good chance it would lead to the Grand Canal. The assumption was accurate; within a few minutes she emerged into the wide ravine of the canal, where the torches had all burned out and the searchers had either given up for the night and gone to their beds to get some rest, or had fallen asleep right in their tracks. She walked down the middle of the canal alone and damp and weary, her dress clinging to her, her thoughts self-involved. After a few moments there loomed before her the white Rialto Bridge, somehow retaining a bit of the torches' luminescence before turning to shadow. It was then that she heard it. She looked around her, trying to find it; it was the sound of the piano she'd listened to the morning before, its notes dropping from the air. She was still trying to figure it out when a gust swept past, and she could hear the sounds of the bicycles, all of them, around her. They had approached from behind and ridden right by her on both sides, now disappearing somewhere in front of her. She was so taken aback that it took her a moment to call. "Wait!" she cried. "Hello!" But they were gone and the music trailed off with them; and she stood there incredulously just looking into nothing when an answer came from in back of her, in the sound of his steps.

She turned there in the middle of the Grand Canal and saw his form emerge, slowly, and stand there before her and open his mouth and stop as though he was afraid to call her name, afraid it would somehow not come out. She waited until he said it—"Lauren," it did come, he appeared grimly relieved—and she gasped a little. "Oh," she just said, and stepped up to him, and reached over and touched his face, and then his hair, which was now completely white. His ravaged eyes did not quite meet hers. They were still fixed on something that time and time again he tried to shut out, only to open them each time and see the same individual horror. His face was not old; he was not jowly, nor was his nose larger; he was not shrunken. But his eyes and his hair were ancient, and indications of a passage from which he couldn't return. She laid her open hand on his cheek and looked at him sadly; and then he turned to stare into her eyes directly, the muscles of his face holding fast. Then he broke down. She pulled him to her shoulder and against the strap of her dress he cried, clinging to her hair with one hand and trying to cover his face with the other.

Over and over he said her name. She led him to the shadow of the bridge and they lay against the bank. He turned away from her; she pulled him back. She took his face in her hands. "Why have you been following me?"

He shook his head. "You were with him," he finally said.

"Not today."

Each time he looked up, he looked away again. "How long . . ." he began.

"Since . . . ?"

"Paris."

"Almost four weeks, I think." She still held his face. "Are you all right?"

But he wasn't all right. "I was on the train a long time," he said.

"Look at me."

"I was confused." His eyes were closed.

"Michel."

I kept count, he said. I marked the days on the compartment walls, the way prisoners do. I filled one compartment and moved to the next. I filled one car and moved to the next. Every compartment was a year, every car a decade and a half. I was in the last compartment of the last car when I got here. I was the only one on the train. They had to come and tell me when we arrived because I kept all the windows closed at all times; I had learned to do that. So I had no way of knowing, I thought we were in Wyndeaux again when we stopped. We were always in Wyndeaux when we stopped.

"Wyndeaux?"

"They always got on at Wyndeaux."

"Who?"

He grimaced, covering his eyes.

"Michel, listen to me," she said. "I have something to tell you."

"I know."

"You don't. I found the house. Your mother's house."

He nodded. "I know."

She pulled him to her against the bank of the canal. His knees buckled and his face slid to her breasts, and she pulled the dress down and pressed his head against her. The Rialto Bridge rose above them in the fog, and the shine of the lanterns came from the nearby passageways. She was hot and his face was hot against her so she dropped her dress completely from her shoulders. She tore at his shirt and opened it, and tore at his belt. Make love to me in your blue coat, she said. She took him in her hand and caressed him. I'm sorry, he said, when he didn't respond, and she put her fingers to his mouth. Tell me about your dream, she said. He shook his head. I don't have a dream, he said. Once you did, she said; and he answered, It was someone else's dream born in me, at the moment it died in someone else. And then it died in me, and I don't know where it went, I don't remember it at all. Lauren told him, I know where it went. She said, It was born again in my child, and it killed him. How do you know that? he said; and she answered, I know it the way we both know that somewhere, sometime, before we ever met, we were together some way. And now the dream is out there sailing the seas in a bottle, for anyone to find. The pulse of his wrists beat against her nipples. Her hair spread out across the bank above her head like plumage. One leg tensed and the other bent slightly when she felt his tongue inside her; she dropped her hands to his snow-white hair. He moved his tongue slowly until her entire back arched against the incline of the bank, her toes curling in the soil. She began to move her head from side to side, and all around her the steam of the canal began to dance with light, like crystal; there flew across her vision a stray gull looking for the water, there blew across her feet the stray scarf of a gondolier looking for his boat. For one fleeting moment she thought water was beginning to trickle back into the channel; and she raised her head to look and saw it was her, that with every flickering spasm of his tongue she released more of herself until her thighs were gleaming in the fog. He slowly brought his hands down and held her from behind, pulling him to her a little more; in turn she pulled him closer, his white hair brushed against her belly. She imagined herself to be another long and dimly lit corridor. She imagined she was lined with lanterns and torches which cast a faded glow for him to follow. The more lost inside her he became, the greater her flow, until she thought she would fill the canal herself. She was caught motionless by his discovery of the volatile moment she carried in her; he touched it and she grabbed his hair and held on. When he touched it again she was flung into the dark looming shadow of the bridge above her. He rested his eyes, and against her blond mound he kissed her where she was enflamed and flooded. He stood and pulled her to his chest, and she felt him reach down and separate her with his hand and enter her standing. He was so hard and burning he seemed to tear his way up through her; she felt herself lifted from her feet and braced against one of the beams of the Rialto. He wrapped her naked body in his coat, and she nestled her thighs against his hips, clutching the nape of his neck. Every so often she would shift, and feel him shift inside her, the tip of him touching something else far up within. From across the canal she could see an old woman carrying a lantern, and they could both hear her footsteps echoing above them as she crossed the bridge. Lauren's breasts bobbed against his shoulders, and he gently bit the side of her throat. They stood like this for what seemed an immeasurable period of time, smoldering at their common core. She pressed the side of her face against his forehead and he stroked her hair. A breeze came down the canal from an unknown direction. I love you, Adrien, she said. Not Adrien, he answered, it was never Adrien. Adrien was a name that came to me that particular dawn. I don't know why, my name isn't Adrien. I love you Michel, she said. He nodded, his eyes closed. Whatever happens, she said, I want you to always remember that I loved you down deep inside me. He nodded again. I didn't want to, she said. I know, he answered. She felt the lining of his old coat against her bare body. You're still so hard and I'm still wet, will it be terrible when we come, will it kill us? Perhaps, he answered. She looked at the side of his face and said, I'll have to be there when he returns. He nodded, never opening his eyes. She touched his lids and watched him, and waited to die with him if that was her fate.

He left her at the hotel where she asked to be alone. She could see how terrible it was for him to be cast back into the fog by himself. But he could see the passages of conflict that wound through her.

So he walked back the way they had come, up the middle of the Grand Canal until he rounded the one bend and saw the Rialto Bridge in the distance. That was where he heard the music, beginning to fade as though the pianist was carried off by the sea. He'd heard it before; it came drifting from a window the morning the race began, when he was standing in the shadows of the station watching her on the steps below. Now he began to follow it. Along the edge of the canal were the remains of old vessels and the paraphernalia of armies; all the way, the music was in front of him. Then he saw them.

They were only feet away from where he and Lauren had been minutes before; their bicycles lined the banks, dropped disconsolately by the wayside. They sat peering through the fog in exhausted confusion. When Michel walked up, several raised their heads at the sound of his steps, and then the rest began to stand. By the time he reached the bridge, they rushed him, only to step back and babble several languages at him. Michel looked from one to the other.

Then he heard the voice from the back. Jason stepped through the crowd, staring at Michel, at his white hair and ancient eyes, and said, "Is it you?"

"It's me," said Michel. "You're lost."

"No shit."

"Haven't you heard the helicopters, seen the torches? The whole city's been looking for you."

"We haven't heard or seen anyone," said Jason. "We took a wrong turn at the beginning, I rode for hours up and down one canal, up and down another. It was like the city vanished."

"You're in the middle of the Grand Canal, in the middle of the city," Michel said. He pointed behind them. "San Marco Square is right up there, at the end—"

"I told you," said Jason, "we've been riding along this canal all day and night. Look, if you know where we are then let's go."

They got their bicycles and followed him back.

She was asleep when she heard the door open; she didn't know, that first moment, if it was Michel or Jason. He dropped his bicycle against the wall. He was bare to the waist, carrying a loaf of bread and a bottle of whisky. He didn't look at her, even as she sat up in bed, nor did he say anything; he only pulled the chair over by the window and intended to eat, and particularly to drink. It was very early in the morning, the light only beginning to seep through the fog outside. Finally she said, "Are you all right?"

He didn't answer. He was exhausted and dirty.

"Where were you?"

He picked up the bread, he took a drink. He stared between his knees, hunched over in the chair, his blond hair falling around his face. Finally he said, "Are you in love with him?"

"Yes."

He nodded. He continued to pick at the bread, as though he

was going to eat it. "He won't be any different, you know."

She said nothing.

"What do you want?" he asked.

"I think we should separate for a while."

"We've been separated for a while. Ten months, a year—"

"Longer than that," she said. "We've been separated longer than that."

He slammed the bottle down on the table; he was in a deep and still rage. He stood up and now looked at her directly, for the first time. "Well," he said, "I can see I'm not number one anymore." He was radiating fury, and she couldn't stand to look at him. He started to leave and she said, "Where are you going?"

"What do you care?"

"But what will you do?"

He slammed the door on his way out.

From his room in the locanda, Michel could see the window of a glass shop across the way. It was before dawn; he had returned to bathe and rest and wait until it was time to call Lauren. He had told Lauren he would call at her hotel, and he intended to, Jason's return notwithstanding. Watching from his room, he could see a vandal at work in the glass shop at this moment; the fog parted just enough that a face and arm were visible, and the breaking glass. Everything was showered in blue; the sound of the glass was inaudible, so each methodic explosion burst like a silent bubble. On one top shelf was a string of glass heads, angelic and seductive; he could see them clearly even from this distance. He became attached to the glass heads and wondered if the vandal might overlook them. The boy was about sixteen; there was no sign of any pleasure in what he was doing. Michel deliberated, trying to decide if it was a political act, like blowing up a train station.

He went down to the lobby of the locanda before noon. When Lauren came to the phone, she was crying. Michel could hear confusion over the line, in the lobby of Lauren's hotel; she couldn't talk. She kept breaking down. "I told him I want a separation." She could hardly say it.

"Is he there?" He was disturbed by how distraught she sounded.

"He left and then came back, and now he's gone again. Michel, where will he go? He has nowhere to go."

"I'm coming over," he said. When he got to the hotel he looked for Jason; he went to her room and knocked on the door with apprehension, wondering if Jason had returned. Lauren answered, alone. She didn't look at him when she held open the door, and he didn't kiss her. She cried for a while, then he held her there on the bed, and kept thinking about what would happen if Jason came back. He won't come back, she said. She was depleted; Michel wanted to take her to his locanda. She muttered, as she drifted, I know he won't come back, if I know him at all. She finally fell asleep, and Michel sat holding her.

When Jason came back he found Michel and Lauren on the bed; the two men just looked at each other. Lauren woke and sat up in confusion. Jason walked to the window, as though going about his business, and Lauren looked at Michel. Jason sat down in the chair at the end of the bed, never quite facing them. None of them said anything to each other, all sitting and waiting, the two men waiting for each other to leave, the woman confronted with her choice.

Finally, in the midst of the silence, Jason shifted in the chair and cleared his throat. With difficulty, he found the words. "Uh, Michel," he said. "This must be particularly difficult for you. I'm sorry." Michel could think of nothing to say in return. Several more minutes passed and after a while Jason finally said to Lauren, "Can we talk?"

She looked at Michel, and he looked at her. Everything inside him was turning. He was terrified that if he left her now, he would lose her; he was terrified of the hold Jason had on her. "I'll call you," she said.

"Will you be all right?"

"Yes."

He left, walking through the lobby of the hotel and back to his locanda, where he waited in his room for someone to knock on the door and tell him he had a call.

After Michel had gone, Jason got up from the chair and walked to the window and from there awaited the passing of the afternoon. He seemed to stand there for hours, as Lauren sat on the bed waiting for him to turn and face her. Outside, the shutters of the village windows were pulled closed as the day grew later, and Lauren thought she could almost hear the sound of the fog in the canals like the flow of the water that wasn't there. The room darkened, its light narrowing to the scope of the burning lamp on the table; and several times she could see his body visibly shudder. His head would shift so that she could see the side of his face, and then he'd gaze back out the window, not yet prepared for what he had to say to her. Several times she thought to ask, What is it? but she did not, leaving it to him to find his own impulse: it wouldn't be the same if she had to provoke him. When the silence was such as to swallow them up, he pivoted finally, almost angrily; and then the anger washed away and what she saw in his eyes appalled her. She could see that in his mind he knew he had lost her, and all that was left was something so desperate he had let his own self go in order to say it. She didn't want to hear it. She was about to shake her head no; and he saw that too, when he blurted, before it was too late, I'll do anything you want. Then he faced the dark again, leaving her with a Jason she'd never known.

Michel did not leave his room. Each time the telephone rang he listened for the sound of the landlady's steps on the stairs; each time he heard the sound of the steps on the stairs, he listened for the knock on the door that would tell him he had a call. Several times the telephone rang, several times he heard the steps on the stairs: the knock on the door never came. He began saying aloud to the ceiling, Please call me. He wanted to walk to her hotel to see if the light was on in their room, but he was afraid he'd miss a phone call, he was afraid she might see him and think he was spying, he was afraid the room would be dark and that she'd be making love to him. He didn't sleep at all. Instead he lay awake and saw to his astonishment the vandal still in the glass shop across the way. One small candle was burning in the window, and all the shelves were sprayed with bits of glass by now; and the boy sat there looking as though he had nowhere to go. Behind him, on the one shelf, was still the string of sculpted heads that Michel had noticed before; they were intact, overlooked in the carnage. It was at this moment that the boy glanced up before him blankly and saw he was being watched; Michel could not help but eye the glass heads, and from across the way the boy could not help but catch the expression of alarm and turn to find its source. He saw the heads. He looked back at Michel and then mercilessly started for them, as though performing an inescapable duty: and as the final bit of destruction was completed, something swept before Michel's eyes. It was an image of a woman's face so powerful that it exploded before him and was lost again: it was like the other memories and dreams he had of his past, except nothing before had been this powerful, nothing had touched him quite like this—not the twins or anything else. But now he'd lost that image: he couldn't place it, he knew it was a woman; but it wasn't Lauren and it wasn't his mother, it wasn't his aunt, it wasn't the girl on the train in the pink dress and bow, and it wasn't any face on the street he could remember. He looked back at the glass shop for whatever it was that had triggered this recollection; the vandal, hopelessly trapped only moments before, had disappeared. The heads had disappeared. Michel worried that it might have been the glass heads that brought this memory back to him and now that they were gone he would never recapture that memory. But then he realized that in fact it was the smashing of the glass that did it: and its light. The strange, refracted sort of light caught in the glass itself, from no other source, from no sun or moon or celestial origin— a light that seemed born of itself, inimicable, contained in itself; and then it came back to him again. The light: and he was in a strange room, with no windows and no door to be seen and there on the wall before him, framed and overwhelming, was the picture of a very young woman. His recollection of this was now as vivid as any memory he'd ever known. Every detail of that picture was clear to him: her sad desolate eyes and full child's mouth, and he realized it was the woman in the film that he had given up for his own film of his mother. Standing there in his own mind, in this unknown room, he stared at the picture a long time and then saw, over in the farthest dark corner, a small old figure with white hair. The man looked familiar. Michel retreated, from the old man, from his own mind, from the memory which ticked in his ear like a bomb. This was one fear he would not actively pursue. But backing away from it as he did, everything in him sank, and left him facing nothing but his own savagery. He now thought of Lauren and of his own emotional violence, and his dark appetites. He wondered if he was no different from Jason.

He lay back on the bed waiting. The longer he waited the more hopeless he felt. He wanted to pick up the telephone and call her, but he wasn't sure what he would tell her. He'd resolved he was going to wait, anyhow—that she was going to call him as she had said. But the phone downstairs did not ring, not until once at three-thirty in the morning; he heard it and believed it had to be her, but the footsteps never came up the stairs and the knock never came at the door. So he waited. By dawn he understood the train from Paris was but a prelude to this; but he was held back from that last complete collapse by his hope and sureness, both of which Lauren embodied to him. It was unfathomable to him that he would lose her. It had all gone much too far for Jason to reverse the course. They were all at a point they would never get back from, and the bond between Lauren and Jason was fatally shattered. Lauren had to see that. Jason had to see that. They would have to see that they could never survive a reconciliation now, because they could never know but that Michel might be around any corner waiting. Jason would have to realize that his list of second chances had expired, he would have to live with the fact that she gave him a chance because he begged for it, and Jason wasn't the sort who could stand something like that. She could never again, whatever happened, be quite Jason's; she could never again give herself to him quite completely; everything would be a little less for him, and Jason wasn't the sort who could stand for less. There would always be that part of her heart where Michel had traveled, there would always be the territory Michel inhabited. Jason could live on it like a squatter, steal his time rent-free; but Michel would have been there once, and she would never forget it, and Jason would never forget it. Nothing would ever be quite the same for Jason again. And that was the only conclusion one could come to about all this, and it had been determined during a moment neither Michel nor Lauren could remember.

But by dawn Michel's will had collapsed. The fatalistic ramblings of the night fell in tatters around him. Now he was bitterly sorry he'd left Lauren there with Jason. Yet he understood she had to make this choice not for him or for Jason but for herself; he also understood that her wisest and best choice truly was neither man. Michel understood too many gold rings had adorned and bound her body too long, and he asked himself if he was offering only another gold ring. He examined his own wrists, his own ankles; he felt for a leather collar around his neck; he felt for a lock on his chest, or a zipper across his heart.

Nine o'clock he walked from his room and stood over the lobby of the locanda. It faced him like an abyss. He sat with an Italian magazine in his lap and gazed at the telephone; the landlady watched from behind the front desk. Occasionally she would nod and smile. Half an hour passed and the telephone still didn't ring. An hour passed.

Why are you doing this to me? he whispered. Then he called her.

When she came to the phone he said, I have to see you.

Yes, she replied, I have to talk to you too.

They spent the day walking around the city. Portentously the fog began to disperse, but the scathing heat was still there, and the canals were still empty. Her face was red and her eyes were swollen. She showed him a note Jason had written her. In it Jason talked about how everything had turned against him, how everything had fallen through and nothing had worked out; the note seethed with a sense of betrayal. The last line was: I had the best woman in the world and I fucked up. Now Lauren told Michel that Jason was willing to do anything. He was willing to be married on her terms; there would be no more women. It wasn't worth it, he told her, if it really meant losing her. He would do anything she wanted. He had never said these things before, and he wouldn't have said them now if he didn't mean them; whatever else was true, Jason wasn't a liar. For Jason to beg her for anything was almost more than she could comprehend. Now she didn't know what to do; Jason himself assumed it was over, that his pleas were useless. Jason could see, she told Michel, that she was in love; but she felt she needed time. In

San Marco Square she cried as Michel held her; by the Rialto Bridge where they had made love she cried. Michel couldn't stand it. He couldn't stand to watch her like this. You can't afford, he said, to take more time: look at you. Look what this is doing to you. I want you but I would rather you chose to stay with him than go on doing this to yourself. Why am I the villain in this? she asked, at the Accademia Bridge.

You're not the villain, said Michel. What makes you think you're the villain? We're not victims. We're all where we've chosen to be. Jason is where he's chosen to be; he's been making that choice for all the years you've known him, just as the choices I've made have brought me here, even the ones I don't remember. Being a victim has nothing to do with it.

They walked on. Having exhausted things to mourn, having nothing left to say, they were left to a kind of calm; and they accepted it. They took in the city as lovers, lamenting the lost water, seeing the palaces and drinking wine in the square. Sometimes they circled around the places they had been an hour before; sometimes they stood together in one place without moving at all. From the high windows of one gatehouse in particular, she could see the mist lifting from the basin of the lagoon; and the heat seemed to turn its floor to glass. This took Lauren back to one of the last things she remembered before burying Billy, which was looking up at Gibraltar and seeing how it shone like a mirror in the sea. Only now instead of watching the land from the sea, she was on land gazing out to where the sea had once been, and in the glass she saw herself living with Michel in a small house high on a fjord near the top of the world. The fjord was jagged and stark, and over its cliffs, which she could see encircling their house, clouds rolled past. Each cloud released another, which released another. At the edge of the fjord she could see many gorges cutting their way through the earth; the bottoms of the gorges were filled with water and in the distance she could see veins of light blue trickling across the dark fjords with their odd streaks of red cast from no sunlight. Living here with Michel it was never noon or night or dawn—only a vague gray solstice tumbling endlessly across the sky. At this moment Lauren was standing outside the house and could spot Michel far off at the foot of the cliffs, his white hair visible against the dark blue and black that was all around him. He kept walking and she couldn't be sure if he was coming nearer or going away, or just treading the curve of the earth. Lauren was quite a bit older, and though he was too far away to tell, she was sure he was quite a bit older too. Through the open doors of the house Lauren could even see some of the things from her apartment on Pauline Boulevard. The room inside looked casually familiar; she was sure that behind the door, which she couldn't see from this high gatehouse window, was an ivory trinket Jason had brought back from a race in New Orleans, and a brown milk pitcher she made in Kansas as a girl, with two sleeping children shown near the handle. It didn't seem peculiar to her that there were also, behind the door, two pictures of Jason—one from their wedding day and one from the period of time they lived in San Francisco; she hadn't even thought to take these down when she assumed a new life. Everything seemed in its place to her, there in the glass bottom of the lagoon, except one thing: and turning now from the gatehouse, descending the steps and walking back with him, she realized what was missing and that was their child. She realized that because of the surgery in Los Angeles she wouldn't be able to have a child by Michel, and someday she was sure he would come to bitterly regret this. He would come to see that in choosing her he had foreclosed part of his future: for a man without a past this might be unbearable. Lauren was too keenly aware of all the ways there were to be hurt by someone. Along this walkway, she could still sometimes see through the buildings the glass bottom of the lagoon; and she remembered something that had taken place on her wedding night years before. It wasn't her first night with Jason of course; she was already pregnant with Jules when they flew to San Francisco, where they arrived several hours before dawn and caught one lone taxi into the city. In their hotel room not far from where they would come to live, she turned from a long doorway mirror to see his reflection out of the corner of her eye, and then to see him before her, as his real and reflected images seemed to glide into one. She could see, in his eyes, not her reflection but his own. She raised one finger and he raised his correspondingly, and they drew a line together down an unseen untouched looking glass that divided them. Together they explored this looking glass, running their hands up and down between them. She was sure it was there. He knew it was there. It was always there with Jason. And, as he always did with her and the others, he stood and waited, tall and nude and blond, waiting for her to step over to his side of the glass and become part of him. At this Lauren stopped and looked around her, to see that they had circled back and now she and Michel were at the hotel; with nothing having been spoken for some time, she turned and looked him fully in the face. In the new light of the village, his hair was even whiter, his face more drawn, and his eyes seemed to swim and sink within themselves. I want to go back now, she said to him. I'm ready to make a decision.

He wasn't there in the room when they arrived. Like the day before, the two of them sat together on the bed, and he held her hand on his lap as she closed her eyes. He caressed her face; like the day before, Jason finally arrived and stood over them looking at her.

"Is she all right?" he said to Michel, and then Lauren sat up. Like the day before, Jason went about his business, while Michel and Lauren sat waiting. Finally Lauren said, "I want to talk to you."

Jason sat in the chair, sullenly.

"I have to make a decision, for all of us."

He said nothing.

"I want to know if you still meant what you said this morning."

"What was that?" said Jason.

"About us, if I stay with you."

He just stared at her; not a single expression flickered across his face. She waited, and after a moment of saying nothing, he just stood up from the chair and sauntered out of the room.

That's it, thought Michel, he's lost her.

Lauren turned to Michel and said, "I have to give him another chance."

He said nothing, but she could see the incredulity in his eyes. She wasn't sure she believed it either. When he couldn't find a response she tried to explain. "Don't you see, Michel? I don't know whether it's that he deserves another chance, or I deserve another chance, or that I simply don't deserve a chance with you. I don't know which of those it is, but I have to do this." Her eyes pleaded for him to understand, but he just sat there looking at her in an almost willful shock. "It was different when I thought I had found Jules again," she went on. "It was different because somehow I've always known that abandoning Jules led to you—I don't know how or why, but I've always known that. When I thought I'd found Jules again, it made it somehow all right to choose you; I think in a lot of ways he was more yours than Jason's, though you never laid eyes on him. But then I lost him again, and my bond with Jason is fast for that reason, and I can't break it for that reason—it's something Jason and I share together, because Jason abandoned him too, from the beginning. So I have to give him another chance because of what we hold in common, as crazy and unreal as that may seem: the loss of Jules makes Jason and me inseparable."

She wanted him to say something. She wanted him to say it was all right, but more than that she wanted some ridiculous sort of reassurance that somehow it all didn't matter. The enormity of what she'd done hadn't sunk in. She hoped he wouldn't hate her, and she could take some relief in that, because he didn't hate her, there was nothing in his face like hatred, only disbelief; he stood up from the bed not looking at her at all; and she suddenly realized he was leaving, and she was simply astounded by it. It simply didn't occur to her that whatever had been done or said could mean he was going to walk away now and be gone from her. It never crossed her mind for a moment that these were the last moments she'd ever lay eyes on him. She reached for him as he turned to go, and he bent down and kissed her gently and quickly.

Michel, she said. She kept looking around as though he would surely appear again. In the hall he walked staring straight ahead, the willful acceptance transforming once more; he was intent only on getting past the washroom where Jason was waiting for him to leave, down the stairs past the lobby and its eventful telephone, out into the lagoon where the fog was no longer enough to hide him.

From the moment he left her, he struggled to maintain his hold. It was strange for him to find himself so near a precipice, and yet to realize so dispassionately what was happening to him: he didn't think it was possible for one to be witness to his own collapse. He found himself driven in such opposite directions with such identical force that he thought he would shatter at the middle if he didn't stop and stand still long enough; yet he couldn't stop. He found himself circling her hotel and then the train station for one more glimpse of her; he found himself waiting around the locanda for a phone call from her, or a visit; he found himself walking as far away as the city would allow him to go, placing as many of Venice's twisting passages and corridors between the two of them as he could. He didn't see her; he didn't get a phone call from her; there weren't enough passages or corridors. Whatever impulse seized him at a given moment, it was defeated as quickly; and when all impulses attempted to pull him one way or the other, then the defeat was just that much more unbearable.

It was clear to him after five or six days that she wasn't going to come; it was clear to him she might not be in the city at all. He couldn't bring himself to call at the hotel to find out; she might suddenly appear with Jason and realize Michel was still waiting and dying for her, and consequently she might dread him or hold him in contempt. Still, he waited: she might just call from Paris or London, to tell him she'd changed her mind and was returning to him. After a while, he didn't think this was going to happen either.

He had no resources now. The money he'd saved those two years he ran the Blue Isosceles in Los Angeles was virtually gone. He had exactly eight dollars, plus the cost of one second-class train ticket back: back the way he had come. So still trying to maintain his hold, he stopped at American Express one more time, watched the window of her hotel one more time from a distance; and then got on the same train that had brought him here. He gripped the armrests of his seat, set his head back and stared straight before him; and with the lurch of the train he found himself hurtling again into darkness. He knew, of course, exactly what his stop would be.

He had come to despise the things that tormented him, and to tire of sidestepping the shadows.

Now he was afraid that some perverse twist of fortune would bypass his destination, having given him so many chances before. The train crawled through the night to Milan, and took the following day to weave slowly along the Côte d'Azur: Monaco, Nice, Cannes, St. Tropez, Marseille, Montpellier; and then that second night along the Pyrenees to Toulouse. He didn't sleep much; the time he did fall asleep he would suddenly shake himself awake after an hour or two, alarmed that he might have missed it. But he didn't miss it: by the second dawn of his trip he was within sight of the coast, though the sea itself was now far away. Biarritz, Bordeaux. The last hour before his stop Michel stood in the aisle watching out the window, eyes narrowed and scanning the horizon, unwilling to allow for the chance that it might slip by him. Finally the train slowed, the station came into view, and he saw the peeling green letters on the station sign.

Walking through the city, nothing came back to him, nothing jarred a memory. The high walls and the garrets, the spires and the belfries—none of this looked familiar; the streets seemed foreign. He wasn't sure whether this disappointed or relieved him. But at the city gates he did recognize, past the dry and empty docks and the hushed cafés, the house in the distance, over-looking as it did what was once the sea. This was not a memory related to his past, but rather to his visions from the train to Venice—only now the house looked like a black flame flickering at the sun, nearly as black as the large, almost perfectly round rock at the base of the house's path.

When Michel got to the house, nothing stirred. Walking slowly up to its front door, none of the manifest ghosts seemed to belong to him. He stood at the door several minutes before reaching over and opening it; then he stepped in and the house seemed to exhale back. He turned, looking at everything, then he stepped slowly through, the walls rising vertiginously as he circled through the house and then up the stairs. On the second level he walked from room to room: his mother's room, with the one bed; the next room, with two small beds side by side; and the third room, off in a corner, very tiny, with one tiny bed that was his. This room he remembered from the movie. He gazed over the room and was about to exit when he lowered himself onto the bed, on his knees, and ran his hand over the wall to find the carving.

There it was. He tried to read it. In the film it looked like A.D. 1957. The A and the D and the 1 and the upper part of the 9 were apparent; but now it definitely did not look like 57. It looked more like roman numerals than any digits he could imagine. He sat there pondering this awhile, afraid the date was significant and that he was missing something. Then he bent down and looked much closer; and feeling foolish and disgusted with himself, he suddenly realized it was not a date at all.

ADRIEN.

For the first time, since that morning in Paris that seemed like forever ago, he knew the name Adrien was no figment of psychic calculus that had just wandered across his mind; and he knew he had been here before, right before that morning. Not here in this room, or this house, but here at the edge of this particular discovery, which now peered at him from around some cold stark corner from which he wanted to turn away. He realized that this discovery would ask more questions than it answered; and that these new questions would cut him to the core: they already once had. So as he always had, he now threw himself into the pursuit of his terror.

He went back to the docks. The bars were empty; there weren't a lot of sailors in Wyndeaux anymore. He came to one café in particular that gave off in the afternoon a faint glow, something incandescent and blue from within the walls. He went inside. At his entrance, a half-dozen older men turned to look at him. He could not have imagined what he looked like to them. His hair was white and his eyes throbbed blankly like small peepholes through which someone could look and see another place. His long blue coat was in shreds. In French, Michel found the words. "I need some men to do some work for me." He stepped to the closest table and put his money in full view. "Eight American dollars. About forty-five francs." He shook his head, trying to find the words. "It's all I have." He shrugged. "It's not much work. An hour. It will buy six or seven bottles of wine; it—" He stopped; he could think of nothing else to say that would persuade them. None of the men moved at first. Then one came up to him, a smaller man with a cap. "What do you want?" he said.

Michel drew him to the window. He pointed out, far on the beach, the rock. The small man couldn't remember how long it had been there, but another recalled when it wasn't there at all, many years before; and another told of the woman who lived in the house on top once, and how one stormy day she came into the village and hired a number of men to do some digging for her.

When their own bottles went dry, the men in the café got their shovels.

He led them down the docks to the beach. The sand, after several weeks in the sun, was dry and hard. After Michel and the six men had pushed the rock several feet away, they began digging. The work went on three-quarters of an hour when they came to something. The discovery of the small casket disturbed the men, but Michel exhorted them to begin another hole next to the first. Another three-quarters of an hour revealed the second casket; Michel had the men pull them up and set them on the beach. Then the men stood away, staring at Michel. The two holes were side by side, one thread of earth separating them.

They were my twin brothers, said Michel. He leaned over the first casket and with the blue sleeve of his coat wiped away the layer of hard sand at the wide end of the box. Then he wiped away the sand on the other. The letters were carved on each. The first casket read: ADRIEN. The second: MICHEL.

Open the caskets, said Michel; but at this the old Frenchmen balked.

Michel reached into his pocket and pulled out the eight dollars; he handed the money to the small man. Still, the men didn't move, waiting to watch Michel take the shovel from one of them and pry open the lids of the plain, simple wood caskets. As the first lid came off, the men turned their heads away, and then glanced back slowly, and stared first at the boxes and then at each other. The second lid came off; both caskets were quite empty.

No bones, no skulls, no remains at all. Some sand in the corner of one, the slight corrosion of salt to each.

They watched him standing above the two caskets, not looking at them but facing the empty sea, his eyes ablaze in the falling sun and the shovel dangling at his side.

The flame that was the house seemed to rise like smoke. He turned and looked toward the hill, not expecting to see Lauren, not even expecting to see his mother standing there in front. Instead, for some reason, he thought he might see the face of a woman in a picture in a room in a light he remembered; he thought he would glance up at that house and see her face framed in the window. But the window was empty, all apparitions vanished with the revelation of the empty caskets, and the sun at the edge of the endless beach was the only thing that vaguely resembled a ghost.

No twin brothers, monsieur, said the small man, finally.

Michel shook his head. N-N-N-No, he said, no t-t-twin brothers.

They left, filing back up the beach. M-M-Merci, Michel said to each one; and then was there alone.

He sat down, straddling the earth between the two graves and watching the sun disappear. He took off his coat and threw it up by the empty boxes. He held the sand in his fingers, his hold maintained.

Lauren, name me now. He knew if he called her she would hear him. He knew if he called her she would answer. Since she had known him from the beginning, she would know who he was at this moment; it was one final thing on which he could count. He began: LLLLLLLLLLLLLLLL—and he lost his breath, forced to inhale again. Swallowing, he tried once more— LLLLLLLLLLLLLLLLLLLLLLLLLLLLLLLL—until his entire body was racked with the effort, as though his tongue was coiled around his throat, strangling him.

He would wait until it came to him. He would say it sometime tonight, or sometime tomorrow, or sometime the following day; he would remain here until he did. Then he would wait for her answer. That night, the sea returned. He could hear it rumbling in the distance, he could see the blue line shaking itself loose. Should the seas ultimately dry up completely, they would nonetheless come back one more time tonight; he would be there when they did. Should she stop at this moment, wherever she was, and hear him calling her, and whisper back a response, the resonance of that very murmur would nonetheless return across the miles no matter how many there were; he would be there when it arrived. He had not come this far to desert all these things simply because of the treachery of his voice; though broken into a thousand shards of sound, each shard was still his. After all of this he would not allow his own lips to betray his talent to speak her name: this vigil was set. He watched the horizon widen before him in a growing gash of blue, as time and time again he wrestled with the name his throat would not give up. Straddling the graves, the Atlantic plains before him bleached in a tawny red light, he felt as though in a womb of haze, anticipating the inevitable cradle.

My dear grandson, the letter began. I have not heard of or from you in some years now and, unsure precisely where you may be at this moment, I can only hope this note finds you. I also hope you can make out the French; I fear an attempt at your language on my part would serve neither of us well. Recent events in my very old life have made it somehow appropriate I try and reach you once more before I die. None of these events directly affects you, but they have unlocked particular memories that do affect you, and they seem to me things it might be well for you to know of, and things only I may have the opportunity to clarify. A young man, about your own age, appeared some time ago with the idea that he would finish my picture, which you yourself took some interest in the last time we were together in Paris, and on which you squandered too much of your own youth, if I may say so. I have attempted to dissuade this young man from the enterprise, as I know, for reasons of my own, that the effort is futile. I say this because I have always felt a measure of remorse over your own sacrifices for me, sacrifices principally of the spirit. I suppose I never told you your contributions were doomed be- cause, as I am with this other young man, I was moved by the generosity of heart and mind which I surely did not deserve. I could not bear to tell you how completely, how totally this failure was my own, and I sensed you left the effort a bit broken, and now it haunts me—one more element of guilt in a generally haunted state such as mine.

I should tell you now I always somehow felt you were more my own son than my son was. I have said this a number of times, but never to you. I am not sure when I first felt this. I suppose it was sometime during our first meeting, in Los Angeles, when you came to find me in my room in Hollywood, and introduced yourself. I had trouble understanding you, and therefore you did not speak much, so the language barrier was academic. Perhaps I had this feeling of you as a son when I showed you the stills from my film and saw how they entranced you, how the entire picture entranced you even though you had never seen it. Perhaps I had the feeling when you took me to the park one day and the black lake reminded me of the village where your mother was conceived and later returned to live. I'm sure I had the feeling by the time you came to Paris, some years later, after Jacques had sent me back. I've wondered if you had this feeling too, never having known your father, and whether that feeling was what brought you to Paris. You still did not say much. I tried to find a way to let you know the film was useless, but I could not; and I wondered if Jacques was unwittingly correct to keep you from me, as he had done so successfully for so long. I think the reason I could not explain these things to you has to do with an incident that took place when you were much younger, five or six years before we met. I never told you of that first time I actually saw you. I was sitting in a crowd of people, and there was no way you would have seen me or known who I was; even your uncle and aunt did not know I was there. It was at your school auditorium, filled with parents who had come to see their children perform in a variety show; you were to recite a poem you had written. I could see it was you as you first took the stage; you began rather tentatively, even meekly, and I wondered if you would finish or run away in the middle of it. Everyone was amused by you. I felt how mortifying it had to be trying to get through the words in front of that many people. I was angry with the school administrators for allowing you to do it, and I was angry with you for allowing yourself to do it, for not having the good sense to keep quiet as you learned to do later on. Then, when you were near the finish, I could tell you had made a decision, and that the poem you had been reciting at that moment was not the one they had programmed you to read. Though I could not understand the lines you spoke, I could tell by the expressions of confusion in all their faces that it must have all been quite shocking. What was surely most abominable for them was the idea that they had lost control of a small stuttering child. Then I was angry with myself for having shared in everyone's condescension toward you. I wanted to tell you now that I was there. I hope you're not embarrassed by this, and that I haven't waited too long to tell you.

The other day I was going through an old trunk I keep here in my room, when I came upon some letters. They were letters your mother had written to me when I was in California. There were only a few, some written in part to your uncle. All of them were more or less the same, not especially lucid, I must say; I hope I may speak about your mother this frankly. They were filled with fragments of news, mostly about your brothers who drowned when you were too small to remember them. This was something she talked about often. I never met those other grandsons, but the tragedy of their deaths was still imparted strongly in the letters, even torturously. I rediscovered, as I said, these letters, and I have read them over. Then I found another, written earlier, which I had dismissed once and forgotten. I am not going to enclose it here, but I want to tell you some of what was in it, because it conveys a different story altogether. For some reason I thought of the incident in the school auditorium when I read it. Your mother speaks of having a son, by a man whose identity she never revealed—probably it doesn't matter. This son she named Adrien; he was not a well child, and he died very young, at the age of three or four. Two years later she had another son, apparently by the same man (who seems to have returned just often enough to sire children). This son she also named Adrien; you were this son. If she ever told you of your namesake, I don't know; but it seems to me it would have been something you would have sensed. Because this version of the facts departed so radically from everything else she ever told anyone, I may well have been initially correct in dismissing it as an individual delirium. Yet as I read this letter over, and as I hear you before that hall of people stammering as though to let something or someone else out, I cannot help but wonder if that someone was another child who came and went before you. Reading over this letter, it all seems rather unjust to me—that sense you must have had of not being a live child but a dead one resurrected back through the same womb. It apparently was not until you spoke your first word that your mother understood what she had done. Some three or four years after your birth, she renamed you Michel.

I hope you will not resent my saying this to you. If you are closer to being my own son than my own son, then I have to say it because I have so much to make up for. I am writing now from my secret little room, where I grew up, and where you came to visit me in Paris. You remember it. The lights don't work in Paris anymore, except occasionally; it doesn't much matter, since this room always had its own light. Nothing works except occasionally; perhaps California is the same way now. It is the zenith of summer, but the winter will come in no time, and the last one was harder than anyone can remember. The world and I seem to be failing together. I will never see you again, we will never exchange anything again. I have never given up so much as this, or attempted to reach as far as I am trying to reach now. I was wrong about you when you were younger, and now I hope you do not stop until the other one is released from inside and leaves you alone. It is not your fault he couldn't make it. In the meantime, the others will have to submit to the rhythms of your speech. I was blind all my life, and they came to call it vision. If you continue to talk to them, who knows? They may someday call it poetry.

Your grandfather, Adolphe.

When Jason and Lauren returned to Los Angeles, they spent the first couple of weeks in a motel not far from the ocean. The trip from the airport on the bus was long and dusty; the freeways were closed, the sites of flea markets and tramp towns; travel was by side streets and whatever boulevards were still operable. Each bus stop was mobbed with people, a sight as prevalent as the abandoned cars by the roadside. People spent hours crossing town, negotiating distances, and transit was limited to what was necessary, since there simply weren't enough vehicles to take everyone everywhere. The buses always got too full, and always ended up passing by huge packs of travelers, until the frustration spilled over into vandalism and violence, people hurling things at the passing windows that wouldn't stop for them.

Jason got a job teaching physical education at one of the junior colleges on the west side of the city. The two found an apartment, one room with a kitchen. Left to herself, Lauren spent those initial weeks untouched and untouchable. Jason would leave her in the morning lying on the couch facing nothing, and find her there when he returned in the late afternoon. There was nothing he could say to her, because he knew why she was this way. Neither had spoken his name once to the other, each hoping he would go away. But he did not go away: she could not get him out of her mind, she could not stop seeing him everywhere, she could not cease living it all again and again. When no one else was around she called to him, out loud.

One day she went to see about getting the furniture from the old apartment out of storage. The terminal was packed with people, shouting and arguing with other people behind long counters about lost chairs, dressers, broken mirrors. The scene was mobbed and chaotic; and baffled by where to go and what line to be in, Lauren finally just left and took another bus to Pauline Boulevard. The street was still filled with sand. She didn't see the cats, and she didn't call them. She hadn't come to see her old apartment, but his.

The landlord remembered her. He also remembered Michel, and there was a letter for him, addressed to M. Sarre; the return address was an A. Sarre in Paris. Irrationally Lauren was certain this was a code for her—a letter sent from Adrien to Michel. She took the letter from the landlord and opened it, and then discovered it was from someone signed Adolphe, and dated almost a year before, and in French besides. She could only make out a bit of it, trying to decipher it on the long bus ride home.

Still, this was her only tie to him now, the only way she knew to reach him. That next day, when Jason left for work, she began writing letters to Michel. Each one cried out that she had done the right thing, she had made the right decision, she was certain of it. She would finish one letter and then begin another, folding it inside the first; in the second letter she would enclose a third; in the third a fourth, and on and on. By the end of the week she'd written him over a hundred letters, some merely scraps of anguish. At the center of this, her greatest Chinese-puzzle-box letter, she ran out of anything else to say, and the final missive only read:

Where are you?

Where are you? she wanted to know. I know I did the right thing, she said, Jason thinks so, I do too. But where are you anyway.

She got a large manila envelope and put the letters-within-a-letter inside, and went to the post office. It was mobbed and chaotic, like the terminal where the furniture was stored. But she waited in line the two and a half hours, to weigh the letter and mail it into the void, to the only address she could think of, which was A. Sarre's return address, seventeen rue de Sacrifice.

The weeks went by. She did not receive an answer. Two, three, four months passed; she saw Michel everywhere, around corners, far down a road, in long blue coats at the front of buses. When the telephone service was in order and their telephone actually rang, she was always sure it was him. But it was not him, and the blue coats were worn by others, and the mail delivery, erratic as it was these days, never turned up anything for her. One year passed, and finally she gave up hope.

Lauren and Jason became good friends. If he cheated on her, she never knew. There were no calls from women begging to speak with him. He was home every night, after work. He worked harder to make her happy than he had ever done before. Their marriage was better than it had been before, and they had nine comfortable years, right up to the afternoon someone blew up the Federal Building on the west side of town and caught Jason in the blast. He hadn't been riding a bicycle; he'd been standing by the road waiting for a bus. These explosions were more common at this time, but Lauren was still shocked that someone like Jason should be touched by one. It was the only night he hadn't come home and before Lauren learned of the news, it still crossed her mind, after all these years, that he might be with another woman. That year she returned to Kansas, something she and Jason had talked about; there wasn't much difference between Los Angeles and Kansas anymore anyway—sandstorms instead of tornados, and an inexorable lethargy. Almost all the way to Kansas on the bus, two concrete walls followed her at each side. These had been constructed in the eighteen months since the Blight had swept the continent, and national guardsmen were still sporadically posted every fifty or sixty miles; when the sky above was bleak and overcast, Lauren had the sensation of traveling down a long gray tunnel all the way back home. Nobody talked much anymore of what might be behind the walls, or of what America looked like. When she reached her destination she was relieved to find there weren't so many walls; they could be seen in the distance, long white lines along the horizon in the west and north and south: only the east was open. She lived in the house where she grew up; it had been left to her. Her parents were gone by this time, and her brothers had moved away. She did not remarry. She got a job at a nearby ranch caring for disturbed children—work she thought of doing one time or another during the past twenty-five years of her life. All these children were bright and talented, but each had a special psychological tic that bespoke something terrible and tormenting deep inside. There was one child who tied things, interminably: shoelaces and cords and clothing and hair, wrapping things in knots and then undoing them. Another boy had memorized every area code in the country from an old telephone book: he could tell anyone who asked that Tallahassee, Florida, was 904, or that Madison, Wisconsin, was 608, or that all locations in Wyoming were 307, all at a moment's notice. Then there was a girl named Kara who renamed every star in the sky, and who recognized them as they shifted from one quadrant of the night to another. These strange talents existed at the expense of an ability to cope with the intellectual and emotional imperatives of day-to-day life, leaving the children outcasts from their own families, friends and neighborhoods, and unable to make the necessary connections with other people. So Lauren became their connection, drawn as she was to the children's one common characteristic, which was that each one was exquisite, with skin like milk and large moon eyes and hair soft and fair, all of them set aglow by their odd visions; having never been devoted to anything but these odd visions, the children became enormously devoted to her. Do you love me? the girl Kara would ask, and Lauren answered yes, and Kara said how much, and Lauren said a great deal, and Kara said can you measure it, and Lauren said no it's much too much to measure; and only then did the child seem satisfied.

When Lauren was an old woman, she would stand on the Kansan desert and watch the leaves. By now the ground was completely white, the dirt and the grass and the high weeds bled of color. Every fall there would arrive from some place unknown leaves that were dark and brilliant blue. They would scatter across her feet and catch against her ankles, and dance in dark blue patterns over the stark white earth; and she would look to the east as though the horizon might yield a series of naked blue trees. But nothing ever traversed the horizon these days but for the sun at dawn; and every other horizon supported only the walls. For several days the leaves would continue to arrive, and then gather in a swarm to the west of her house, where her porch faced, and they disappeared, perhaps turning at the wall and circling south and returning to wherever they came from. Then she would be left only to surmise the empty expanse and guess at its loneliness, counting to herself the very small white hills, no larger than earthen mounds really, that filled the dead fields. It was several autumns before she actually walked out to one of the small hills, and just turning over a few handfuls of dirt she found the rail of a small bridge, and recognized it as a moonbridge, like the ones that were in California years and years before. Now the moonbridges were buried and forgotten, though nothing invited one's gaze at the moon like the clear and brilliant skies of Kansas.

The nights the grown teenage Kara came to Lauren's for supper, it was her gaze that found those skies, a mass of starry light

for which the girl still had a thousand names; Sargasso and Lab-
yrinths and Hopscotch and Dispossessed and others. All of the
names meant something to her but nothing to anyone else, which
was her intention. Lauren's talent was understanding which secrets were to be shared and which weren't; consequently Kara
could tell her anything, and withhold anything. Lauren would
fix a simple meal and they would eat on the porch when it was
warm enough; by November they ate upon a plain unembroidered
tablecloth in the main room. Lauren asked about Kara's parents,
who lived in Chicago. Kara asked Lauren if she had ever married.
Lauren told her she had a husband and child once, and outlived
both. Kara wanted to know their names and all about them. Jason
and Jules, Lauren told her; and talked about each as long as Kara
seemed interested. Kara was captivated by the image she had of
both of them; she was fascinated by what they might have meant
to Lauren, just as every young person is fascinated by the notion
of old people having once been children. Lauren denied having
photographs, but the girl persisted, seeing through the lie; and
finally Lauren produced them, a small box, and she watched
from one end of the couch as the beautiful Kara wondered at
how beautiful Lauren once was, and how beautiful Jason was,
he always having been the incarnation of the chaste but impas-
sioned dreams of too many young girls. Not long after that,
Lauren realized that Kara had fallen in love with Jason too, just
like all the others.

Kara progressed, as all Lauren's students progressed, communicating and extending herself and allowing her unique manifestation of genius to become less important. With the girl's
parents far away, and not so much unconcerned as despairing of
a way to reach their child, Kara became surrogate daughter to
Lauren and Lauren surrogate mother to Kara: everything was
exchanged. Kara, from the precocious yet limited perspective of
an adolescent, saw Lauren as a self-sufficient woman undisturbed
by and fatalistic toward past losses, in control of those things
considered and felt. Lauren tried not to allow herself to get too
close to the girl, knowing the parents would one day want to
claim her back, once the teacher had done her work. The balance
was fragile, and shocked by the smallest things; Kara felt betrayed,

for her own sake and Jason's, to come into Lauren's home one night and find Lauren staring out into the night in a reverie, her face and fingertips pressed to the glass, murmuring the name of a stranger. Michel, the old woman whispered to the window, can you measure it?

So Kara, shaken, went back out and found all her stars again. It had been a while since the sky had turned; everything was in a different place. It had been a while since the girl had kept such track; she hadn't cared about stars lately. It was when she saw, coming down the road, the headlights of the brown bus that would take her back to the ranch, and it was when she heard behind her Lauren swing open the kitchen screen door, its corner hitting the tarnished metal ring around her ankle, that Kara came up with a star she simply couldn't account for. She sat in the chair looking at this one star, which was very low on the northern horizon. Here comes the bus, she heard Lauren say behind her, in the voice Lauren always used, not the one Kara had just heard inside the house; and Kara bolted·from the chair not to run to the bus but toward the unaccountable light. Lauren followed, slowly behind, as the headlights grew nearer and nearer. Kara kept running toward the star, realizing soon enough it was not a star at all but the glint of something in the white earth; she arrived at it just as the bus pulled to a stop not a hundred feet away from her. The light was lodged in the dirt, without any indication how it might have gotten there or how long it had been there. There's something buried, cried Kara to Lauren, looking over her shoulder at the woman; and she brushed away the sand and with her fingers dug the object from the small hill before her: the bottle had been caught, it turned out, in the railing of one of the old buried bridges.

The girl was mildly fascinated to hold the bottle up and, in the light of every star she knew in the skies above, see two blue eyes blinking up at her. They seemed old, nearly blind, and very sad.

But it was not a star, after all; and she was disappointed. She turned to the bus and the superintendent of the ranch who stood on the roadside waving at her, and then she turned to Lauren behind her. But Lauren was walking away, without a goodbye;

and it was only at the final moment that Kara decided not to bury the bottle back in the sand but to keep it, since it was odd there were two eyes watching her, and since they were so sad, she thought. Tucking the find beneath her arm, she ran to the bus.

ABOUT THE AUTHOR

STEVE ERICKSON attended the University of California at Los Angeles, where he won the Samuel Goldwyn Award for fiction. For three years he wrote the "Guerrilla Pop" column for the *Los Angeles Reader*; he has also written for *Esquire* and *Rolling Stone*. His second novel, *Rubicon Beach*, was published in 1986. He lives in downtown Los Angeles.